The Hagenspan Chronicles

Book Six

Owan's Regret

Widows and Successions

Robert W. Tompkins

Owan's Regret

Widows and Successions

translated from the original tongues by

Robert W. Tompkins

Owan's Regret

Book Six: Widows and Successions

being chiefly concerned with the events

which occurred during the forty-third year

of the reign of Ruric III, called Serpent's-Bane

The turning of the page,

the waning of the moon,

the crispness of the leaves as they crackle 'neath my feet.

How long has my bower been barren?

Has it been as long as that?

Once was my bed full—

full of the sweat of a man and

panting laughter and sting of love

and the promise of babes to my breast....

Once was my bed full.

The turning of the page,

the bleak ebony night,

the rattle of the leaves as they blow against my window—

my window, drawn and shuttered against the night's biting wind—

How long has my bower been barren?

I would say, "Where have the years gone?"

if it hadn't been that I had been

secretly watching them creep along, creep away,

full of stealth and shadow.

I would say, "Where have they gone? Where?"

The turning of the page,

the waxing of the moon,

the gold and white of buds as they burst upon the branch.

How long has my bower been barren?

As long as that?

> *I will throw back the shutters*
>
> *and allow the light to pass—*
>
> > *to come into my room with its*
> >
> > *fickle promises of warmth, of sight—*
>
> *And if it be that I am stricken blind ...*
>
> *well, then ...*
>
> *so be it.*

The turning of the page.

Chapter One

"This is not our skin!" cried Ruric the King. "What have you done with our skin?" Feebly he sought to throw off the bedclothes that weighed him down, but even that modest effort was draining to the old man, and he began to cry. "The arms of the king should be strong," he whispered sadly.

Maygret, his wife—Queen Maygret—rose from the velvet-cushioned chair where she had been dozing, and bustled to his side. "Your arm is still strong, O King," she said, her brow furrowed with concern. "An evil dream has overtaken you."

"Why are we still abed, woman?" he said, uncertain that he recognized her. "Is there not a court to be held?"

"Yes, Sire." She stroked the loose, wrinkled skin of his arm. "But Herm can hear the complaints of your people today. You should rest and gather your strength."

"Why?" he asked in a faint voice. "Are we ill?"

Maygret continued her soothing caress of his arm, and smiled sorrowfully at him, but he had already nodded off again, and was whimpering softly in his sleep.

The king was indeed ill, Maygret somberly reflected. But his illness was not one that could be cured with potions or physics or balms.

A few moments later, the king woke without opening his eyes, and whispered, "We dreamed that we had been bewitched, a powerful enchantment. An evil vision it was…. Are you there, Maygret?"

"I am here."

"We dared not open our eyes, for fear … fear that it was not but a dream." His voice dropped so low that Maygret had to strain to make out his words. "Swear to us."

"What is it?"

"Swear to us on your crown … swear on your noble blood."

"Anything, Majesty."

"Tell us truth, Maygret…."

"Anything." Tears formed at the corners of her eyes. The king's own eyes remained shut against the gray glow of morning that seeped past the draperies of his window.

"Are we … are we *old*, my Queen?"

She did not immediately reply, but her lower lip began to quaver. The king opened his pale, rheumy eyes and read the answer in her trembling chin.

"When did that happen?" he said in a voice filled with wonder. "When we went to bed last night, were we not young and full of vigor? And now, this morning…." His thought trailed off, and he stared distantly past the curtains on his window as if he could see completely through the heavy fabric, but the distance he beheld was not a matter of space but of time. "How many years have passed like a breath of wind? How many…."

His slight whisper became another soft breath of wind passing from his memory, and Maygret realized that he had fallen asleep again.

A girl cleared her throat from the doorway, and said, "I beg your pardon, Your Majesty, but may I bring you tea?" Maygret half turned her face toward the girl and nodded. At her periphery she saw the shadow of the girl curtsey and depart. A nice girl, polite and respectful and not very pretty.

Maygret sighed, frowned. There was a day when she would have been intensely jealous of any woman prettier than she serving anywhere near the king, for Ruric had ever been a man of wandering passions. But he was the King, after all, and concubines and courtesans were his birthright.

But Maygret also knew that none of those others were ever the *Queen.* Ruric's Queen, his jewel, his prize—not merely bedded, but wedded.

She took scant comfort from that fact now, for she was tormented with apprehension for her husband, whom (she realized with a bit of surprise) she loved. She had sat by the old king's right arm for decades, had heard his counsel, had occasionally offered her own. Sometimes he had even listened to her. Every now and then, Ruric had visited her bedchamber, and once, many years before, she had borne him a son, a prince, who had died as a babe. Since that time, she had often been cold to the king, had occasionally raged at him, had sometimes snapped and snarled and sniped. As the years passed, and Ruric had tolerated her poor behavior and never unseated her from her position in the throne to the right of (and just lower than) his, she grew to accept him, then appreciate him, then approve of him.

One day she realized that she was beginning to feel … *affection* for him.

And now, when after all the tumultuous years of their union, she longed to love him at last … he was leaving her. Not all at once. Sometimes still he was warm and cheerful, and still able to shuffle about the courtyard and greet his men, and eat and drink and joke and laugh. And rule. But more and more, lately, the king would fail to recognize Maygret … fail to recognize, even, himself. The duties of ruling Hagenspan were left in the hands of Ruric's Prime Minister, Herm, who had long been a favorite of the king, and then been dishonored some years back, and had gradually gained favor again. Maygret tried to remember why it was that Herm had been dishonored, but there seemed to be a cloud of some sort over that part of her memory.

The old man lying in the bed stirred a bit, and his eyes fluttered open. Finding Maygret with his gaze, he smiled and said, "We believe … that we are the king."

Earnestly she responded, "You *are* the king! You are Ruric Serpent's-Bane, and you are the father and glory of all Hagenspan!"

He closed his eyes and nodded, still smiling. His head sank back again into his pillows, and his breathing slowed, deepened. The girl appeared in the doorway again bearing a steaming pot of tea, and Queen Maygret brushed a tear away from her cheek.

Chapter Two

Hess Boole slowly rode his fine stallion Chancy around the perimeter of the Lady Hollie's lands. It was a beautiful spring day in the broad valley between the craggy Sayl Mountains on the west and the gently rolling Senns to the east; Boole could feel the sun burning the top of his slightly balding head, and he smiled. As Captain of the Guard at Beale's Keep, he was in charge of the security of this serene land, but he was happy to note that his position had become largely ceremonial, due to the absence of any real threats to Hagenspan's peace. In the dozen or so years that he had served Lady Hollie, as his belly had grown larger and his hair thinner, the land had prospered more than in any time in recent memory. Crops were abundant, cattle were plentiful, and wild game thrived in the woodlands. Beale's Keep had been barren when Hollie and her company had inherited it, but patience and the blessing of God had proved it to be some of the most fertile farmland in all of Hagenspan, and fish and game were so plentiful that the Lady of the castle was able to provide a virtual feast every time her table was set.

Hess Boole loved Hollie Roarke; there was no denying that. Even as he rode his horse around the borders of the valley, ostensibly keeping watch for any danger to the land, his mind kept drifting back to her. Once songs had been sung celebrating her great beauty.... He supposed that they still were, perhaps, in the taverns in the east, but he hadn't heard them in, he supposed, several years. Almost unconsciously, he began to hum.

The years had done little to dim her beauty, though it was a loveliness more mature now, more elegant perhaps, than the fierce radiance of her youth, which had caused men's jaws to drop, the breath to catch in their chests, hearts pound like anvils, words stopped stupidly on their tongues. Now the golden luster of her hair had faded somewhat, becoming intermingled with white. Tiny wrinkles had formed at the corners of her eyes, and she had grown just the slightest bit thicker across her midsection.

But in Boole's generous eyes, there was still none fairer in all the country, none even close. And he knew—even though she did not permit him to share her bed—that she loved him too. There were smiles upon her lips that belonged to him alone; there was a light in her blue eyes that sparkled only for him.

He dismounted at a small brook rippling with clear, cold water that reflected the glittering sunlight like a bed of dancing diamonds. He dropped Chancy's reins to the ground, stepped a few paces upstream, knelt, and drank. Splashing ice-cold water over the top of his head, he shook, blew, and sputtered, sowing crystalline droplets everywhere like seed.

He spied someone walking in his direction from across the field, and for a second his heart lifted, thinking that it might be Hollie. But a moment later he recognized the waddling gait and the florid face of Aron Millerson, the priest of the Amendicarii. He smirked to himself—imagine mistaking fat Aron for his beautiful Lady! Feeling just a little disappointed that it wasn't Hollie approaching, he was pleased to see the chubby young cleric anyway.

Aron drew up to Boole, mopping his face and smiling ruefully, his legs heavy with the exertion of his hike. "Blessings of Iesu be upon you," he panted.

"And on you," Boole replied. "A fine bright day He's given us."

Aron nodded thoughtfully. He was a solemn young man for the most part, though he was capable of bursts of delighted laughter when the mood was upon him. He had been only a teenager when he had been commissioned by Lord Cedric Roarke of Blythecairne to go to the Amendicarii to study and learn the Words of God. The ensuing years of preparation with the priests in Mount Tendor had increased his knowledge, though he was still confused about many things. In fact, on the day of his sending forth from the mountains—over four years ago—he had protested that he was ill prepared to take God's Words to the people of the land. But Matthias, the chief priest, had assured him that he was as ready as God needed him to be, and that whatever was lacking in his preparation would surely be filled up by the experiences he would soon have.

There had been twenty priests in all sent forth from the Amendicarii. Three of them had been boys from County Bretay; they were Aron and his friends Gosse and Spence, who had formerly been guards together at Castle Blythecairne. When the three had finally parted ways, it had been a bittersweet event, for they had been companions for many years, and it was likely enough that they would never see each other again. Gosse had gone home to be the vicar at Blythecairne; Spence, who had quickly learned the language of the southlands, had wistfully headed in the opposite direction of home, to live among the people of Sonder Westen. And Aron Millerson had trekked north and west, at last arriving in the valley which was the home of the modest castle called Beale's Keep. He had been remembered fondly and warmly received by the Lady Hollie, who bade him stay and be the teacher for the folks who dwelt with her there—an invitation which he eagerly accepted.

Aron had been rather slender when he arrived at the Keep four years earlier. The simple fare provided by the Amendicarii had reduced his youthful roundness to a healthy trim, and that leanness had only been augmented by the long trek from Mount Tendor to the Lady Hollie's valley. But once he got to Beale's Keep, he rediscovered the joys of a bountiful table, and he ate with great gusto and gratitude. When he had been sent forth from the Amendicarii, he wore a coarse brown robe— the humble uniform of his office—and he had a spare robe as well so that he would never be without clean vestments. But after a year or so of Lady Hollie's plenteous board, he found that both of his robes had become so uncomfortably tight as to make him unable to breathe freely. Finally he had spent a humiliating day sequestered in his room cutting apart his garments and remaking the two into one significantly larger robe. Though some of his friends noticed his suddenly expanded capacity, they respectfully refrained from mentioning it.

It was with the intention of washing his robe today that Aron had come to this little creek so far from the castle. He had been surprised to find Captain Boole there, but not disappointed; he enjoyed the Captain's company (even if he was a bit bawdy), and he could always come back some other time to wash his robe.

"You've come far from the Keep," Boole commented, making conversation.

"Aye," Aron said, and he couldn't hide the sheepish grin that crept across his face. "Sorry, Captain Boole, I'm not trying to hide anything from you … it's just that my, ah … I had a rather personal reason to … I was intending to do a bit of bathing, is what it was."

"Ah," said Boole, understanding, "so you needed a private place to show your priestly bum to the sky, without any prying eyes to spy." He grinned, pleased with his rhyme. He thought of another one, and quickly added, "As you try to dry your sopping hide."

Aron chuckled, and said, "Well, not to be indelicate—but, yes."

"No need to say another word," Boole said, holding up his hand. "I'll be on my way immediately, and leave you to the privacy of your bath. Though I'd be careful of what parts I'd dip into that frozen water! It's so cold it'd shrivel your pod clean through to your backbone!"

Aron's cheeks flushed pink, but he smiled gratefully at the older man.

Boole laughed. "Just give me a few minutes to get Chancy over that knoll yonder—I don't want to risk your Iesu striking me blind just because I happened to see the pasty white flesh of one of His chosen pets, goose-pimpled by the breeze, and knocking in the knees!" He tipped his head back and laughed again—another rhyme!

Aron shook his head, still smiling. He wasn't sure sometimes just how reverently Hess Boole held the notion of Iesu … but he was a good man nonetheless, trustworthy and loyal. "I'll see you back at the castle for dinner?"

"I'll save you a spot," the Captain affirmed. "Until later, my friend."

Aron held up his hand in a parting salute as Boole galloped away with a wave.

Chapter Three

"Good shot, Owan!" Alan Poppleton cried. "Really remarkable!"

Owan Roarke was indeed becoming a notable marksman. Alan had been schooling the boy with the sword and the bow ever since Owan had been strong enough to lift them, and though the slender blond-haired lad seemed to shy away from swordplay, with the bow he was something special.

Alan wondered sometimes about Owan's reticence with the blade, wondered if it had something to do with the death of the boy's father, the Lord Cedric Roarke, who had slain three dragons with a sword, but not the fourth. But Alan did not ask, and neither did Owan volunteer the information. Instead, he spent hour after pensive hour practicing his bowmanship, seeming to take joy in the flight of the arrows that he created, though seldom did he smile. He experimented with ways to produce shafts that were true and straight, and also did tests with feathers of various weights and stiffnesses to try and optimize their flight, but so far, he hadn't come up with any real improvements over the shafts that the old guards made.

Still, though, Alan was impressed with the boy's resourcefulness.

He suspected that Owan was destined for great things, even discounting the obvious fact that he would one day be Lord of Beale's Keep. After all, the boy's veins flowed with blood that was both noble and heroic. His father was Roarke the Dragon-Killer, his mother the great Lady Hollie, who had killed the dragon her husband had been unable to. The two greatest heroes in the history of Hagenspan, Alan thought, though in the decade since the last dragon had been vanquished, people talked about it less. And the two Dragon-Killers had united to produce this one son, Owan Roarke, who was slight and somber and inquisitive and thoughtful. Might his glory not, perhaps, exceed even theirs? A small smile played across

Alan's face. At least there were no more dragons. Any glory Owan might attain would have to be of a different sort than his parents'.

Owan turned his solemn gray eyes toward the small castle of Beale's Keep and squinted slightly. "Who's that coming?"

Alan followed his gaze and said, "Don't know—looks like a messenger, maybe. But he's coming this way, so we'll know soon enough."

Owan turned back and sent one more shaft hurtling through the air toward its target, and grimaced when it missed its mark by an inch or more. Then the two friends shouldered their bows and waited for the messenger to arrive.

A moment later, and Alan could make out the features of the man's face. He thought that the fellow looked vaguely familiar, and tried to remember where he may have seen him before, but could not. The dust of the man's journey clung to his clothing; it must have been a matter of some urgency that drove him.

The man strode up to Alan and Owan, glancing at the boy's face and nodding noncommittally, but then bowing on one knee in front of Alan. "Lord Poppleton," he said.

Alan chuckled nervously and said, "Stand up, friend. You've missed your target by a hundred leagues! Lord Poppleton is my father."

"I've come from your father," the courier said, as he rose to his feet, and suddenly Alan realized where he had seen him before. "He sends for you. His illness is grave, and it is time for you to become who you are—to fulfill the destiny of your blood."

An icy fist of fear clenched itself around Alan's heart. He had not seen his father in more than a year, and had not been aware of his illness—what could that be? Then an acrid thought occurred to him: his father had become *old*. "I'm sorry … I know we've met, but I don't recall your name."

"Fret yourself not, my Lord. I am Hallna Bennker, one of your father's trusted friends."

"Yes, of course," Alan replied, though he was unsure he had ever heard the name before. "Tell me of my father."

Bennker glanced at Owan again, and asked Alan, "May I speak freely?"

"Of course," Alan said testily. "This is the future Lord of Beale's Keep: Owan, the son of Lady Hollie and Roarke the Dragon-Killer."

"Forgive me," Bennker said with a self-conscious frown. "I did not know."

"That's all right," Owan said softly. "I'll go gather our shafts." Before Alan could protest, Owan trotted off toward the targets, fleet as a deer.

"Tell me of my father," Alan repeated.

"My Lord," Hallna Bennker said with a nod. He spoke with a faint accent that suggested he was not originally from Ester. "Lord Poppleton had been confined to his bed for nearly a fortnight before he sent me to find you, and it has taken me a fortnight again to arrive here. He is quite pale and trembly; his right hand shakes cruelly with no exertion at all, as if it is beyond his ability to control." Bennker smiled apologetically. "My old friend fears that the time is near for him to depart and go where spirits go. I know not if he is mistaken or correct. But his holy wish is for you to come home and assume your mantle as Lord of Ester, and spend at his side whatever time remains for him."

Alan hesitated only for a fraction of a moment, and then said, "Yes, of course." He immediately felt a guilty pang of regret. Owan, Hollie, Hess Boole, Aron Millerson, even Alan's dearest companion Brette, who had ridden with him to the War of the Last Dragon—all of his friends lived here at Beale's Keep, and parting from them would be bitter. But he had always known that this day would someday come … and he did love his father, too. "We can leave first thing in the morning, if that suits you."

"Where are you going?" Owan said, panting slightly as he returned with a fistful of arrows.

Alan looked at the blond-haired boy sadly. He had no wife or son, and he had loved Owan as his own, ever since the boy had been old enough to stand. "Master Bennker," Alan said, "would you please return to the Keep and wait for me there? I must have a word with Owan."

"Certainly, my Lord."

Owan looked at Alan uneasily, a shadow of foreboding darkening his eyes.

"Where are you going?" he asked, his voice tight in his throat.

Chapter Four

She knelt in the dirt of her private garden, humming softly, cherishing the tug of defiant resistance that the weeds made as she pulled them from the earth between her flowers. She breathed in the scent of the moist earth, the perfume of the colorful blooms that glistened with dew. She touched the soft pink petals with the backs of her hands, and smiled when a dewdrop rolled from the curled edge of a petal and disappeared between her muddy fingers. She felt the sun warming her back, her shoulders, her bare feet, and was glad.

This cherishing, this caring, this *noticing* … it was a gift from Cedric, she knew. Even now, after—what was it? fourteen years? sixteen? Even now, after so many years had passed, she still recalled the time when she had first been gazed upon by the eyes of the man who would become her husband, and the father of her son.

Hollie had sat across the table from him that evening in the murky twilight of Kenndt's Public House, while poor Will had sat next to her, chattering nervously about whatever came into his head. And Lord Cedric Roarke (though she had not known his identity then) had sat in virtual silence, with the whispers of a pleased smile playing upon his lips, and had ravished her face with his eyes. She had never been *noticed* so completely in her life—she, whose beauty was almost legendary in the small dark prison that her life was.

She had been accustomed to being used to satisfy men's black hungers, being torn apart as if she were a piece of meat, consumed to answer the bleak demands of their lust. Cedric had had a hunger, too, after a fashion … she had felt as if she were being consumed that night, too … but not ripped apart like meat; it was more like she had been drunk like a slow glass of wine. And she had drunk of it, too. It was a heady, giddy experience, each sip savored and caressed by the tongue, then swallowed and sent on its burning path to her stomach. She had offered to lie with him that night—after all, he had paid for the privilege—but he had declined, tenderly, regretfully.

On that very night she had begun to suspect something … she had begun to suspect *love.* It was a thought that had never occurred to her during any encounter she had ever had with a man before, and when the thought did occur to her, she couldn't identify it, couldn't give it a name. And even though it took several frustrating months for her to surrender to the implications—that she could love, that she could even *be* loved—at last she did.

These were the things that she thought of when she remembered her husband's eyes. And she wondered if he could see her yet. The warmth of the sun on her back said yes … so she lifted her face toward the clouds and smiled.

It had been many years since she had lain with a man. After Cedric had been slain by the dragon, she had not had any desire to go to that place again—that panting, sweating exercise that had left her exhausted and bored, discontented with everyone except Cedric. There had been several men, though, who had offered to take her there, and to their credit, she thought, some of them had been as concerned for her welfare as they were anxious to indulge their own lust. She thought of her poor brother-in-law, Haldamar Tenet, a widower now, and shook her head with a sad smile. She thought of Esselte Smead, now Lord of Thraill, red-faced and generous, who had offered her marriage and honor. She knew that, no matter whatever else might happen in her life, she would never marry another man as long as Esselte Smead lived, just in case it might break his heart.

And she thought of Hess Boole, jovial and boisterous, with twinkling eyes and booming laughter that echoed through the halls of Beale's Keep. She smiled again, just thinking of that unruly laughter. Hess was different from Cedric in many ways, quite different. Where Cedric had been quiet and sensitive almost to the point of insecurity, Hess was self-confident almost to the point of absurdity! Bawdy and irreverent, he would wink at her from across the room even when there were others present, and occasionally pat her rump when she wasn't prepared to defend herself. She allowed him to kiss her from time to time when there was no one else around, and once in an unguarded moment she had allowed him to cup his hands around her bosom. But she had never been intimate with him, not in a physical sense, and she was content for it to stay that way. But she knew that Hess desired more … and it gave her a warm little stirring in the hollow of her stomach to realize it.

For she knew that she loved him, too. She loved him. How odd, she thought, that she should love two such very different men in her lifetime. But then, she reflected, they were really more alike than different, after all. They were both courageous and strong and noble, willing to sacrifice their own comforts for the sake of others; to deny themselves for a greater good.

She smiled heavenward toward Cedric again, and willed him to know that she meant him no disrespect, that she would always love him … but that she loved Hess Boole, too. She hoped that was all right. And anyway, she was in no hurry.

ξ

She was still among the flowers when she saw Owan pass beneath the iron portcullis that led from the castle courtyard to the walled garden. She knew that sometimes he retreated here when he wearied of the company of his friends, Tully and Joah and Windy. No one was permitted to enter the garden but Hollie and Owan and their invited guests.

She held her peace, in case her son was hoping for a moment of privacy. But then she noticed that Owan seemed to be crying, and she rose to her feet and stepped toward him.

He saw her then, turned his back to her, ashamed of his tears, and dried his cheeks with the back of his sleeve.

"Owan," Hollie said quietly, "I don't mean to intrude." She laid a hand on his shoulder, noticing too late that her fingers were still stained with dirt. "May I help?"

He shook his bowed head once, no, and said, "It's—" and then stopped, afraid he was going to blubber. He wrestled with his emotion, regained control, and choked, "It's Alan. He's leaving."

"Really?" Her maternal concern was mingled with curiosity. "Why?"

"His father." Owan turned his head slightly so that he could sense his mother's face at the periphery of his vision. "He's sick, and he wants Alan to come home and be the Lord of Ester."

"Oh." Hollie felt the stinging wound of her son's pain; she had known intimately the anguish of loss herself, and she had tried to shield her boy as much as possible from that despondent sense of bereavement. She drew his slight frame close to her and put her arms around his chest. "Your father," she said, her voice soft and slow, "sometimes spoke of how we never quite seem to have enough time with each other during our lives here and now. He hoped for another country—a gift from God—where we are never old, and nevermore parted."

"The same one Aron talks about," Owan said dully.

"Yes." He didn't seem to be uncomfortable in her embrace, so she continued to hold him. She murmured, "I have that hope, too."

"I wish—I wish I had known him," Owan said, and a fresh reservoir of tears burned his eyes.

"I know you do, sweetheart." Hollie pressed her cheek against his blond hair, and kissed him.

"Alan was the closest thing I ever had to a father."

"I'm sorry," she said. "There's still Captain Boole," she offered tentatively.

"He's more interested in you than in me," he said without bitterness, and Hollie felt a moment's alarm that Owan had noticed. "Boo's fun, and he's a good man and everything…." He stopped, not needing to add, *but he's not Alan.*

Hollie kissed his head again. "We always knew that someday Alan would be called back to Ester to take his rightful position. He's the son of a Lord—just like you."

"I know," Owan said, "but I wasn't—I wasn't ready, not yet."

"When is he leaving?"

"Tomorrow morning, I think."

"Then," she said, "let's feast him tonight. We'll honor him with all of the honor that Beale's Keep can bestow. You can sit next to him if you like." Owan nodded silently. "There will always be friendship between Beale's Keep and Ester, between Lord Alan and Lord Owan. You can visit him someday if you like."

Owan nodded again, and said, "But it won't be the same."

"No," she agreed with a whisper. "No, it never is."

Chapter Five

Chancy crested a small hillock just north of the castle, from which Captain Hess Boole could look down across the field and faintly see Hollie's private garden shimmering in the distance. Sometimes he could discern the top of a blonde head moving about in the midst of the greenery and blooms, and even though he couldn't make out any of her features, it always gave him a warm thrill to know that he was seeing *her*.

He smiled and shook his head, almost imperceptibly. He still felt the same way about Hollie, still the same after a decade and more. As if he were some kind of moon-faced lad who had never slapped the rump of a barmaid, who was still panting for his first feathery kiss. But this bit of foolishness, this unforced childishness, made Hess Boole glad.

He was, he figured, more than forty years old by now. He could have married, several times, if he had had the inclination, and Hollie would have willingly let him. But … no. He knew that, if he had succumbed to the occasional but fleeting temptation, it just would have turned out all wrong. He supposed he could train himself to love another woman, and he figured he could probably discipline himself into some kind of conjugal fidelity. But he knew that there was a part of his heart that would always belong to Hollie. He was as sure of that as he was sure of the horse between his legs. And that just wouldn't have been fair, not to his wife, not to Hollie, not to himself.

Hess Boole had accompanied her when Hollie had come out of the westlands from Castle Thraill to claim her reward for killing the last dragon of Hagenspan, along with a small company of guards and friends who loved her.

That reward had been the decaying castle of Beale's Keep, along with some of the surrounding lands, which had all been blasted and befouled by the malevolent hatred of the vile serpent. When Hollie first saw the prize she had won, she nearly turned back in despair, but Captain Boole had steadied her, supported her, encouraged her.

When the day came for Hollie to mark out the boundaries of her land (in accordance with the king's edict—all of the land she could traverse in one day's walking), she had taken no companion with her save Hess Boole. Boole had carried food and water for her, had kept on striding purposefully alongside her, urging her along, willing her to obtain as great an inheritance for herself as she could possibly get.

At dawn they had begun walking, southward, past the edge of the dragon's defile, on through the windblown plains, to the edge of a forest. Hollie had thought to turn eastward then, but Boole had urged her into the woods, explaining that her people would have need of good timberlands too. When the sun reached a certain point in the sky, which Hollie could not even see because of the trees, Boole had said, "That's good, my Lady. We'll turn east now." And in the ground he planted a stake, one of four ceremonial rods that had been sent to Hollie from the king in order to mark her boundaries.

For several more hours, they had picked their way through the forest, heading—Hollie supposed—eastward. She lost track of time, she lost track of where she was, and as she grew wearier she even lost track of why she was doing this thing. She only focused on Hess Boole's back in front of her as he beat his way through the brush, making Hollie's path as easy as he could. After a time he bent, pounded another picket into the ground, smiled at the weary woman breathing raggedly with her hands on her knees, and said, "Back out into the sunshine now, my Lady."

Northward they went then, and Hollie did indeed feel refreshed when she stepped out of the shadowed cloister of the forest into the bright midday sun. "Step lively now, my Lady; we've miles to cover before dark." And so she tried to keep up with his stride, but soon she feared that she was becoming exhausted, and became concerned that Boole had chosen milestones that were simply too far for her to reach before sunset.

"Sunset?" Boole cried with a laugh. "Why, a day stretches not just from dawn to dusk, does it? I thought a day stretched clear from dawn to dawn of the next!"

She nodded, understanding, but a glazed look lingered in her eyes. "But when shall we rest?" she murmured.

"Time enough for rest tomorrow, my Lady," Boole said gently. "This is for you, and for Owan, and for your people—this little stroll we're taking today." He looked at her tenderly. "But if you want to stop now for a short meal, we can do that. You just need to be ready to walk again when I say 'Walk.'"

Hollie nodded gratefully, and Hess Boole handed her the water-skin while he prepared a simple cold dinner. After they had eaten, Hollie looked at her brawny companion hesitantly, and asked, "Is it time to go?"

"Aye," he said, but he did not rise. Looking at Hollie with a tumbled mixture of emotions playing in his eyes, he said huskily, "First ... I believe I'll kiss you, with your Ladyship's permission."

Hollie was shocked—perhaps—and she wondered where her voice was that should be commanding him to stop. But that voice did not speak, and she found herself in his arms, being kissed, and returning that kiss, at first hesitantly, then with somewhat more enthusiasm. After a long moment, their lips parted, and they reluctantly loosened their embrace. Boole smiled at her, embarrassed but triumphant, and she said, "Captain Boole ... you have probably cost me two acres of land." He laughed then, and she had said, red-faced, "Thank you."

Then they had walked again, long into the dark hours of the night, Boole leading the way with a flaming torch. Sometime in the night, Boole had pounded in the king's stake, and then they had turned toward the west, trudging on for interminable hours more until Boole knelt and drove the king's last stake into the earth. Hollie lost track of everything then, apparently losing consciousness as well, for sometime later she wakened to the first rays of dawn beginning to streak the sky with their orange paint, and found to her surprise that she was being carried in Hess Boole's arms.

"We're nearing the Keep now, my Lady, my love," Boole had said softly, trying to keep from panting, gasping. "You'll have to walk this last bit yourself, in order to certify your claim."

"Thank you, Hess. I can walk," she said, and he dropped her feet to the earth, the pain of exertion surging through his spent arms like the coursing of the River Eldric. "Thank you," she repeated, and kissed him—their second kiss.

Arm in arm they covered the last bit of wilderness that the dragon had ruined, crested a small knoll, and in the gray morning light they saw the broken castle in the distance. Ruefully untying the knot of their arms, they walked toward the Keep together, chatting innocuously about things that didn't matter. As they arrived in the dusty courtyard, Owan (still just a small child) had run to his mother, wrapping his arms about her weary legs, and Alan Poppleton had walked toward the pair, accompanied by Sir Faultnor, who had been charged with certifying Hollie's claim to the land she had encircled.

As Hollie knelt and took her little boy in her arms, Faultnor asked Boole about the journey the pair had made, and where he could find the boundary posts. When Boole told him, he looked fairly astonished, and said, "You vow that you planted all four stakes yourself, and gave them to no other?" When Boole did so affirm, Faultnor asked, "And you covered all of this ground afoot? You had no horses placed along the path to aid you?"

Hess Boole answered truthfully, "Every inch of the Lady Hollie's border was covered by the foot of man, not beast."

Sir Faultnor looked uncomfortable, but summoned a weak smile and said, "So much land! The king will be … impressed."

Hess Boole thought of that day as he looked down into the valley toward the blooms of Hollie's garden, and reflected for the hundredth time that that had been the best day of his life. *So far*, he reminded himself. There were many days yet to come … and maybe there would be even a better day than that one among them.

He smiled, chirped a command to Chancy, and rode down toward the castle.

Chapter Six

The feasting had been completed for over an hour, and most of the assembly had drifted off to their sleeping quarters, after having bidden farewell to Alan Poppleton with hugs, with kisses, with tears. The only ones left at the table were Alan, his longtime friend Brette, the Lady Hollie, and Owan.

Hollie listened to the subdued talk of the young men as she studied the patterns painted on the tablecloth by meat juices dribbled off platters, and by wine goblets upended when careless arms reached across them toward more food. *Young men.* Hollie reflected with a moment's surprise that Alan and Brette were not so very young anymore; they must be thirty! Neither of them had married yet, though Hollie figured that Alan would have to soon, now that he was going to be the Lord of Ester. Children must be produced, an heir elected.

She knew that Alan had wished to wed one of her own two nieces, the daughters of Cedric's sister—Piper and Jesi Tenet. But headstrong Jesi had married another, and heartbroken Piper had vowed that she would never take a husband, for the love she had borne for poor Willum of Blythecairne. So far that vow had kept her, cheerless and unrelenting, and it had been several years since any young man had even attempted to thaw the cold winter of her heart. Hollie wondered idly where then Alan Poppleton would find a bride. Probably some pretty young virgin of his own land, she decided. Most likely his father had already assembled a sizeable harem of potential consorts for him to choose among. She wondered if that would please Alan's innate male vanity, or if it would distress him—like any man, he probably hated to make any choice that he didn't feel was his own.

Her thoughts wandered unbidden back to her own wedding day, high in the mountains of the Amendicarii, so many years ago. She tried to remember Cedric's face, but found that her mind's eye was seeing something that looked more like Hess Boole, and she decided that perhaps she had had too much wine. Taking a deep breath, she prepared to stand and make her way to her bedchamber.

She looked at Owan, thinking to tell him that it was time for him to turn in as well, but then she saw how earnestly he was hanging on each of Alan's words, wringing every last golden drop of companionship that he possibly could from their relationship. No harm in letting him stay up late, she decided. Tomorrow was going to be miserable enough for him.

She pushed her chair back from the table and stood, and the three young men deferentially stood too. "Well, Alan—Lord Poppleton," Hollie said. "Words can scarcely suffice to tell you what a blessing you have been to me these many years—both of you," she said, including Brette, who would be leaving in the morning with Alan. "Beale's Keep will miss you." She smiled sadly. "*I* will miss you." Her face brightened then, as if the clouds of her transitory sadness had parted, and Alan marveled at how beautiful she still was. "But the next great adventure of your lives awaits! You will rule wisely, and bravely, I am sure. And you will go no place that you are not covered by my prayers, that the God of all the universe will regard you with favor, and deal kindly with you."

Alan, grateful, tried to think of something appropriately ceremonial to offer in reply, but could only come up with, "Thank you, my Lady."

"Be sure you are well-provisioned for your journey. Anything you need is yours."

"Yes, my Lady."

"The two of you stop and see me before you leave tomorrow."

"We will."

Hollie nodded at him, and said, "Well, good night, gentlemen." She tilted her head toward the three, saying, "Brette. Owan."

"Good night, my Lady," said Brette and Alan. Owan watched his mother leave, grateful that she had not treated him like a boy in front of Alan and Brette. Suddenly he felt that he had been granted to steal one step closer toward manhood himself.

As Hollie passed through the short hallway to her bower, she wondered what it was that Owan would say to Alan, now that she had departed. Then she decided that it wasn't important, probably. What was important to Owan was probably not what the last word would *be* ... just that it would be *his*. And that was a gift she could give her son gladly.

ξ

It was a week later, and Alan and Brette, accompanied by Hallna Bennker, had covered about half of the distance from Beale's Keep back home to Ester. They had traveled due south through the foothills of the Sayls until they found the King's Road, which led westward to Raussi, through the county of Fennal to the small city of Sarbo, and then at last to Ester on the sea.

Alan had nearly chosen to go north around the mountains and then west to Castle Thraill in order to pay a visit to his friends there before heading home, but that journey would have taken perhaps a week longer than the one he had decided upon. Besides, he thought, the number of friends that he still had at Castle Thraill had diminished with the passing of the years. Many of the people he had first known there had ended up following Hollie to Beale's Keep, leaving only a few of Sir Cedric Roarke's old comrades behind at his old holdings. There was Master Smead, of course, who was either the Lord or the Steward of Thraill, depending on how you looked at it; Alan suspected Smead wasn't entirely sure himself. There was Haldamar Tenet, Roarke's brother-in-law, but visiting him was a cheerless affair since the death of his wife. As far as Alan knew, Piper was still there; at least, he hadn't heard otherwise, but it had been a couple of years since he had known for certain. The one that Alan would most have wished to see, Jesi Tenet, was gone—that he knew. For after a few years of tempestuous, intermittent courtship, Alan and Jesi had parted in frustration, and then later—*my God, it's been five years*—Alan had heard that she had been swept off her feet by charming Tayson Bost, the son of the Lord of Thrimball. Married and gone, still farther into the northwest, almost all the way to Haio's Port. Probably with children by now. Alan felt no sting of bitterness, just a blunted sense of grim regret. Anyway, there was no real reason for him to stop at Castle Thraill, not anymore. Besides, his father wanted him home.

They had just completed a cold midday meal beside the road, and were preparing to mount up again and cover a few more miles toward Ester. As Brette gathered their gear, he noticed his friend staring wistfully off toward the north. Though they didn't talk about the girls often anymore, Brette thought he understood what Alan was feeling. "You miss them much?" he asked.

"What?" Alan said, startled from his reverie. "Who's that?"

"The Tenet girls," Brette said. "I was wondering if you ever missed them."

"Oh." Alan replied sheepishly. "I guess I was thinking about them at that."

"Amazing how many days have passed, since those days," Brette said with wonder. "They sure do speed past."

"Yes, it's a pity about the Tenet ladies," joined Hallna Bennker from the other side of his horse. "Lovely young things, but full of sorrows."

"Yes," Alan agreed somberly. But then he asked, "The Lady Jesimonde? What sorrow has she?"

"Perhaps you had not heard," Bennker said hesitantly, unsure whether it was his place to impart these tidings to his new Lord. "Her husband, the Bost lordling, suffered a fall from aback his horse, some time ago. Perhaps a year has it been. He lies at death's gate, unwilling to cross over, but unable to come back."

"How … sad," Alan said after a moment, and he did indeed feel sadness that it had been necessary for Jesi to bear this sorrow. A memory of her flashed through his mind, dancing gaily at the end of his arm and laughing, and then another—her storm-filled eyes flashing with anger and spoiling for a fight. But he had no pictures in his memory to suggest that she had ever borne heartache (except perhaps for the passing of her mother), and it grieved him to imagine those fiery eyes filled with tears and despair.

"Yes, sad it is," agreed Bennker cautiously. "If my Lord would care to send condolences, that can be arranged when once we return to Beedlesgate."

"Thank you, Master Bennker. That will not … perhaps that would not be appropriate," said Alan, his brow furrowed.

"As you say, my Lord." Bennker mounted his horse, a roan with a wide white blaze on its face. "Shall we be on our way?"

Alan nodded tersely, still wondering at this news about Jesi, and hoisted himself skyward.

Chapter Seven

Aron Millerson knew he wasn't a very good priest. He knew that he was inattentive in his prayers, and that his discourses on God were oftentimes poorly researched and uncertainly delivered. He knew that his own softness and flabbiness was another indictment against him, magnifying his indolence and sloth. And lust! How many times had he secretly stolen glances at the Lady Hollie or one of the young women? Not to pray for them, to bless them in Iesu's Name, no—it was to filch an ill-gotten glimpse of their feminine beauty for *himself*! When he thought of all that stolen beauty, which he had taken without regard for the consequences—for him or for them or for God—it filled him with a dull, uneasy shame, almost as if his stomach were ill from too much greasy food. He wished that he could cry, releasing a torrent of repentant tears toward God, but he only felt that dull, stupid regret. Impotent guilt. Lazy. His eyes remained dry, and that only increased his sense of shame and unworthiness.

He tried reading from the large volume of the *Iesuchristion* that he had brought with him from Mount Tendor, and for a few minutes he labored over the strange writing that he had to translate anew every time he read it. He had hoped that his acumen with the difficult language from across the Great Sea would increase with familiarity, but so far it had not. So he sweated and strained over the words, hoping to wrest some meaning from them, either great or small, and often forgetting what the beginning of a sentence had said by the time that he reached its end. He considered writing the words out in his own language, but the translator from across the Sea had said that it was not to be done. This Aron Millerson could not comprehend; if God wanted His people to know His words, why then would He write them in a language they could not understand? But Aron obeyed, even though he felt vaguely uneasy about it. He pressed on, trying to read another line of the text, and a moment later realized with a start that he was staring out the window at a bird singing from the stone wall. Balling up his fist, he struck himself on the thigh, punishing himself for his woolgathering. He would have to beg the Lady Hollie for a room without a window.

But the sun was shining, and the sky overhead was clear and blue, and that bird just *would* sing. Aron longed to be out there in the midst of it all—God's beautiful creation—instead of shut up within the clammy stone walls of his room. *And what would be the problem with that?* Aron silently asked himself, and then batted the thought down as quickly as it had occurred to him. He gave his thigh another buffet, and tried to reapply himself to his reading.

Another frustrated quarter of an hour passed as Aron studied. A bead of cold sweat appeared on the line of his brow, and he chastised himself angrily. *Why can't you understand? Why* won't *you understand?* He tried to remember the things he had learned from Matthias and the brothers in the mountains—how clearly he had thought he perceived God's deep mysteries! But now that he was alone, with no one to teach him, he couldn't remember what it was that he had learned, and what he had only imagined. And he felt that the answers that would comfort him were beyond his reach, beyond the reach of his damnable stupidity in translation, the stupidity that mocked him every day.

He remembered something Matthias had once told him: that Roarke had been able to glean most of the essence of the message of Iesu from just the three scraps of God's Words that he had been granted in his lifetime. That Mankind was rebellious and deserved punishment, that Iesu had taken that punishment in Man's place, and that Man's responsibility now was to do justice, love mercy, and walk in humility before God. The simplicity of that message gave Aron hope. Then he looked again at the volume of the *Iesuchristion* with its multiplied thousands upon thousands of words, and involuntarily shuddered. Well … he would do the best that he could, he vowed, and then hope that God was as merciful as his teachers had said that He was.

He bent his neck again over the carefully inscribed pages, and tried to make himself grateful, earnest, and studious. He read a sentence, read another sentence, and a moment later he recognized that (though his eyes were still following the words) his mind was now fully engaged with thoughts of a young dark-haired woman of the castle named Sirina, who had occasionally smiled at Aron in a way that he thought was invitingly familiar. "Aagh!" he groaned, and tensed his thigh in preparation for another pummeling.

ξ

Herm, the Prime Minister of Hagenspan, stopped at the doorway of King Ruric's bedchamber and nodded to Sir Herbert, who stood guard at the entrance.

"How is His Majesty today?" he asked with concern.

"Naught has changed, my Lord," said the slender knight, who was surprised that Herm had deigned to speak with him. Usually the Prime Minister would bustle past the knights on guard duty without as much as a glance. "He seems not to recognize Queen Maygret."

Herm clasped the knight's arm with a grim look on his face. "What a sad day this is for the kingdom," he murmured. Herm's once-black hair was shot through with threads of gray now, making him look more respectable and wise than he had in his youth, when he had been merely handsome, eager, and bright. His chest heaved with a regretful sigh, and he said, "Well, perhaps His Highness will recognize me." Smiling ruefully at Sir Herbert, he patted his arm once more and stepped into the king's bedchamber.

Queen Maygret nodded somberly to him from her seat beside the sleeping monarch. "The king should rest," she whispered.

"Yes, my Queen," Herm said softly. "I understand completely. Actually, it was *you* that I wished to see."

Maygret looked at him with a question in her eyes.

Herm continued, "A delegation from Lispen across the Sea is near to arriving in the city. They have sent their messengers requesting an audience with the king. I believe," he said, "that they wish to discover our strength of arms, to see whether Hagenspan is capable of a defense, should they wish to steal our bounty for themselves." He looked at Maygret uncomfortably. "For them to find the king in such a state as he is would be ... unfortunate."

She nodded curtly, and frowned. "What is it that you would do?"

"By Your Majesty's leave, I would do this: Freely admit that the king is in failing health and is unable to attend. But *you*, O Queen—show yourself to be strong, vigorous, and full of resolve. Show that you will yield no quarter to any who would spoil fair Hagenspan, and that your armies are equal to your determination."

Maygret looked at him thoughtfully. "But how could these men possibly be intimidated by one old woman, no matter how many soldiers she boasts?"

"If I may, Your Majesty?"

She nodded impatiently at him.

"Your noble lineage is renowned, O Queen. It is spoken that the blood of your Feie ancestors runs still in your veins, and I believe it must be so. For—forgive me if I am speaking out of turn—for a woman to have attained your number of years, but still be as vital and fair—nay, so comely, so lovely!—as Your Majesty, there certainly *must* be something enchanted about her blood. Dear Maygret," he said, and she did not chastise him for the informality, "you are doubtless the equal of any woman in Hagenspan, in Lispen, or all the world!"

She thought that his praise must certainly be absurd, but nevertheless, a small smile curled at the corners of her lips. She was not immune to flattery.

"And, my dear Queen," Herm continued, as his cheeks flamed with apparent humiliation, "it would be my greatest honor to stand at your side as Prime Minister, to lend any strength that I may add to the occasion. Though I am certain that you would not need me."

"No," she whispered, as the king stirred in his sleep, moaning softly. "What you have spoken is good. Assemble and outfit the guard in their most impressive array, and I shall receive our visitors. And you shall be at my side."

"As you wish, Your Majesty," Herm said deferentially. "It has ever been my desire to serve you." He bowed toward her with a sweep of his arm, and then turned and left the room, the traces of a smile playing beneath the corners of his moustache.

Chapter Eight

Hollie frowned over the parchment scroll that was spread on the desk before her, with stone weights at the edges to keep it from rolling itself back up. She wasn't sure what to make of the words, but she felt certain that nothing good would come of them.

"Even such a look as that on your brow does nothing to diminish your loveliness," came a voice from the doorway.

She smiled slightly, though the troubled look of concentration lingered in her eyes. "Good day to you, Captain Boole," she said.

"So formal today, my Lady!" he laughed. "What troubles you, o dear one to my heart?"

"Hess," she softened. "Please come in and bless me with the benefits of your wisdom."

"Oh, I'm in trouble now!" he teased. "If such a one as you is needing wisdom from such a one as me, then it's a sorry day for wisdom in Beale's Keep!"

"Nevertheless," she smiled. "Come in."

He remained in the doorway, and a cautious tone sounded in his voice. "You'd be best to have a care, my Lady, for I'm feeling a bit wanton today," he warned. "If you're to invite me in again, it would have to be with the clear understanding that I won't be leaving without a kiss."

"I see," she said. "Well, perhaps I'll have to muddle through somehow, availing myself of nothing but my own wits, then."

"Well, since you put it that way," he said, stepping into the room, "perhaps I'll come in at that, and give you such humble wisdom as I have to offer, and then take my chances with the kiss."

"Well chosen," she said, and smiled at him.

He stepped over to where she sat, saw the parchment spread before her, and asked, "What troubles you, my dear?"

She nodded at the scroll and said, "Read that, and tell me what you make of it."

"May I sit?"

"Please," she said, and made room for him on the bench where she sat—but not so much room that he could sit freely without touching her. He seated himself next to her, thigh-to-thigh, and draped his arm around her waist. He pressed his lips to her cheek, breathed in deeply, and said, "You smell lovely, my love."

"Thank you," she smiled softly. "But I really do want you to read this."

"Of course," he agreed, remembering the distressed look on her face when he had seen her from the door. "Now be patient with me, for I'm a slow reader."

He leaned over the desk, peering at the words through squinted eyes, and a cloud passed over his own features as he read, understanding what it was that had troubled Hollie.

> *To Hollie, Lady of Beale's Keep and widdow of Roarke Lord of Thraill and Meadling:*
>
> *It has come to the attention of His Majesty that the debt incurred by your late husband the Lord Roarke at the time of his last visit to Ruric's Keep some years ago was never repaid the crown. The king apologizes to Your Ladyship that this matter has lain dormant for lo these many years, and it is with sincer'st regret that he does at this time require payment of your husband's loan.*

The crown wishes not to cause Your Ladyship any undue hardship, and realizes that the land the king generously granted Your Ladyship is but a humble plot. Therefor, the entyre sum shall not be payable immediately, but His Highness graciously grants you a year to repay the full am't.

Please send to Ruric's Keep at your earliest convenience the sum of fifteen thousand gold rurics, or the equivillent thereof in other coin of gold.

(signed) Herm, Prime Minister, for His Highness Ruric King of Hagenspan

Boole finished reading, and looked at Hollie dolefully. "That's the money Lord Roarke borrowed to buy your freedom, isn't it?"

"What else could it be?" She looked as if she wanted to say more, but her thoughts remained her own, and Boole did not want to force open doors best left closed.

"Didn't it ever get repaid?" he asked in disbelief. "It doesn't seem like Lord Roarke to have borrowed a sum and not settled up."

"Well, I *thought* it had been. It never occurred to me that it hadn't … it wasn't really my business." Another thought suggested itself to her, and she spoke it. "Maybe it *was* paid back, and Herm has somehow expunged the payment from the king's records, in order to create this new bit of trouble for me."

Boole had heard of Herm and the story of his possession by the dragon spirit. "But I thought he was, um, all right now—Herm, I mean? That after he got set free from the dragon's hold, he was just as sane as you or me, and he apologized to everybody and, uh, repented of his things that he, uh, that he did?" He grimaced, and said, "God, I sound like a blathering idiot. I fear I'm out of my depth here, my Lady."

Hollie gave him a squeeze, and said, "It's alright. I am, too."

"So," he said, after sitting in silence for a moment, "what are you going to do about it?"

"I don't know," she sighed. "Fifteen thousand rurics. We don't have that, not within ten thousand."

"No," Boole agreed. "That's a trouble."

She laid her head on his shoulder. Sometimes it was almost too much to ask of her to be a Lady, without a Lord at her side. Without a *man*, who could be strong and resolute for her, so that when she only wanted to cry, she could cry. Hess Boole sensed something of that need, and held her securely in his arms, not speaking for a few minutes.

"Did you want me to help you find an answer, or did you just want someone to share the news with?" he asked at last.

She considered his words. "If you have an idea, I'd like to hear it."

"Well," he said slowly, "there doesn't seem to be any way that we could raise fifteen thousand rurics, no matter what we did. If we sold every grain of wheat from the next five harvests, we probably couldn't do it."

"No."

"But you do still have friends—friends who owe you a debt of gratitude, even if it weren't for the love they bear you anyway."

"Esselte Smead."

"Yes, Smead, and the folks from Blythecairne too."

"Yes, I thought of that." He waited for her to continue. "I could probably ask them, and they would probably give it." A tear escaped her eye, and made a glistening path down across her cheek. "It almost feels like

I don't belong to myself any more. Like the freedom that was bought for me all those years ago has suddenly been revoked."

Boole said earnestly, "Let me ride to Thraill then, my Lady, and let me send a rider to Blythecairne, and we will make your case for you. Surely Master Smead and his counterpart at Blythecairne will know whether they paid the king or not! And if not, we will see how much they still love you, and we will purchase you back from the king again, so that you will belong to yourself alone!" He rested his bearded cheek against the top of her golden head. "Unless," he said more softly, "you would care to give yourself to one who has always loved you, so that you would belong to him." Lest she misunderstand, he clarified, "Me, that is."

She nestled in closer to him, her cheek against his chest, breathing in his honest man's scent. "Let me think for a day about sending riders to our friends. But whoever we send, it won't be you." She closed her eyes. "What would I ever do without you?"

He kissed her head, grateful for the words that were like sweet music to his soul. "Are you, ah…?" He was almost afraid to ask. "Are you ready now to give me your heart, dear one?"

She was silent for a long moment, and he almost thought that, at last, she was going to say yes. "Will you wait for me a little bit longer?" she whispered.

His heart sank then, and he could feel his face grow sad, a tangible sensation that both surprised and disappointed him. But for the sake of the one he loved, he forced his voice to be cheerful. Well, a little cheerful, anyway. "I've waited for you this long. Waited and served you and loved you. I guess another couple of days won't hurt too bad."

"I'm sorry, Hess," she said, hearing the fresh wounding in his voice despite his best effort to hide it. "Do you still want to kiss me?"

"Well, yes, I suppose so," he said, "if it's not too much trouble."

She slapped his arm. "Turn your head down here, you great oaf, and I will give you the best kiss you've had in fifteen years. Unless you've had a few that I'm not aware of."

"Not that I recall," he said with a sad smile, and though the kiss that followed was long and moist and tangled and soft, there was something about it that was more bittersweet than passionate.

Chapter Nine

Alan paused at the doorway to the chamber where his father rested, peering into the darkened room, trying to discern whether the old man was actually sleeping or merely lying awake in the dark. He wasn't sure what to say to his father—Sir Charles Poppleton the Worthy, Lord of Ester. They had never shared too many words together, and Alan hadn't spent very many days with him in more than a decade. He wasn't sure why King Ruric had given him the name "Worthy" when he had made him a knight, but he felt certain that his father was worthy enough in his way. But Charles Poppleton had never been particularly close to his son, concentrating on the affairs of his government instead, and leaving the raising of boys to others less profitably engaged. After a moment Alan heard a soft snore coming from within. He considered walking on to see if he could find his mother, but then stepped into his father's room and seated himself next to the sleeping man's bed.

He gazed at his father's face. A few white wispy threads of hair covered his scalp, and Alan wondered when it had gotten so thin. His father's hooked nose was as prominent as ever—no, more so—for his cheeks were sunken and withered and mottled with red. Even his eyebrows, which had been a flamboyantly snarled tangle of hairs, seemed less substantial, as if his father's whole face were somehow in retreat from the vibrant life that it once knew. Charles breathed through his mouth, and his jaw hung slack, revealing long yellowed teeth with several gaps where a decayed few had been extracted by the surgeon some years ago. Looking at his father, Alan felt sorrow, felt pity, searched his heart to see if he found *love* there ... hoped so. He bowed his head and listened to his father's gritty breathing.

Alan had never particularly resented Lord Poppleton's detachment from his son, for his father had things to do, important things, and Alan had plenty of studies to occupy his time, and friends and tutors and sisters and a mother to occupy his heart. Somewhere during the course of his youth, he and Brette had discovered each other, and they had been best friends for twenty years since. In fact, Alan felt a closer kinship with Brette's father Jerl than he did with his own, a fact that caused him to experience a pang of discomfort now.

He remembered his tutor Gavoreck, who had trained him in reading and counting and the little bit of medicine that he knew. He remembered Brison Cairl, the Captain of the Guard at Beedlesgate, the castle of Ester—Cairl had taught him the ways of warriors, of sword and spear and shield and bow. And he remembered sitting at a table with Brette and Jerl, learning how to drink beer while Jerl taught him magic tricks. If he had ever wished during those years that it had been his father who had been teaching him those things, he no longer recalled … though a part of him wished that it had been his father, now.

When he had been readying to leave with Brette for Solemon, intending to join in the battle against the last dragon, Lord Poppleton had stopped him, embraced him, his face wet with tears, and had told his son how very proud of him he was. Alan had been surprised at the time; in the insensitivity of his youth, he had not known that his father had held him in his heart, even though they spent but little time together. When he returned home to Ester after the dragon was finally dead, Lord Poppleton feasted his son and declared a holiday in his honor. Those had been happy days … but very shortly, the white-haired Lord and his son had run out of things to say to each other once again, and restless Alan departed for Thraill and then Beale's Keep to serve the Lady Hollie.

A decade had flashed by like an instant. Alan had attempted to fill part of the gaping void left by Owan Roarke's dead father—though not with the Lady Hollie, of course, who was quite devoted to Captain Boole. It had been widely assumed that Alan would someday wed young Jesi Tenet, and Alan had indeed wished for that to happen. When Jesi suddenly married Tayson Bost instead, though, he had been heartsick and humiliated. To cover his embarrassment, he threw himself even more headlong into his relationship with Owan, investing precious hours with him, training him earnestly and affectionately, being for young Owan Roarke everything that Charles Poppleton had not been for him.

Now, suddenly it seemed, years had passed, and his world was about to change forever: Alan was going to assume the Lordship of Ester. He hoped he would have enough time with his father for him to learn the things he would need to know. He wondered if Hallna Bennker would be a helpful aide … he wondered if Brison Cairl was still the Captain of the Guard. He wondered if somehow he would be able to thank his father for … something. He wasn't sure what. But he felt beholden to the old man for something, for the Lordship, for his very life perhaps. Because now, now that Alan was a man, now that his father was old, he desperately wanted to love him. To have some point of contact between the two of them that said, *You mattered to me.* Despite the proximity of the sleeping man, Alan suddenly felt quite alone.

The old man coughed, woke, smacked his lips and blinked in the dim gray light of the bedroom. Suddenly aware that someone was in the room with him, he turned his head, spied his son, and smiled. "Alan!" he said in a voice that sounded as weak as he looked. "You've come home. How I've missed you, my boy!"

Tears sprang to Alan's eyes. And he spoke words that he suddenly realized were very true: "I've missed you, too, Dad."

ξ

"You're off your game today, Buds," Joah commented with a quizzical look at his friend.

Owan ventured a sheepish glance back at his companion, and nodded. His marksmanship today had indeed been subpar. He thought he might make some comment about the feathers on his shaft not being trimmed properly, but he knew it was really his own listlessness that was causing him to miss the mark.

"What's wrong, anyway? You've been moping around for a month!"

Owan shrugged his sullen shoulders. Mustering a small spark of new determination, he said, "Here. I'll show you." And he drew back on his bow again to send an arrow hurtling through the air toward an apple sitting on the gnarled post of a distant fence. A fleeting caprice of wind caught the shaft at the last moment, though, and it scudded along the earth yards past its mark, coming to rest against a clod of dirt, its tail feathers suspended quivering in the air.

Joah whistled. "*That* showed me, all right! I couldn't even tell that that helpless apple was in danger, but you defended it, right and proper! There's probably a knighthood to be had for you." He gave his friend a playful shove. "What was it—a spider?"

Owan cursed, an adolescent mimicry of an adult soliloquy.

"Here, let me help you," Joah said, and proceeded to unleash an enthusiastic torrent of equally foul language. In a moment the two boys were chuckling at each other, jostling and pushing.

After Joah had exhausted his middling vocabulary of curses and oaths, he stole a curious look at his friend and tried to press his question again. "So," he asked, "*is* there something wrong?"

Owan grimaced and said, "Oh … you know. I guess I just miss Alan."

"Well … you've still got me and the boys," he said, meaning their other friends Windy and Tully.

"I know. It's just … well, Alan was the closest thing that I had to a father."

"Yeah, I know the two of you were real close. But there's still Hess Boole."

"That's what my mother said," Owan frowned. "Not the same, though."

Joah sat on the ground, plucked a blade of grass and placed it between his teeth, then stretched out on his back and watched the cottony clouds waft across the azure sky. "Seems to me," he said after a pause for thought, "that the father that you *did* have was a pretty good one. If you believe the tales, he was maybe the greatest man in the history of Hagenspan."

Owan sat and hugged his knees to his chest, the breeze riffling through his straw-colored hair. He closed his eyes, feeling suddenly weary, and let the sun warm his arms and face. "Maybe."

"Roarke the Dragon-Killer?" Joah demanded. "What more could you have hoped for?"

"What's that to me?" Owan said sourly. "If he'd been a farmer or a fisherman instead of a knight—" He stopped his thought mid-sentence.

"What?" Joah insisted. "If he'd been a farmer, then what?"

Owan glared at him, a flash of confused frustration blazing in his eyes. He shook his head, and shook it once again. He stood, gathered his bow, and began walking off toward the fence to collect their arrows.

Joah scrambled to his feet and jogged after him. "Hey, I'm sorry, Buds. I didn't know you felt that way. Not so much, anyway."

"You're an idiot," Owan grumbled.

"Yes, that's true," Joah agreed, and threw his arm around his friend.

Chapter Ten

Lord Charles Poppleton sat on a chair of stuffed deer-hide in the grassy courtyard at Beedlesgate. His arms and shoulders were wrapped in a shawl, and he was nodding drowsily in the summer sun. Alan, his son, was seated next to him, fending off a momentary ennui, patiently waiting for his father to reawaken and impart a few more scant words to him. Because his father's words were few and finite, they had become precious to him.

Lord Poppleton snored loudly, a startled snort, and woke back up again. He grinned sheepishly at his boy. "Can't seem to get warm enough," he rasped.

"Do you want another blanket?" Alan asked.

"No, no, that's alright," the old man demurred. He blinked up at the sky, trying to clear the fog from his eyes. "It's cloudy, is it?" he asked uncertainly.

"No … it's quite bright and clear." Alan looked at his father with concern.

"Heh! Don't worry about me, my boy. It's just sleep's covered my eyes and shivered my bones." His cheeks lifted in a smile again, making his hooked nose dip like the beak of a bird. "It's good to have you home."

Alan smiled hesitantly. "Yes. I'm glad I'm here, too."

The old man chuckled. "Later on, we'll have to go to my private den, and I'll show you my collection of treasures. They'll all be yours soon." He had just done this two days earlier, and it suddenly dawned on him that he probably had. "We've done that already, haven't we?"

"That's alright," Alan replied, "I'd be happy to see them again."

"Good, good," his father agreed. "Did you know I have a gemstone that Kenyan the Lord of the Fairies gave to the first Lord of Ester?"

"Amazing. What a treasure!" Alan said encouragingly.

"And, let's see … there's a short iron sword that was given to Finngal, your grandfather five times removed, by Sempal the king of the dwarfs. When Ruric Serpent's-Bane saw that piece, he coveted it for himself, and I barely was able to hang on to it. I never showed him Kenyan's jewel."

Alan nodded, politely feigning that he had never heard this story before.

"And, oh … there's a hide-covered shield that was carried by Karalog the Loud when he went to do battle with the dragon at the Cave of Mendor, and escaped with naught but his tunic and that shield. I may be the only one left in Hagenspan who knows that tale. Remind me to show that to you."

Alan nodded again. He looked up and noticed a dusty rider entering the gates to the courtyard.

"And of course there's the hauberk made of gold ringlets—just for show, of course. One of them was given to each of the Lords of Hagenspan by King Elken to celebrate the great wealth of his reign. He was—eh? What's this?"

The rider had drawn up to Alan and Lord Charles, and dismounted with a leap and a thud. "My Lord, forgive this intrusion. I am Tobia Oundland, one of the princeps of Thrimball; my father was cousin to Lord Bost, and my mother is sister to Lady Lillias."

"How very impressive," Charles Poppleton said, stroking his chin. "What brings such an honored guest to the gates of lowly Ester?"

His face reddening, Tobia Oundland bowed his head and said, "Forgive me, my Lord, if I sounded proud before you. I only wished to establish my credentials."

"Forgive *me*, young princeps," Charles said with a small laugh. "My own vanity is twice the sin of your pride, for it was me who wished to humble you. Forgive an old man his conceit, I beg you." Laying his wavering, blue-veined hand on Alan's knee, he continued, "And may I present to you my son, Alan, Lord Poppleton of Ester. I am merely his advisor now."

"Thank you, my Lord, you are kind," Tobia said. Turning his attention to Alan, he began, "Lord Poppleton, I bring word from Lord Bost of Thrimball. I have a delicate issue to discuss, regarding the succession to Lord Bost's throne."

"What is there to discuss?" Alan asked. "His heir is his son."

"That is the sad news that I have to impart," Tobia said with obvious regret. He glanced to the left and to the right, making sure that no ears could hear his words that were not attached to the heads of noblemen. "After a long illness, Lord Bost's only son Tayson has died—a result of injuries sustained when he was thrown from his horse. As you may know, Lord Bost has been particularly fruitful in producing daughters—but of sons, only the one." Tobia continued talking softly, but Alan lost track of his words. *Jesi Tenet was a widow!* Fighting to suppress thoughts of the dark-haired girl he had once loved, he forced himself to concentrate on the princeps' message.

Tobia was saying, "—of your kin who are of noble birth." He looked at Alan expectantly, and when Alan didn't answer, they both glanced uncomfortably at Charles Poppleton.

Charles looked curiously at his son, and said wryly, "Do you need me to translate for you, my boy?"

"Forgive me," said Alan, trying to mask his agitation. "Your report has, uh, taken me by surprise. Sad, very sad. Can you—can you repeat the last thing you said?"

Tobia Oundland drew a measured, disapproving breath, and recited his mission again. "After a long illness, Lord Bost's only son Tayson has died—a result of injuries sustained when he was thrown from his horse. As you may know, Lord Bost has been particularly fruitful in producing daughters—but of sons, only the one." Alan nodded; that was the part he had heard before.

The messenger continued: "Lord Bost has sent seven of the princeps out to the seven castles nearest Thrimball. In addition to receiving gifts to assuage the grief of the family during this time of great mourning, Lord Bost is also offering to give a gift of his own away—something most precious.

"A youth of noble birth from northwest Hagenspan is required by His Lordship to enter into the covenant of marriage with his oldest virgin daughter Bennita. In this way, even though Lord Bost no longer has a son, at least he may be assured that someone of his bloodline shall continue upon his seat. Applicants for this position of unique honor are urged to present themselves to Lord Bost at Thrimball at their earliest possible convenience. This message is hereby delivered to you, Lord Poppleton of Ester, and any of your kin who are of noble birth."

"I see," Alan replied solemnly. "I regret to tell you that, like Lord Bost, my father sired but one son, and I am already committed to the lordship of Ester. I, uh, I have some cousins, though. Would they suffice, if they are not yet wed?"

"I believe so," Tobia said, grateful that his mission would not prove entirely fruitless.

"Then," Alan said, "I shall send for them, however many of them are of suitable age and availability, and you may tell them your tale."

"Thank you, my Lord." He stood before the two Poppletons, waiting to be dismissed.

A faraway, cloudy look passed over Alan's face, and his father murmured, "The princeps waits."

"Oh, yes," Alan said. "Forgive me once again, sir. I fear that I have much to learn regarding the proper decorum for a Lord of Hagenspan."

"Not at all," Tobia lied diplomatically.

"May I ask—" Alan began uncertainly. "May I ask you a question?"

"Of course, my Lord."

"What is to become of the Lady Jesimonde, your Lord Tayson's wife?"

"That has not yet been determined, I understand. She may either live out her days as a widow in the house of Bost, or she may return to the house of her father. The Lady Jesimonde is one generation removed from proper nobility, I believe, or she may have been allowed to produce a son in surrogate for Lord Bost. As it is, though, she is of little use to him—not meaning to sound unkind."

"No, of course not," Alan murmured. He blinked, took a breath, and said, "Well! I shall send for my cousins, then. Find a largish man named Brison Cairl—he's the captain of our guard—and tell him I said to give you a meal and our best bed."

"Thank you, my Lord." Tobia Oundland bowed and led his horse away toward the stables.

Charles Poppleton regarded his son curiously.

ξ

Hess Boole knocked on the sill over the door to Owan's private chamber, and boomed, "Owan! A moment for a visitor?"

Owan was on his bed, staring at the ceiling, a discolored scrap of paper lying beside him. "Hiya, Boo," he said without inflection, not shifting his gaze.

"What's the matter, boyo? It's a grand day outside, and here you lay abed!" Owan shrugged noncommittally and didn't reply.

Boole stepped into the room, his face shadowed by a frown, and said, "Your mother is worried for you." He took two steps closer and said, "Is there aught that I can do for you? Something I could help you with?"

"I guess not."

Boole seated himself on the edge of Owan's bed, causing it to list heavily in his direction. "What's this you've got?" he said, making conversation, indicating the browned piece of paper.

"It's the letter my father sent me before he died," Owan replied expressionlessly.

"Ahh," Boole nodded gravely. "Your mother told me that you had such a thing. I've often wondered what it was he told you."

"Read it if you want."

"It would be an honor, if you don't mind."

"No." Owan sighed. "I don't mind, I guess."

"Then, with your permission." Boole picked up the fragment of paper, and began reading aloud:

To Owan Roarke, my son.

The greatest regret of my life is the fact that I was not able to spend more time with you. But I just want you to know that in the moments we spent together, you were loved, my boy. Listen to your mother and Master Smead, and wear your name proudly. I will be watching you and waiting for you in God's country.

Cedric Roarke

The letter had been dictated to Alan Poppleton the night before Roarke went to fight the dragon that ultimately killed him, and it had been signed with a flourish by Roarke himself. Captain Boole reverently laid it back down next to the boy. "Ah, that's a fine memento," he said. "Your father always had an agreeable way with words."

"I guess."

"I knew him well," Boole continued, wondering what might be the key to releasing the grip of the boy's iron-fisted melancholy. "Oh, not so well as your mother, perhaps, nor Master Smead, but somewhat better than most, I'd say."

Owan did not respond, but he did look at the big man's back, idly noticing the sunburned skin on the back of his neck peeking through his pale, thinning hair.

"I remember one time, back before Lord Roarke left seeking God's Words and came back with your mother. Back before I was Captain of Dawn Company, too. It was a harvest-time celebration we were having back at Thraill, with eating and dancing and fights and footraces. It was a grand time," Boole said wistfully. "There was nobles and knights from all the land roundabout, and they all come to Thraill to buffet each other and show off their skills with the bow and the sword, and to drink your father's beer.

"Well, the lads had them a contest to show who was the best swordsman, and, to shorten up the tale a bit, a great hulking brute named Parmalee of the Clenched Fist took the prize. He was from off toward Sarbo-town, someplace. Well, this Parmalee won the contest, as I said, and as your father was approaching him to give him his reward, old Clench-Fist was yelling great swelling words full of pride and boasting to the whole crowd, about how he was the greatest swordsman in the land, and other such nonsense. The crowd was cheering him on, and he was lapping it up like a cat at a saucer of cream, roaring out his swanks. Well, your father just presented him with his prize, smiling all benevolent-like, and congratulating him heartily and never telling him he was an idiot.

"Later that night, after the feasting was done, your father beckons to this Parmalee, and leads him out to the practice yard where the boys of Castle Thraill did all their training. No crowds around, though a few of the guards were there. I was, myself. Well, Lord Roarke and Parmalee starts sword-fighting, and don't you know? In about two minutes, Parmalee's sword was laying on the ground and he was rubbing his wrist, and his face was the color of a turnip. And your father just tells Parmalee something about a little humility being a good thing, and he makes all the boys who seen them fight promise to never tell about what had happened there. I never did, neither, not until now. That's the kind of a man your father was."

He patted Owan's leg affectionately. "The next day, Clench-Fist Parmalee was leaving the games, and the mob was still chanting his name, and he just ducked his head in shame. But your father stopped him, and shook his hand and clapped his shoulder, and yelled out to the crowd, 'Let's raise one more cheer for our champion!' And they did, a mighty swell, and Parmalee's about fit to bust out weeping by now, and Roarke just smiling at him, and I swear there wasn't anything but kindness in his smile. So then Parmalee yells out to the crowd, 'And let's have two cheers for Lord Roarke, who's a better man than me!' And so they did."

Boole fell silent for a moment. Owan could hear the drone of insects outside his window, the drowsy sound of bees among flowers. Somewhere in the distance a crow cawed. With a stifled groan, Boole rose from the bed, straightened, and stretched. "There's chores waiting for me, I expect. Better go earn my meat." He towered above Owan, seeming to fill the entire room, and smiled down at the boy. "If you ever want someone to talk to, just come and find me."

"Thanks," said Owan, and the captain turned to leave. "Boo?"

"Aye?" He turned back to the boy.

Owan searched for a word to say, and found nothing to express exactly what he was feeling. "Thanks."

"Any time."

Chapter Eleven

Ruric Serpent's-Bane, the father and glory of all Hagenspan, woke from a pleasant dream. He had been waging war single-handedly against a giant leathery bat that breathed fire, which swooped down upon him time after time only to be gutted by the sword held in the king's mighty right arm. As the acid blood dripped down upon Ruric's flesh, scalding him, purifying him, his limbs turned to burnished gold and he grew in stature until he filled the sky. The bat quailed before him, and he suddenly realized that it was not a bat—it was the dragon, the last dragon of Hagenspan. As the dragon fled the king's wrath, seeking a cleft in the rocks in which to hide itself, Ruric brought down a huge golden foot upon its neck. Suddenly the neck he was standing on became the back of a whale, and he was riding along on the crest of the waves, feeling the cold salt spray pelting him in the face like the salty kisses of beautiful maidens. He laughed, and the sound of his mirth echoed off the mountains, and all the people of Hagenspan laughed for joy to hear him.

"Are you all right, dear?" said a white-haired, wrinkled old crone, who looked at him with pity raining anxiously like autumn from her gaze. "You were whimpering in your sleep."

"What happened to the whale?" Ruric croaked.

Maygret's breath caught in her throat for a confused moment; then she said, "What?"

"Damnation, woman! You know what I mean! Where's the bat?" Ruric cried in a febrile voice.

"I don't understand." She shook her head and looked helplessly at Herm, who was standing beside the king's velvet couch.

"Herm!" the king cried, recognizing his Prime Minister and friend. "You're looking well."

"Thank you, Your Majesty," Herm replied in a voice smooth as silk. "You are very kind."

"Who's that woman?" the king whispered hoarsely, even though Maygret still sat at his side. "Is it your mother?"

"No, Your Majesty," Herm answered quickly, almost before the queen could feel the sting of the verbal wound. "This is the greatest friend your kingdom has ever had, the lovely Maygret, daughter of the Feie, who has graced fair Hagenspan as her queen for all the long days of your glorious reign."

"Maygret," the king smiled. "We remember her, just a lass, with all of the fire and fury spitting out of her like a thundercloud. God, what a beauty she was." He paused a moment to consider the implications of what he had said, and then turned his eyes to look at the elderly woman. "Are these Maygret's eyes looking back at us?"

The queen held his gaze, as her eyes pooled with tears. "Forgive me, Your Highness," she whispered.

"What has become of your face?" Ruric asked in wonder, and then, finally, he understood once again. "Oh." In a voice blunted and gray, he apologized—not the apology of a king, but of a man. "Forgive *me*, my dear queen." He wanted to say that he was sorry, that he loved her, that he regretted leaving her alone while he was away riding the waves of the sea on the backs of whales. But even if he had been able to summon the words, he could not have uttered them, not while Herm was standing over them. "We dreamed we were strong," he whispered to her confidentially. "We dreamed we filled the sky."

ξ

Alan sat upon his father's leather-appointed throne, shifting his weight from this side to that, trying to find a position that was comfortable; his rear end was still slightly sore from the long ride home from Beale's Keep. He would be adjudicating the complaints of the citizens of Ester for the first time this afternoon, and—though his father would be close at hand to advise him—he was just about terrified at the prospect of passing judgment on things about which he knew practically nothing.

A voice came from the foyer of the great hall. "It looks like the seat fits you just fine, my Lord." The speaker was hidden in shadows, but there was none that it could have been save Brette.

"Come in, my friend," Alan commanded. "I've missed you lately." Most of Alan's time recently had been consumed learning the things his father and advisors needed to teach him, or sitting with his mother, regaling her with the adventures he had had, or listening patiently as old Lord Poppleton showed him things that didn't seem to matter at all, but were somehow important for him to share. In any case, he had not had much time for his friend Brette, who had probably been catching up with his own family, Alan hoped.

"I am yours to command, my Lord," Brette said with a sweeping bow and a smirk.

"Yes, you are," Alan smiled back. Sobering, he continued, "I do have a charge for you, if you'll take it. I won't force it upon you. But there's none else that I'd trust with this task."

"You intrigue me," Brette said.

Alan took a heavy ring from where it hung on a silver chain about his neck. "Ride, if you will, to Castle Thraill, and see how it stands with Jesi Tenet. Tell her that I am Lord in Ester, and that I require a bride—" here he reddened, "—and that it would fulfill my fondest wish if it should be she." Something about the construction of that sentence sounded wrong. "If it should be her. She. Well, say it however it sounds right."

Brette hesitated, did not extend his hand for the ring. "May I speak openly?" he asked.

"Always, unless the etiquette of court proscribes it."

He chose his words carefully. "I know you have loved the Lady Jesimonde, for … for a long time," he began, his eyes troubled. "But, Alan … she's no virgin. How will that sit with your father? Your mother? Bennker? Cairl? The priest?—I've forgotten his name."

"It's Fuller," Alan said, referring to the man sent from the Amendicarii to Ester. "And I don't know what they'll think. And for all I know, she'll refuse me anyway. But … this is the rest of my life we're talking about. These are the only days I'll ever have to live in, as far as I know. Who could I possibly want at my side for all those long years … but Jesi?"

Brette frowned. "Surely one of the virgins of Ester would serve you better, my Lord—one chaste and gentle and white as a lily. Jesi Tenet and you … you've always been a bit like fire and water, you know. Lightning and thunder."

Alan looked at his friend, frustrated but not angry. "Of course … what you say is probably true." Brette was only looking out for Alan's best interests; he would make a fine counselor. "Will you take this charge?"

"What if she has a child already?" Brette asked.

"She must not," Alan said thoughtfully. "Otherwise, they wouldn't have sent out the princeps advertising for an heir. I suppose she could have had a daughter." At that disagreeable thought, Alan frowned. "If she has already borne a child, then you are released from your duty." He extended the chain to his friend, with the ring dangling, spinning, its jewel glittering in the faint light of the hall. "Will you take this charge?"

Brette looked into Alan's eyes for a long moment, and then said, "If I may be permitted to pray that she turns you down."

"You may," Alan agreed. "And I will pray that she does not, to balance you out. Then we will see which way the winds of Providence blow."

Brette reached out and snatched the ring from Alan's hand. "I love you, you know. Even if you are a fool."

"Fools like me need friends like you. Need them badly," Alan said with a grim smile. "Thank you."

"Hmmp," Brette snorted. "What if she says yes? Then your troubles will have just begun."

"Yes, you're probably right," said Alan, Lord Poppleton of Ester. "So ride. Ride like the wind for Thraill! Before I change my mind."

"At your word, my Lord." Brette snapped off a brisk salute. Then he turned and strode from the hall. Alan shifted his weight on the leather chair, trying to find a position that was not *too* vexing for his bottom.

Chapter Twelve

Lady Hollie studied the walls of her judgment hall, noticing with approval where her masons had plastered over the crumbling stones. The walls of Beale's Keep had been cracked and collapsing when she had inherited them, fractured by the irritable thrashings of the dragon that had dwelt there for a hundred mouldering years. The room was the largest in the Keep, with only the dining hall to rival it, and it was here that the dragon had apparently inhabited during the greater part of her fitful slumber. When Hollie had taken her first torch-lit glimpse into this room over a decade ago, she had found the throne of ancient Lord Beale splintered and fouled by the serpent, fit for little more than kindling. She had had Yeskie, the craftsman who had traveled from Blythecairne to join her, make a stout table of oak for the judgment hall, after the fashion of the one her late husband had commissioned for Blythecairne. Yeskie had worked some of the wood of the old Lord's throne into the table's design, too, out of respect for the dead, in case his ghost should have some opinion about the new inhabitants of his Keep. It was a piece of singular beauty, the last work of its kind that old Yeskie was destined to shape. Hollie ran her fingers over the aged wood now, remembering white-haired Yeskie and wondering about Beale's ghost.

"My Lady—may we enter?" Hess Boole was standing in the doorway, and behind him were the messengers he had chosen to carry her letters to Blythecairne and Thraill, the two provinces formerly ruled by her husband.

"Yes, Captain Boole, please do," she replied, and was rewarded with a smile and a wink from the big man. Entering behind him, oblivious to the wink, were two guards: Kelly, a slender, quiet man who had come from Thraill, and a somewhat younger man—a large, clumsy fellow of an irrepressible good nature with the unlikely name of Feather. "Be seated, gentlemen."

The three sat across the table from Hollie. She began, "Has Captain Boole informed you of the task for which you have been chosen?"

Kelly shook his head solemnly, and Feather said, "No, my Lady," in a voice mixed with bewilderment, curiosity, and pleasure. He had never been chosen for an assignment of any particular importance before.

"Part of the reason you boys were picked," Boole interjected, "is that you're both men without wives. This chore you're elected to, it'll take some good bit of travel. You may be away for several weeks."

"Will we be traveling together?" Feather asked hopefully.

"There shouldn't be any danger," Hollie said softly. "And it's a matter of some delicacy. If you are brave enough to risk it, I would like you to go separately, one to Thraill and one to Blythecairne." She looked at each one of the young men intently, and it seemed that they drew courage from her gaze.

"At your word, my Lady," Feather said, embarrassed for fear that he might be thought a coward.

Kelly asked, "Can I take my dog, Captain?"

"I don't see any harm," Boole replied, looking at Hollie, and she nodded in agreement.

"Thank you," Kelly said. "May I ask what our assignment is to be?"

Hollie nodded again, and drew two letters from her sleeve. "There are two messages I need to have delivered. I will read one of them to you, so that you understand the gravity of your mission, and then I will seal them and entrust them to your care."

Unrolling the crackling paper, she began to read.

To Master Keet, Steward and Lord at Blythecairne:

You once said that, should I ever encounter any great need, the resources of Blythecairne would be at my disposal. I regret to inform you, that day has come.

King Ruric of Hagenspan has demanded of me repayment of a loan he once made to my husband, your Lord Cedric Roarke. It is in my heart that this payment may actually have been made long ago, but it seems no record of it exists. It would seem fruitless to argue the point, since it is Herm his minister who bargains for the king, and Herm bears me no goodwill.

The total sum due is fifteen thousand rurics. Beale's Keep shall contribute three thousand, which will tax our treasury sore. I am asking if, out of your great kindness, you might contribute six thousand, and I am asking Lord Smead of Thraill if he might contribute six thousand as well. Beale's Keep would be willing to repay your kindness with a yearly tribute from our land's increase, if that should be agreeable to Your Lordship.

Eagerly awaiting your reply,

Hollie, Lady of Beale's Keep, and once Lady at Blythecairne

She concluded, "The other letter is identical, except for changing the Blythecairnes for the Thraills, and the Smeads for the Keets." She rolled the missive back into a cylinder, and put a small pan of wax over the flame of a candle to melt it for sealing. "Do you understand why haste and discretion is required of you?"

Kelly nodded grimly. Feather was bursting with questions, but he observed Kelly's silent acceptance of his mission, and decided to keep still.

He nodded too, and blurted, "Yes, my Lady." He could ask Kelly his questions later, if they had time before they left.

Hollie dribbled the melted wax over the edge of the letter she had read, then pressed a seal into the brownish glop and held it there for a moment as it cooled. She handed that letter solemnly to Feather, and then repeated the process with the other message, which she handed to Kelly. "Captain Boole, will you see that our two friends are properly outfitted for their task?"

"Of course, my Lady."

"Then, go," she said, rising to her feet. "Go, with God's speed, and may He be your covering as well."

The two messengers bowed their heads, mumbled their thanks, and turned to go.

"I'll be with you in just a flick of a tail, lads," Boole said.

Hollie shot an uncomfortable look at him, waited until the men were out of earshot, and said, "Do you think we should send a couple of more men with them?"

"Why?" Boole said, slipping an arm around her waist.

She allowed him to draw her near, but said, "Don't you think there might be danger for them?"

Kissing her quickly on a rose-colored cheek, he said, "What danger? They've been out in the woods a time or two before."

"Yes, but—" she grimaced. "It's Herm. It's Herm. There's something I don't trust. I can't explain it. But there's still something wrong with him."

"You mean the spirit of the dragon? But I thought Sir Willum drove that out of him."

"I know." She rested her face against his chest. "Maybe he's just bad. Why else would he have written that letter in King Ruric's name?"

He patted her shoulder comfortingly. "I'll tell the lads to keep an eye peeled for trouble. Maybe there's another dog we can send along with Feather, to keep watch for him."

"That would be good."

Captain Boole stayed a moment longer, cherishing her woman's softness wrapped within his arms. He thought he should be releasing her and following the young men to the storehouse to get them equipped for their journey, but then he reconsidered, deciding to linger in the moment for as long as he could draw it out.

"Hess," Hollie murmured, "people will begin to talk."

"Well, it's about time. People ought to be talking," he said, a faint smile gracing his swarthy face. "Who's to say they ain't already talking?"

"Get you gone, Captain Boole," she commanded with mock sternness, as she disentangled herself from his embrace. Softening, she said, "Come back to me after you've seen them off. Bring me tea. Bring some beer for yourself."

"At your command, my Lady." He saluted, wheeled, and strode from the room, starting to sing a bawdy song he had learned recently from a traveling bard.

Hollie thought about calling after him and ordering him to stop singing. Instead she just smiled and shook her head.

Chapter Thirteen

It had been several years since Brette had been to Castle Thraill, but the familiar sights and sounds of the little community around the castle grounds made him feel almost as if he were coming home again, much the same as he had felt a few short weeks ago when he had actually *been* returning home.

He nodded and tipped his cap to a bare-armed woman who was seated on her stoop, sweating over her butter churn, and he greeted several urchin children who ran up to watch him, slack-jawed, as he passed by on his horse. He turned from the village and made his way through the long grainfields that led to the castle itself, stopping once to exchange tidings with a small knot of farmers who were lazing away the afternoon, hiding from their wives. In a short time he came to the clearing in front of the main gate to the castle, where he was greeted by a guard he did not recognize, who had flowing dark hair and a smooth-shaven jaw.

"Halt and dismount, rider, if you please," said the man, and Brette had the impression that it was an order, not a request.

"Certainly," Brette said, and did so.

"State your name and your business," he said crisply, and something about the way he said it suggested that he resented his duty, or disdained his guest, or felt otherwise disagreeable about something.

"Brette, son of Jerl, from Beedlesgate Castle. I bring news from Ester in the land of Fennal, and I seek audience with Lord Smead. My business is that of Lord Poppleton of Ester, and I will reserve the details for the ears of Lord Smead."

"You've a sharp tongue in your head, haven't you?" said the other. "Well, you don't pass this gate unless you've been granted leave by Bascan."

"Castle Thraill used to be a friendlier place," Brette said, annoyed. "Who is this Bascan?"

"Bascan is me," said the longhaired man, "and I am the Captain of the Guard for Day Company. As to whether this used to be a friendlier place, I'll not hazard a guess. But it is what it is, and my word is my word."

"Why should a Captain of the Guard be standing watch at the gate like a common peon?" Brette wondered.

"I know not how it was in the friendlier day you claim to remember!" Bascan retorted. "But in this day, the six captains all share each of the tasks of their charges, whether they be stately or base." He took a long, scornful look at Brette. "Whether you are a friend to Lord Smead, or just a wandering saddle-bum, we shall see. For the moment, unless you can prove yourself to my satisfaction, I believe I will turn you away."

"Captain Bascan!" came a voice from within the gates, which was quickly shown to belong to a shuffling snowy-haired man. "Do not treat our guests so rudely, I pray you." Brette tried for a moment to identify the voice, which was familiar to him in the sense that one recalls the misty details of a dream, and then realized that the white-haired man approaching him was Haldamar Tenet, father of Piper and Jesi. "You're Brette, unless I miss my mark—the friend of young Poppleton."

"Yes, sir," Brette said, enthusiastically grasping the older man's hand. "I am happy to see you again!"

"And I you, my boy," Haldamar smiled. "Let's see—the last time I heard, you were with Hollie at Beale's Keep. Is that where you've come from?"

"No, sir. Lord Charles has stepped to the side in Ester, and called Alan home to assume the lordship. That's where I've been."

"So that must be the news that you bring! Well, come in, and we'll go to old Smead and let him know."

"Master Tenet," Bascan began sternly, "I have not—"

"Tush, boy," Haldamar dismissed him. "Toss us in the brig if you will, and then let Smead know where we are." He began leading Brette away.

Brette caught Bascan's eye and nodded grimly, silently casting him a shredded scrap of self-respect, then followed Haldamar Tenet within the gates.

"Actually, sir, my reason for coming to Thraill involves a member of your own family."

"Oh? Which one?"

"I've come with condolences for the Lady Jesimonde, if she's here. Otherwise, I'll just pay my respects to you and the Lady Paipaerria and Lord Smead, and then continue on to Thrimball."

"No need. She's here, while she decides what to do next with her life." Haldamar Tenet cocked a bushy white brow at the younger man. "It seems that your pity should have been delivered to Thrimball right from the beginning, though, if you wanted to console old Lord Bost for the loss of his only son."

Brette's voice dropped to a subdued tenor as he said, "Well, sir, what I've come bearing isn't so much consolation as it is proposition."

"Hmm." Haldamar strode thoughtfully across the courtyard toward the stacked stones surrounding the entry of the castle itself. Before he neared the doors, though, he paused under the balcony window of his daughter Piper. "Let me tell you something, Master Brette."

"Sir?"

"This spot we're standing on … it's where young Sir Will used to throw pebbles up at my daughter's terrace, to get her attention in the dark of the night. She used to steal down the stairs as quiet as a shadow, to meet her beloved and share a few lonely moments in the garden, and maybe a kiss or two. Then … then he off and got killed by the dragon, like so many good boys did, and he left my little girl a widow. Oh, they were never married, I know, but Piper gave her heart to Sir Will, as sure as she's still barren as a wall today." Haldamar sighed. "It's a rare day when she smiles.

"Now, Jesi, she's always been a spirited girl … but you know that, I expect. I always rather supposed she'd marry your Alan, and I expect that's what you're here for now. But she didn't do that, no. She off and married Tayson Bost, who was a beautiful boy, just beautiful, but vain as a peacock, and no horseman either. So he gets throwed by a horse that was just too much for him, and now she's a widow too.

"Two widows, and both of them not a day over thirty." He paused to peer at Brette. "I don't know why I told you all that, except to let you know that they've both known some tears. And that they're not too liable to be the answer you're looking for, unless you're as gentle as a moth with them. Or maybe I don't know what I'm talking about. Is that what you come for, or not?"

Brette drew a slow breath, and then answered, "Lord Poppleton—Alan, that is—has got it in his heart that he won't be happy with anyone but Jesi. I tried to tell him … well, I advised him against it. But he insisted that I come and at least ask."

Haldamar Tenet nodded. He assumed a faraway look, as if he were hearing the whispers of something spoken long ago, and he said softly, "You have to at least ask, don't you? Otherwise … you'd never know. And you'd always wonder. Asking is better, even if you turn out to be a fool for it."

Brette didn't understand, but he nodded anyway. He wondered who Haldamar Tenet had asked, and what it was he had asked for. But before he had a chance to ask, Haldamar said, "Well, come on. Let me show you to Smead."

ξ

Esselte Smead sat on a large couch, and he covered most of it. His already impressive bulk had more than doubled in the several years since Brette had last seen him. "Pardon me for not rising," he puffed, "but it's something of a hardship for me." He peered dimly at his guest. "Who is this, Hal? He has the look of someone I should recall."

"This is young Brette from Ester; you remember—Alan Poppleton's friend."

Brette knelt before Smead and took his hand, saying, "I'm honored to see you again, my Lord."

"Nonsense," Smead said, pleased. "A swollen old bag who can scarcely see."

Brette could think of no way to respond to that, so he remained silent, knee bowed before the old steward of Thraill, who had been made Lord upon the death of Cedric Roarke.

"Well, get up," Smead commanded happily. "Draw up that chair, and tell me your news."

Brette told him of Alan's assuming the lordship of Ester at his father's insistence. He mentioned that Alan had sent him north to Thraill in order to offer his sympathies to Jesi Tenet. If Smead deduced anything deeper than that, he made no mention; he was eager to hear the stories of Brette's time at Beale's Keep, being especially interested in the welfare of the Lady Hollie. Brette assured him that she was healthy and happy, and was much loved by the people of County Temter, which he absorbed with a satisfied nod.

When Brette finished his narrative, Lord Smead looked in his direction thoughtfully. "You know ... you may be an answer to my prayers, young man."

"My Lord?" Brette did not wish to be the answer to anyone's prayers—he just wanted to return home again—but he liked and respected Esselte Smead.

"I am dying, Master Brette."

Haldamar Tenet started to say something in protest, but Smead continued, "It's true, Hal, and we both know it. We always knew it would happen someday, and there's no harm in acknowledging it when it's on its way." Haldamar frowned, but made no more objections.

"As I was saying, young man, the days that remain to me are but few. I wouldn't want you to think that I grew this round just by eating! No … there's something wrong with my body that's beyond my control. Something growing inside me, choking me off, stealing my wind." As if to punctuate that statement, Smead panted for a moment, a ragged wheeze. He mopped his brow and continued. "I need to break a promise. And I need someone I can trust to deliver that broken promise for me."

Brette shook his head faintly and smiled with concern. "I'm afraid I don't understand."

"Can you write?"

"Yes, my Lord."

"Then I will dictate some words to you, and you shall write. Haldamar, you stay and be witness to these words."

ξ

Once, many years ago, Brette had been present when a dying man had dictated two letters—one to Hollie and one to Owan. Only that time, the dying man had been Lord Cedric Roarke, who was going to face the dragon the next morning in the shattered town of Solemon, and the setting for the recitation had been a cheerless night in the hollow of an open field, not the sweaty cloister of a red-faced, gasping old man. And the one who was the scribe for those long-ago messages had not been Brette, but his friend Alan—Brette had only been an onlooker to that bleak transaction. But as Smead began speaking, saying, "First— to Lady Hollie Roarke," the memory of that day swept over him so eerily that he shivered.

"Let me know if I'm going too quickly for you," Smead wheezed, and Brette nodded his understanding. "All right, then. Write this: I promised your husband Lord Roarke that, upon my death, the lordship of the lands of Thraill would pass to Owan Roarke, his son and yours. I find now that the span of my days is not going to be as great as I hoped, and Owan—who has not visited these holdings for many years—is not yet of an age to rule this people. Additionally, he is not at this time able to dwell here at Thraill, being bound to you, his mother, who must needs tend Beale's Keep." He stopped for a moment to catch his breath, and order his thoughts. "For these reasons and more, I am reneging on the word that I gave Lord Roarke … but only for a time. Upon my passing, the lordship of Thraill shall be granted to—" he paused, as if to make absolutely certain of his decision, "—Owan's cousin, the Lady Paipaerria Tenet."

Haldamar blurted something in surprise, and Brette stopped writing, the quill poised hesitantly above the parchment. Smead held up his hand, and said, "Write it down, Master Brette. I've prayed much over this matter, and I'm decided. Write: —the Lady Paipaerria Tenet, who must leave the lordship to Owan upon her own passing, or at such time as she should choose to surrender the province of her own will." A fit of coughing overtook him then, and he hacked and choked for nearly a full minute, until tears streamed down his crimson cheeks. Finally he raised a jeweled goblet to his lips and expelled a blackish clot of mucus and blood into it.

Feebly he said to Brette and Haldamar, who were looking on in horror and pity, "As I say … there may not be much … time left."

Brette said sadly, "Is there nothing that can be done for you, Lord Smead?" The bloated man smiled weakly, and said, "I will tell you in a moment. First, make a second copy of that letter ... except change it so it's fit to be sent to Piper instead of Hollie." As Brette began that task, Smead sighed, "I had thought to say more ... but it takes so much wind." The only sound for the next few moments was the scratching of the quill against the page, and finally Brette signaled that both copies were complete. "Let me sign them, my boy," Smead rasped, "and then the two of you sign them as well, as witnesses."

After the three men had made their marks upon the pages, Smead said to Brette, "Now, one final duty you can render to me."

"Anything, my Lord," Brette said, without stopping to consider what that might mean.

"You may offer your sympathy to poor Jesi, as you have been charged by Lord Poppleton," Smead said, his eyes closed against a spasm of pain, "and then, allow me to impose upon you for a month of your time."

Brette swallowed, and said, "Yes, my Lord."

"Deliver that letter to the Lady Hollie for me ... and tell her all the things I meant to write, but didn't have the breath for."

"My Lord?"

Smead opened his eyes, smiled softly past the ache of his body, and whispered, "You've seen her. You must know what I mean."

Like a flash of epiphany, Brette thought he understood. "You love her."

"Of course, my boy." The faint thread of a smile still played upon his lips. "Don't we all?"

Brette glanced at Haldamar Tenet, who was silently studying something on the floor. He said, "Lord Smead, it would be an honor for me to deliver your message."

Chapter Fourteen

The sun blazed down upon Owan's face, and the gusts of wind felt as if they were flaring forth from some forge or furnace, or maybe from Hell itself. He walked past sunburned field workers who were wincing in anguish from their heat-intensified labors, their tunics soaked through, wringing wet, their eyes squinting against the stinging rivers of sweat that flowed from their foreheads. As he acknowledged their croaked greetings—"Good day, young Lord"—he pitied them for their pains, and vowed to do something, someday, to make their labors less stressful, if he remembered.

Right now he was headed to meet Tully and Windy and Joah at a place where there was a bend in the stream that was overhung by three stout willows, making a shady pool for swimming and fishing. The other three had been there all morning, Owan supposed, but he had had studies to complete, and his mother had not released him until he had put the last touches upon them, even though the room where he received his lessons was oppressive and airless, and neither Owan nor his teacher wished to be there. "The price for privilege," his mother had scolded, though, and so he had learned logic and jurisprudence and the history of the kings of Hagenspan, and old Dreo (his tutor) had not allowed him to leave until he had recited the whole lineage of Hagenspan's monarchs, right from Hagen all the way up to Ruric the Third. This took longer than it should have, because Owan always seemed to forget Tamdar son of Elken, who was king for only one day, almost a hundred years ago. Why he should have to remember Tamdar, Owan did not know, but Dreo insisted, and suggested there was a lesson of some kind to be learned there, but Owan had not yet grasped its significance.

He drew near the creek, and craned his neck, straining to locate his friends. Probably they had spied him coming, and had secreted themselves in the tall grass or behind the tree-trunks, waiting to leap out at him in mock attack. It was a game the boys often played, pretending they were defending Beale's Keep against foreign raiders like the Va-Keen, or some other enemy indigenous to Hagenspan, like the trolls that had been subdued by King Kender of the Far Sight, generations ago. Owan had learned about the War of the Trolls from Dreo, and had shared that terribly interesting information with his three friends; since then, they had been fighting trolls for most of the summer.

He felt like calling out for the boys to show themselves. There was something eerie and a little bit frightening about being watched by invisible eyes, even if he knew they belonged to his friends. But he refused the urge to acknowledge his fear, and hoped that he looked relaxed and casual as he walked. His nerves tingled with the anticipation of his friends springing out upon him with a whoop, and he hoped he wouldn't do anything embarrassing. He felt a sudden urge to urinate.

A dozen trudging steps later he was among the trees, still expecting to be startled, but perplexed a bit that his comrades had held their silence so completely. He looked up into the shadowed branches, peered around behind the trunks, and felt his previous exhilaration being replaced by the dull throb of disappointment, like the slow deflating of a balloon. "Joah?" His voice sounded very small. The only answer was the gurgle of the stream, and he realized that he was alone.

There were signs of the boys having been there earlier in the day: trampled grass, an apple core, a broken bough where one of them had probably tried to hang out over the water. *Windy*, Owan thought—he was always doing something too marvelously stupid to succeed. He felt no bitterness toward Windy; he just wished he had been there to see it. A momentary flicker of resentment against his mother and Dreo tried to flare up, but Owan squelched it. He picked up a rounded gray rock, and tossed it into the water with a *plunk*. He did it again without enthusiasm, looked around for another rock, saw one, but didn't bother.

He slumped to the earth, drawing his slender legs up against his chest and resting his back against the cleft trunk of one of the willows. He stared vacantly at the wrinkled water of the creek, idly watching the blinding light dance its hypnotic spell across the glittering swells. A wordless, impotent dissatisfaction filled him. Somewhere beyond the periphery of his thought, he gradually became aware of the droning of insects, felt an ant crawling across his ankle, a bead of sweat trickling down from his temple. Drowsy and discontented, he nevertheless fought the seduction of sleep. He blinked his eyes several times, trying to make them focus.

The cool water splished against his feet. On a whim, he spoke.

"Alan used to tell me tales, back when I was a boy," he said to the stream. "He told me that there were once spirits that lived right in the waters, that nurtured them and everything that lived in them. Beautiful fairy spirits—lasses that would steal the wind right out of your breast, they were so lovely." He paused a moment to see if there would be any response, but if the burbling of the creek were the speech of some nymphlin tongue, he could not interpret it. "If there's one of you living there now, in this stream, I'd be obliged if you'd show yourself to me. I'm a mite sad, you see, and it would cheer me ever so much to see a beautiful fairy lass." He waited another long moment, his eyes straining to see if any of the brilliant diamonds of reflected light began to coalesce into any other form. He almost thought they did once or twice.

"I am Owan Roarke, son of the Lady Hollie Roarke who is ruler of this land, and I command you to appear." The water danced on, the sunlight shining off the ripples like laughter. "Please?" He waited again, and for a moment more, suffering another swell of disappointment, though he wondered what he had expected anyway.

"You probably weren't really real," he said sullenly. "It was probably just a story." He picked up a twig and pitched it angrily toward the water, but some caprice of the breeze caught it, and it fell short of its goal, mocking him.

"*You* probably aren't real either," he said to God, and he ducked his head unconsciously, reflexively. When there was no answer—no thunder, no whisper, no word—he dared to continue. "My mother believes You're there. And so does Aron." *Boo doesn't, I think*, thought Owan, though he didn't say it aloud. "But she's a woman. And so is he, practically. What do *they* know about—" and then he couldn't think of what it might be that they didn't know anything about, so he let the question hang in the air.

"All I can think is, if You're real, You're not near as nice as Aron wants me to think You are. He says You created all this whole world, and it all belongs to You. Well, what I'm thinking is, if it all belongs to You, why don't You take care of it a little better then? Why do You have to let good men die fighting Your enemies, instead of just coming down and fighting them Yourself? Or maybe You're not as powerful as Aron says, either. Maybe You *need* men like my father to do Your business, because You can't do it on Your own." Owan wanted to curse, but he couldn't quite bring himself to curse toward God, even if he didn't believe He was there. "And in the end, You had to have a *woman* do Your work," he blurted, immediately feeling a guilty pang of shame that he was showing disrespect to his mother. "If You were just going to kill my father—not to mention all those other men—why didn't You just send my mother *first*?" His eyes grew hot with tears, and he said defiantly, "So that's why I don't think You're real, no more real than the fairies. Or maybe You were once, and now You're gone ... like the fairies." The muscles of Owan's face felt strange, unnaturally strained from the contortion of his frown. "Damn," he said in a softer voice, and reflexively ducked his head again.

"I'm sorry," he said a moment later, and he was no longer talking to God, but to his father. "I—" He had so many things to say to his father, or so he thought, but his heart was too full to shape them into words. "I'm sorry," he whispered, and began to cry softly, his tears pouring forth like the stream he sat beside ... weeping like the willow that sheltered him there.

After a time, he became quiet, still. He rested his forehead against the arm draped across his knees, and sat listening to the splashing of the water.

A breeze caressed his shoulder like the touch of a hand, like the touch of his father's hand. Owan reached up to grasp it, but it was gone.

Chapter Fifteen

Brette heard the low growl as he neared the trees, and reached for his blade. He didn't know what kind of threat was announcing itself—a wolf? —a bear? He had a sudden and irrational fear that it was the dragon, the great and terrible dragon that had been killed by the Lady Hollie, back from the dead to wreak its vengeance upon those it had left behind. Brette had been one of those; he had known the terror of cringing on the ground while the fearsome serpent towered overhead, screaming its rage. His hand trembled upon the haft of his sword now at the remembering, and his cheeks reddened with shame. He silently slid the sword from its sheath, and readied to meet this new challenge.

"Steady, Pup," a voice spoke its low command to the growling animal hidden behind the trees, and then in a louder voice said, "Are you friend or foe?"

"Friend to many, and foe to a few," Brette said guardedly. "Why do you hide yourself in the wood?"

"Aren't you Brette? Poppleton's companion?" Kelly stepped out of the trees, holding his own sword cautiously before him. A bristling black dog stood at his knee, continuing to rumble a low warning. "Forgive me for this rudeness, but I am on a mission of, ah, some delicacy, and there may be those who would wish to hinder me."

"Why, Kelly, you've known me for years," Brette said in an injured tone. "I've served the same mistress you have for most of my adult life!"

"I know," Kelly said, and the tip of his sword wavered, but he did not immediately lower it. "The question is, would you serve her still?"

"Of course!" Brette replied, hoping suddenly that that was the correct answer. What was going on here, anyway? "I'd still be living at

Beale's Keep myself, if it wasn't that Alan was called back to assume the lordship."

"Well, what are you doing out here, then, riding this dark path alone so far from Beedlesgate?"

"Fair enough," Brette acceded. "The truth is, I'm on my way to the Lady Hollie with a message from Lord Smead of Thraill. It's a matter of some delicacy on my part, too, now that I think about it." He slid his sword back into its sheath, hoping to show Kelly that he meant him no harm. "And—now that I think about it—what brings *you* out all alone on this lonely road so far from home?"

"Well ... I carry a message from Lady Hollie to Lord Smead." He smiled pensively. "Kind of funny, us meeting like this, if you think about it." Kelly finally lowered his blade. "Forgive me, my friend, but this has been a bit of a harrowing trip, and my dog's been nervous the whole time. Kind of gives one the jumping frights, with him growling all the time, and being given a charge that Lady Hollie feared might be dangerous."

Brette got down from his mount. "Dangerous? What danger? Isn't the land at peace?"

"So it would seem. And that just makes it seem more sinister, somehow. Wondering all the while what the danger might be, and not knowing if you'd know it, even if you saw it face-to-face." He smiled ruefully. "That's why I was suspicious. It was nothing personal."

"Alright," Brette nodded. "Care to share a camp tonight?"

"That'd be most welcome." Kelly smiled at last, and the tension that had hung between the two like a thundercloud dissipated somewhat. "It's good, Pup," he said to the black dog, who finally stopped growling, and wagged its tail, licked its jowly chops.

ξ

Brette and Kelly leaned back on their elbows gazing into the crackling fire. Kelly had a pipe with him and some tobacco, and they passed it back and forth, drawing the aromatic but bitter smoke into their mouths, then releasing it in swirling circles. The embers in the pipe's bowl glowed red when they drew breath. The two men spoke but little—they were listening warily for any sounds beyond the snapping of the campfire. The black dog lay sleeping contentedly against Kelly's thigh.

They had already shared a relatively bountiful dinner. Brette had offered some jerky that he had been given at Castle Thraill, and three apples he had picked earlier in the day from astride the back of his horse. Kelly's contribution had been some cold chicken and radishes from Beale's Keep. And, despite the sensitivity of the missions they were each on, they had ended up confiding most of their business to each other as they shared their meal. That imparted information was what made them uneasy now; Kelly was distressed upon learning that Smead was dying, and Brette was disquieted with the news that Herm was apparently up to some kind of mischief in the king's name.

"Want to sleep first?" Kelly murmured as he tapped out the ashes from his pipe. "I'm still feeling kind of alert."

Brette nodded solemnly, and lay down, staring for a moment at their leafy ceiling before closing his eyes. The light from the fire made the shadows dance on the undersides of the leaves like mischievous sprites, and Brette had to work for a minute to dismiss the notion that he was being watched by faery eyes.

As he waited for sleep to claim him, he recalled his recent meeting with Jesi Tenet—Jesi Bost, that is. She had wept when she saw him, wept for the passing of the years perhaps, or the passing of her husband, or perhaps she had wept for joy at their reunion. Brette couldn't tell. But she had composed herself and made polite small talk about his family before hesitantly inquiring about Alan.

Brette said, "He is well, and he has returned to Ester to receive the lordship from his father's hand. He sent me to Thraill especially to find you." He didn't mention the ring Alan had entrusted to him hanging around his neck, not yet.

"Oh?"

"Might I ask—" Brette could think of no way to ask diplomatically, so he just pressed onward. "Do you have children?"

Jesi's cheeks flamed red, and a defiant spark glittered in her eyes, but she thought she understood the importance of what Brette was asking. "No, that pleasure has been denied me."

"I'm sorry," Brette said, and he was sorrier for embarrassing her than he was that she had been denied the pleasure of offspring. "Alan would like you to visit him at Beedlesgate."

"I see," she said in a low voice. "I am in mourning."

"Of course," Brette replied, unsure what to do next. "For how long?"

"I have lost a husband, not a pet bird!" she flared, and then softened. "Forgive me. Forgive my temper ... but your manners are not very courtly."

"I'm sorry," Brette frowned. "Beale's Keep is not so civilized as Thrimball, I guess. I've grown used to speaking my mind."

"It seems we are forever either snapping at each other, or apologizing," Jesi said sadly. "Brette—I've lost my husband. And though you never knew him ... I *did* care for him, a great deal." She laid her hand upon his. "Would it be correct for me to assume ... does Alan wish to make me his wife?"

Brette nodded grimly. "He sent you a token." He began to reach for the ring.

"Keep it, for now," she urged. "When you come back from your journey to Beale's Keep for Smead, I shall have mourned for days enough to show proper respect to my father-in-law. When you return, you may give me Alan's token, and I will accompany you back to Ester. I'm not saying I will marry Alan … but I will go to him, and see what may be." She smiled sadly. "I'm surprised that Alan still is interested. It will be something of a scandal for him to take me … if I let him."

"Well, he's always loved you," Brette said, and wished he had not. But he continued, "I tried to talk him out of sending me, but he thinks none will make him happy save you."

At that, the lines in Jesi's forehead smoothed somewhat, and her smile was reflected in the softening of her eyes. "Thank you, Brette. My heart still grieves for Tayson … but at least you have given me something to look forward to." Brette nodded.

Jesi continued, "Come back quickly, if you may. My father-in-law, the Lord Bost, has made it clear to me—secretly, of course—that he would be willing to marry me himself, in order to provide himself his own heir. I … do not wish that."

"No," Brette agreed. Though he understood what Lord Bost had proposed— Jesi was young and attractive, and the old lord's wife Lillias was well past childbearing age.

"Brette?"

"Yes."

"Would you please give me the token Alan sent?"

Wordlessly, he retrieved the ring and placed it in her hand.

"Thank you," she said. "Is it Alan's own ring?" Brette nodded.

"I will keep it close to my heart until you return," she said solemnly. "Brette—do hurry."

ξ

Aron Millerson pounded upon the two rough timbers with a wooden mallet, trying to get them to fit together where he had hewn out a joint for them. They didn't quite mate properly, though, and Aron decided with some consternation to just wham them together as best as he could, and then lash them fast with a rope.

An oily coating of sweat covered him as he knelt at his labors in the dirt, and whenever he laid a hand on the ground to brace himself, the dirt clung to his sweaty hand, creating a thin layer of mud on his palm. A trickle of sweat ran down the crack of his round behind, which was uncomfortable and a little bit humiliating. Sweat ran into his stinging eyes, and when he reached to rub them without thinking, he smeared gritty mud into his face at the corners of his eyes. "Aggh!" he groaned. *Almighty—why do You mock me, when I'm trying to do something to honor You?*

"What are you building?" Owan asked, as he walked toward Aron from the fields. He had not known the plump priest to be this industrious before.

"Greetings, young Lord," Aron panted. "This is called a *cruce* in the tongue of the *Iesuchristion*—we would call it a cross. It is what Iesu the Lamb of God hung upon when He died for your transgressions, and mine."

"Hmm," Owan said, interested only a little. "How do you know what it looks like?"

"Well," Aron said, wiping his forehead with the back of his arm, "I don't. But it must've been something like this. I'm building this just to help us remember what Iesu did."

"What are you going to do with it?"

"Set it up in the courtyard, if the idea pleases your mother."

"Oh, it probably will," Owan said dismissively. "She's a great lover of Iesu."

"Yes," the priest said, looking at Owan curiously. "Are you, ah—is something bothering you?"

"It just seems that your God doesn't take very good care of those that especially love Him," he said.

"What?" Aron said, dismayed at the blasphemy it sounded like he was hearing.

"From what I've been told, no one in Hagenspan wanted to follow God more than my father," Owan reasoned. "And he was killed by the dragon, God's great enemy—and so were a lot of other men, who all had wives and children and said their prayers before they went to battle."

"Well—"

Owan continued, "And your Iesu. The Son of God, sometimes you say. The Lamb of God, other times. Well, if God can't even save His own Son, who *can* He save? What kind of saving can He even do?"

"Owan," the priest began, and was suddenly acutely aware of his sweatstained robe, and the mud in his eyes. "It's not like that."

"Well, then, what *is* it like?"

Aron Millerson stared dumbly back at the blond-haired boy. His tongue felt thick and stupid, and his mind was startlingly blank. He smiled helplessly at Owan, and prayed silently, *God! Help me!*

"Seems like a pretty poor master. That's all I'm saying," Owan declared, and turned to go.

"Owan," Aron blurted, "I don't have an answer for you, not right now. But I promise you, I'll pray, and I'll study, and I'll find you an answer that will suit you. Will you give me that chance, before you give up on the faith of your father? And your mother?"

Owan regarded the fat, sweating man in his filthy brown robe, saw the earnestness in his eyes, pitied him for a moment, until he realized that Aron was feeling sorry for *him*. He nodded once. "All right." He walked back to the castle, sought the cool solitude of his own room.

Aron stared after him until he was out of sight. Then he looked down at the cross lying unevenly in the dirt, his own poor workmanship, and hung his head.

Chapter Sixteen

The charcoal sky was filled with bats. Black, screeching bats that flew pellmell at Ruric, overwhelming him as he waved his sword wildly in the air. The ground smoked all around him, and he was all alone but for the diving leatherwinged fiends. *Herm! Maygret! Where are you?* he cried, but he couldn't hear his own voice, just the screaming of the bats.

From time to time his sword found purchase, but it seemed that no matter how many of his enemies he struck, their number never diminished. Dead bats piled up around his legs, but they kept on coming at him, coming, and coming. He felt the sword wrenched from his hands, and he waved his arms helplessly against the vile creatures, tried to shield his face.

They were laughing at him, slapping him about the head and shoulders, suffocating him. Ruric collapsed to his knees amid the dead bats, bowing low to the ground like a wretched penitent. Bats covered him, buried him. He couldn't breathe. The mocking laughter sounded familiar, somehow … sounded like Herm. *Herm, why are you laughing?* the king asked with his failing breath, but there was no answer. Just blackness, just heaviness, just laughter. Just bats.

ξ

Queen Maygret sat wearily beside the king's bed. She watched as Ruric, unconscious—never conscious now—fought for a breath. A minute passed. Another breath. Another minute, another gasping breath. Ruric's mouth hung slack; his skin stretched tight across his nose, his cheeks. He only had a few yellow teeth left in his gaping mouth … a few white whiskers on his chin.

Maygret, exhausted, could no longer remember what he had looked like when he was young and strong—could remember no moment when it was not like this.

Still she kept watch, a fatiguing vigil for one more breath, one more breath.

She heard voices in the hallway. *Herm.* She straightened up in her chair, patted her cheeks, smoothed her hair. She drew in a deep breath, exhaled slowly through her mouth.

"Your Majesty," Herm said in a hushed tone.

"Come in, please."

Herm came and stood respectfully by the queen's chair. He did not look at her; he just gazed sadly, tenderly (Maygret thought) at the face of the sleeping monarch. He looked quite handsome today, she thought, and immediately felt a pang of remorse. But then, she reflected defiantly, why should she *not* think that Herm was handsome? Ruric had certainly had his share of dalliances over the course of the last fifty years. She was a little shocked to discover herself thinking such thoughts, and a little bit pleased. A couple of spots of color appeared in her pallid cheeks.

"Has His Highness stirred?"

"No, not really," Maygret replied. "Every once in awhile he whimpers a bit, as if he is dreaming foul dreams."

"How sad," Herm lamented, and he sighed a deep sigh.

"Once or twice … I thought I was certain I had seen him breathe his last." Her emotions were tangled, conflicted. "But then he fights for another. He fights like the warrior he is."

"Yes," Herm agreed.

She drew another slow breath, and exhaled with a shudder. "I … I don't know what I would have done without your help, my friend, during these dark days. I will need you much, when … when—"

"How hard it must be for you, Majesty," Herm said mournfully. He wrenched his gaze from his fallen king, and turned his eyes directly at Maygret, eyes full of torment and pity. "How I have longed to comfort you, my queen, my … queen."

For a moment Maygret had thought that he was going to say something else. *My darling. My dear.* Something. And for a moment she had wished it so. Blushing slightly, she said, "Thank you, Minister Herm."

"Forgive me, Your Majesty, if I have spoken out of turn," Herm said with a sorrowful expression on his face.

"No need," she whispered. "The day may come when I shall welcome your comfort." At that her cheeks glowed a furious red.

"Yes," Herm nodded solemnly, and he turned his gaze respectfully back toward the king. And imprisoned in the fluttering cage of his dreams, Ruric the warrior king was fleeing deeper, deeper into the smoking darkness, fleeing from the wrath of the bats, the maniacally laughing bats.

Chapter Seventeen

The yellow dog that Captain Boole had given Feather to accompany him on his trip to Blythecairne was a source of some vexation to the florid-faced young man. Feather was somewhat uncomfortable around dogs (though he could hardly have admitted that to Captain Boole!), and this particular dog was always staring off into the distance, before and behind, muttering a low growling complaint.

Even at night the dog growled almost without ceasing, and though it permitted Feather to pat it tentatively, it never wagged its tail, and Feather was always a little afraid that it would suddenly turn and snap at him.

On this dewy morning, Feather had slipped when he was attempting to mount his horse, bashing his face against his saddle and splitting his lip. Tears had immediately sprung to his eyes, but he felt no shame, with no one to see him save the yellow dog. He did curse himself for his clumsiness, though, as he wiped the blood from his throbbing, swollen lip with a whimper. The dog looked at him curiously with unblinking, impassive eyes, and Feather quickly lurched up into his saddle, in case the dog had a taste for man's blood. It was an irrational thought, he knew—but it still felt safer up here than it did on the ground next to the baleful, muttering canine.

After that morning misadventure, they had trotted onward, eastward toward Blythecairne for several hours. The sun was a white, piercing glare in Feather's eyes, and his lip hurt. He took to riding with his eyes closed, or at most narrowed to slits that he could peek through, and he sucked his salty lip, worrying his tongue across his stinging wound.

They had passed by the town of Katarin a day ago, Feather and horse and dog, but had not lodged there, even though Katarin's chief administrator Padallor Clay had been known to be a friend of the Lady Hollie. But Feather, mindful of his mission, did not wish to get distracted by the comforts of board and bed. The most direct route to Blythecairne was due east, across open ground. If he had taken the King's Road from Katarin to Goric, toward Fairling, and then north to the castle, it would have cost him an extra day, maybe two, and there may have been more potential for being accosted by highwaymen along the way, too. So he had spurned the civilized paths for the rough corridor of the wilderness. He hoped he could find the way without too much more trouble.

ξ

Glassrood of Celester grimaced through his facemask at the approaching figures in the distance. He had little stomach for his duty, not any more. There was a day when his ambition was enough to motivate him from chore to unpleasant chore, from one distasteful task to the next, but he had been growing increasingly restless as the years passed with no satiation for the hunger of that ambition. His master had promised him the lordship of Celester when he became king, but that had been over a decade ago, and still Ruric lingered on.

Glassrood had once been entrusted with a mission on behalf of King Ruric, along with his former mentor, Sir Tiler of Raussi. They had been tasked with going to Castle Blythecairne in the northlands and trying to retrieve some tokens of the dragon that Cedric Roarke claimed he had killed, and that turned out to be something that Herm had no intention of allowing. Sir Tiler had been an old man, and honest to a fault; he never would have deviated from the mission King Ruric had given him. So Herm had come secretly to Glassrood … and what Glassrood had eventually done in pursuit of his own cursed ambition shamed him now.

He had not returned to Ruric's Keep; he had not been able to think up a plausible-enough story of what possibly could have happened to Sir Tiler, and he felt certain that his duplicity would be unmasked. So he had wandered Hagenspan for a time like a vagabond, hiding in the forests, lurking in the alleyways, subsisting on acts of petty thievery. Somehow, though, after a while, Herm had found him. What black arts Herm had used to locate him among all the thousands of Hagenspan, Glassrood could not guess. But Herm had once again promised to make him Lord of Celester, if only he would continue to serve him, at whatever small tasks the Prime Minister found for him to do.

So Glassrood had obeyed Herm for these past ten years, and the beatings and intimidations administered by his hand had multiplied, and the murders. Glassrood had become a man without a soul, he felt, and had taken to wearing a suit of black plate armor, not shiny but dull, so that he could blend more completely into the nothingness from which he appeared, and to which he returned when his foul deeds were done. There were whispers throughout the land of a Black Knight, and powers were ascribed to him that were both mystical and dread. But what Glassrood longed for was the day when he could bury that black armor beneath the dirt of Hagenspan, and return to his homeland of Celester as a benevolent lord—though he had long ago stopped deceiving himself that there was anything the least bit noble about his behavior.

For some reason—Glassrood did not care why—his master Herm wished to hinder this messenger from reaching Blythecairne. *Blythecairne again*, he mused with a bitter frown. He notched an arrow to his bowstring, and readied himself for yet another craven assault. He would meet the man face-to-face, for at least there was some small smattering of honor in combat, but first he would dispatch that dog. Glassrood did not like dogs … though he once did, he seemed to recall. He wondered why. He wondered why he did not, now.

ξ

The yellow dog stiffened, its hair bristling along its spine, and it snarled, teeth bared. Before Feather had a chance to wonder what on earth was wrong with it now, the dog gave a startled yelp, leaped into the air, and then fell with a thump, collapsing silent upon the darkening ground with a quivering shaft jutting from its breast.

Feather gasped, terrified, and jumped down awkwardly from his horse, fumbling to unsheath his sword. He could see nothing in the direction he thought the dog had been pointing toward, and so he turned frantically around in a circle, trying to see where the attack had come from. A small sob of fear escaped his swollen lips, and this time he was ashamed, for he knew that he was watched.

He could not find his enemy; everything he could see anyplace within bow range was mottled and shadowed by brush. He realized that there must be many hiding places nearby, for the land was nothing but small hills and knolls, almost as if it were a colossal scrap of earthy parchment wadded up by the hand of God, and then smoothed back out again. Gathering his shards of courage, he summoned voice enough to shout, "Show yourself!"

A dark form stepped from behind a tangle of brush—the form of a man, Feather thought, but black and empty as the pit of Hell—perhaps it was some kind of a demon. He nearly swooned, but fought to maintain his balance, and breathed a quick thread of a prayer to the God he had heard about from Aron Millerson.

A voice came from within the black helmet, a man's voice, muffled but commanding. "Lay down your sword, and I may permit you to live."

Feather did not immediately comply. He was steadied, somewhat, at hearing the voice of the man who stood between him and his destination. At least it wasn't a devil. He swallowed, said, "You are the Black Knight," and tried quickly to measure his opponent.

"Some have called me that," Glassrood admitted.

"I have heard of you—though I did not believe the tales." He judged that the Black Knight was somewhat smaller and lighter than himself, which probably meant that he was also quicker afoot. And much more determined, and cruel, too, if the tales were true. Feather felt the urge to drop his sword, and nearly did. But … he had promised to deliver Lady Hollie's letter. Perhaps this dark adversary was just a common thief, looking for gold or jewels, but somehow he doubted it.

"I don't know what the tales are, but if they encourage you to hold onto your weapon instead of obeying me, you have misunderstood them."

"I'm sorry, Sir Knight, but I don't think I shall. I don't think I may. I'm not my own man—I'm under orders. Can we reason together?"

Glassrood chuckled grimly. "It has been tried. But my purpose is sure, and you may be certain that I shall not be dissuaded."

"All right, then," Feather said uneasily, and wondered what the Lady Hollie would wish him to do if she knew. He did not wish to lay down his life for the sake of her message, if she didn't really want him to. "What is it you want?"

"You have some kind of a letter from the mistress of Beale's Keep to the Lords of Meadling, I believe."

"It's so," Feather admitted. He had been right about the other's intentions.

"If you will give me that letter and then turn back the way you came, I will allow it, for I am tired of killing today," Glassrood said matter-of-factly. "If you will not, then I will shake myself from my weariness, and send you off to Hell."

Feather was unsure what to do. "You killed my dog," he said.

"So you see, I am not afraid to kill," the other replied testily. "Drop your sword."

Suddenly Feather gave a great shout, and charged toward the Black Knight as fast as his stout legs would carry him. Glassrood was startled, for the younger man's armor was markedly inferior to his own, and he didn't appear to be possessed of any extraordinary courage. He brought up his own black sword to meet this unexpected challenge, but his adversary must have been faster than he seemed, or else some bewitchment was upon Glassrood that slowed his responses, for before he could defend himself, he was dealt a ringing clout upon the side of his helmet.

The next thing Glassrood knew, he was lying on the ground with his black helmet off, and the other man was standing over him. Some moments seemed to have passed, but he could not think how. Glancing up at the Lady Hollie's messenger, he became aware of a dark stain on the other man's leggings, and said with a chuckle, "You've pissed yourself."

"Aye, it's true, and for that I'm shamed," Feather said grimly. "But you might know that this was my first fight that wasn't just for play, so I don't feel that I've done all that poorly."

"No," Glassrood admitted. "You appear to have gotten the better of me."

Feather looked down upon his vanquished foe, and said, "Question is now, what am I supposed to do with you? I don't have no way to bind you, and I don't suppose your word of honor is worth the breath it would take you to blow it."

"Probably not."

"I'd awfully hate to have to kill you," Feather said remorsefully. "I might just have to deal you a good buffet aside your head, and hope that would do to black you out for a spell."

"Yes, that might do," Glassrood agreed, "though my head's still ringing from that last little tap you served me."

"I've already took your sword," Feather reasoned, trying to find some way besides violence to resolve his conundrum. "If you swear to let me go in peace, I could probably just ride off and leave you."

"No, I'm afraid if you don't kill me, I will have to kill you," the Black Knight said. "I too am not my own."

"No, you don't mean that." Feather shook his head, wondering who the man was beholden to. "I've got your blade, and I've shown you mercy, and you're going to permit me to ride on in peace."

"As you say."

"I'm sorry to have troubled you," Feather apologized. "Now you just lay there on the grass until I've gone, and then you can get up and be on your way. And—" he said, "and don't be bullying up no more on people that's done you no harm."

"Thank you," the Black Knight said, mustering as much sincerity as he could. "Tell me your name, young man."

"My folks named me Feather." He was pleased to have been asked. "May I know your name, Sir Knight?"

"No," Glassrood shook his head gently. "If you're going to let me live, it won't do for my name to be known."

"I suppose not," Feather replied sadly. "Well, thanks for the adventure."

"It was a pleasure."

"Now, you just stay there until I'm gone," Feather repeated. "All right?"

"Yes."

"All right, then." Feather backed away from the man in the black armor, and he tripped and fell on his rump with a jarring thud. His face blazing red, he gathered up the sword he had dropped and scrambled to his feet, apologizing.

Glassrood stayed rooted to the earth, as still as a shadow.

Feather walked gingerly to his horse, mounted with care, and rode off eastward without another word, but he did take one shame-faced glance back at his foe, and wondered how such a great oaf as he had ever prevailed in that confrontation.

Glassrood waited a few moments, rubbed the side of his neck where his head had been wrenched by Feather's blow, and then sat up cautiously. He saw the young man heading away on the horse, not too far away yet. Rising to his feet, fighting a wave of vertigo, he stumbled over to the bushes that had concealed him when Feather had first ridden this way. He found his bow lying propped against the twisted branches of the scrub, and shook his head in wonder that the boy had not thought of it.

He fitted a shaft to the string, blinked his eyes, raised the bow, took aim, let the shaft fly.

Chapter Eighteen

Paipaerria Tenet sat on her bed, fingering the silky material of the black gown she needed to put on, a black gown she had worn too many times. She had worn it for a year, once, when her beloved Willum had died, along with her cherished Uncle Cedric and many more of the youths of Hagenspan. That had been the War of the Last Dragon, and it had been many years ago now, but for Willum she mourned still.

Then, a few years ago, her mother had passed away: Ronica Tenet. Piper and her mother had had an often-tempestuous relationship, and it had always disappointed Ronica that her lovely daughter had never married. Ronica had liked Sir Willum well enough, but if he was dead, there was no real reason that she should not marry another, was there? Piper could almost hear her mother's voice even now, and it made her smile, made her frown. It had been just a short illness that had claimed her mother, and it had shocked all of Castle Thraill that Ronica, with her iron will, had succumbed. And it had meant another eleven months draped in black for Piper.

When her sister's husband died just weeks ago, Piper had had Patricia, her maidservant, pull the black gown out of her wardrobe and mend it where it had become worn, and where moths had spoiled it. And so she had worn it again for the first two weeks following her sister's return to Thraill, and it seemed she had only just put it away when this new sorrow visited itself upon her.

Lord Smead, her great friend, was dead: Esselte Smead, who had been a close confidant to her Uncle Cedric, the true Lord of Thraill. Smead, who had listened to Piper's heartache and offered her no reproof or useless advice, but had unfailingly given her his sad, understanding smile, and a soft shoulder to lean upon. Smead, who had become closer to her, almost, than her own father.

Cedric Roarke had named Esselte Smead—who had been his steward—the Lord of Thraill upon his departure, with the provision that Smead should pass the holdings on to Owan, Cedric's son, upon Smead's death. Now, that death had come, and even though Smead had been quite an old man, Piper had not been prepared for his passing. She should have been, she chided herself; he had been growing increasingly ill even before he had stopped appearing outside his own chambers, and that was some time ago. She was sorry that she was unable to shed any tears for her old friend; perhaps later, she thought. Though sometimes she thought she had cried all the tears she ever could, for Willum and Uncle Cedric and her mother.

She lifted the black fabric to her cheek, felt the soft caress against her skin. She breathed in the smell of the gown, the stale scent of so many dreary months of mourning. She wondered idly if Owan would be coming back to Castle Thraill, and what it would be like to have her cousin as Lord. She had not seen him in several years, had not heard about him in months, had not even thought about him in weeks. He would be—how old now? thirteen? fifteen? Oh, God, had it been *that* long, since.... And she remembered Willum again, and a tear sprang to her eye, and she quickly recalled Esselte Smead, now joining him in death, and dedicated that tear to him.

There was a knock at her door, her father's knock. "Come in, Daddy."

Haldamar Tenet entered the room, garbed respectfully in black and gray save for one bright green scarf hanging from his neck. Piper cocked an eyebrow quizzically at her father but refrained from comment. Haldamar asked, "Are you nearly dressed? We should go down soon."

"Nearly."

"That's good. Your sister is almost ready, too." He seemed distracted somehow. "You remember how you used to help Esselte with his duties, and how he'd let you make decisions, from time to time, that were more than just ceremonial?"

Piper nodded solemnly. She had spent many hours at Smead's side, occupying her moments with busyness instead of wasting them on grief. "He was dear to me. I learned much."

A faint smile played across Haldamar's face, then vanished as quickly as it had appeared. "You will have opportunity to put that knowledge to use."

"I suppose Owan will need some help when he comes," she sighed. "Perhaps I can be of assistance to him, if he will allow it."

"I don't believe Owan will be coming to Thraill." Piper looked up at her father with mild surprise. "Not right away, at least."

"Then … who … who will rule in his stead?" she asked, confused. Then she thought she understood. "Will it be you, Daddy?"

"No, my love," Haldamar smiled gently. "It will be you."

She smiled quickly, startled but pleased, and then frowned. "But how can that be? I—"

"Esselte did not wish me to tell you until now, but he made the decision a fortnight past. He sent a messenger to Beale's Keep to beg Lady Hollie's pardon … and he named you as his heir to the lordship—to the ladyship, that is."

"Is that … is that all right?" Piper asked, her brow furrowed with concern. "Uncle Cedric intended that Thraill should pass to Owan."

"And so it shall, when he is of age. You are charged by Lord Smead that you shall leave the lands to Owan when you die, or earlier should you choose. Here," he said, holding out the letter Smead had dictated to Brette. "It's all written here."

She scanned the page, nodding from time to time as she read the words, then read them again. The color slowly drained from her cheeks as the recognition of her new responsibility filled her. "Daddy," she said weakly, "I am not ... enough."

"You'll do splendidly, sweetheart," he said, stroking her shoulder. "If it ever becomes too much for you, you can always hand it over to Owan. But you'll do splendidly."

"Doesn't this ... doesn't this need to be certified by the king?"

"Esselte assured me that it will be. There will be no problem unless Smead's will should be challenged by your cousin. And unless the Lady Hollie is much changed since we last met, there will be no problem."

"I see." Piper took a deep breath, and another. She composed herself, and became—Haldamar could see it—Lady Paipaerria of Thraill, in a twinkling instant. "If you will excuse me, Daddy, I will finish dressing now. We must have a ceremony of some kind to celebrate my office, I expect ... but first, we must say goodbye to our old friend."

"My Lady," Haldamar bowed, and then left her room, closing the door softly behind him.

ξ

"My friend," Haldamar said to Esselte Smead, whose body lay on its pallet, covered with a purple drape, composed as if in sleep. "You were right, about Piper. She'll be fine. Perhaps even better."

There was no one else in the darkened room where Smead was prepared to lie in state, where soon all of the people of Thraill would parade past their old Lord and dab their eyes regretfully, stifling their comments about how large he had grown, until they were safely outside the castle.

"There aren't many of us left now," Haldamar said softly, "not from our generation. Not too many. Just Helkin, and Bettles, and me, and not too many more. Oh, and that other fellow in Dusk Company ... Lauffer. Not too many left, though, older than us." He fell silent again, glanced around at the shrouded windows, the flickering candles making their dim protests against the dark. "You always loved the sunlight. Seems a shame to have you lying here in this gloom. But it probably wouldn't do for your people to get too good a look at you—no offense."

He turned back to his old companion, and studied the faint strands of his thin white hair, which had been oiled and neatly combed. "Piper will be down soon. That will brighten you up, I'll bet." He was surprised at the seeming absurdity of his own statement. "I expect you can still see ... can't you? If you're still here, somehow. Or maybe you're just gone. That would be a shame, though, a damned shame. God could hardly be so cold."

Haldamar nodded toward Smead in agreement with himself, and then turned, started to leave. "I'll go fetch the girls, my friend. Then the spectacle will start, and you'll be the center of it all. I hope everyone realizes just what they've lost. You've been a treasure, old man."

Before he left the room, he turned back once more. "If you see Ronica about anywhere, would you please tell her that I miss her? Terribly? Tell her I wish I had been a better husband, though I did the best that I could, nearly." Smead did not answer, and Haldamar took that to mean he would do what he could. "Thank you, old friend. You've never failed me." Haldamar nodded again, and was mildly surprised to find tears in his rheumy old eyes. "Well, goodbye. I'll stop and see you one last time, when everybody has gone." He left the room, shuffling toward the stairs and his daughters, more aware than usual of the pains in his knees and how tired his back felt.

Chapter Nineteen

Tully swore, "You got rooked!"

Windy joined in. "Fleeced!"

Owan had nothing to say in reply; he had conflicting feelings about the news he had shared with his friends, the news that had just been delivered to Beale's Keep by the hand of Brette: that when Lord Smead should die, the lordship would pass to Paipaerria Tenet instead of him.

Joah was of a different mind. "What are you saying, guys? What did you want him to do, move off to Castle Thraill? It's best this way—he still has Beale's Keep, and he'll probably end up with Thraill someday too."

Tully was undeterred. "Yeah, but if he had got the lordship of Thraill, he could've took us all along with him, and made us his advisors!"

"Yeah," snorted Owan. "*That* would have happened."

"Well," Tully replied cheerfully, "you got rooked, anyway."

"You got fleeced," Windy contributed.

"Why would you want to go to Thraill anyway?" Joah demanded. "You don't know anybody there, and you're scared of meeting new people besides."

"Am not," Tully blustered. "I figured the place would just be crawlin' with pretty girls."

Owan laughed. "What would *you* do with a girl?"

"I know what to do with a girl," he replied defensively. "I just ain't seen one that's pretty enough yet."

Joah asked, "What makes you think there's pretty girls at Castle Thraill?"

"Well, that's where the Lady Hollie came from, ain't it? Tell me *she* ain't pretty."

"That's my mother you're talking about," warned Owan. "And besides, she didn't come from Thraill anyway, not at first. She was from Ruric's Keep, or someplace close by."

"Well, it don't matter anyway," Tully concluded, "because whether there's any pretty girls at Castle Thraill or not, there ain't none here."

Joah asked, "What about Sirina?" He was sweet on the dark-haired woman who was almost twice his age.

"Too old. We might as well be talkin' about Owan's mom."

"How would you like a pop on the nose?" Owan asked politely.

"All right. But I'd rather have a pop on the lips from some sweet young thing."

"You're an idiot," Owan retorted, and the others agreed.

"What about Bleuthe?" Joah asked, still trying to defend the honor of the girls of Beale's Keep.

At that, Tully and Windy started making snorting and woofing noises.

"Hey!" Joah protested.

"How about Melita?" Owan suggested.

"Well … not too bad, I guess," Tully conceded reluctantly.

"*I'd* kiss her," Windy said.

The other three boys laughed, and Joah said, "Yes, but would she kiss you?"

"Why, of course she would, if I was to ask. But I'm too much of a gentleman." The boys laughed again.

After a moment, Tully asked Owan again, "Are you sure you don't know of *any* pretty girls up to Thraill?"

"How would I? I was only a baby when we came here." He considered for a moment. "There's just my cousins, that I know of. And they're old, almost as old as my mother."

"Are they pretty?"

"Who knows? Last time I saw them, I wasn't big enough to be wondering."

"Well," Tully concluded, and the four fell silent.

"To be fair," Owan said, after a few minutes' contemplation, "I'm not ready to be Lord yet anyway."

Joah nodded in agreement, but Tully said, "What is there to know? Your mom don't do anything except throw dinner parties, does she? You could do that."

"It's probably harder than that. She's probably doing stuff while I'm at school."

"Yeah, like kissin' Captain Boole."

"I really am about ready to give you a pop on the nose," Owan said, and brandished a threatening fist.

"I saw him give her a pat right on her bottom once," Tully insisted. "She pretended she didn't like it, but you could tell she did."

"You know, you *really* don't want me to become Lord," Owan said, "because the first thing I'm ever going to do is to throw you in the stockade, and when I do, I'm going to have Bleuthe bring you your food every day, and it won't be nothing but piss and flies."

"Ahh, you know you love me," Tully grinned.

"Sometimes he does," Joah interjected, "but you really shouldn't talk about Lady Hollie that way."

"I didn't know she was your sweetheart," Tully retorted. "I thought you was in love with Sirina."

"What if I am?" Joah's face reddened. "There's no reason to be disrespectful."

"Who's disrespectin'? I'm just gossipin'."

"I'm telling you—piss and flies," Owan said in a menacing tone.

"Yum," Tully said, grinning and rubbing his belly.

Chapter Twenty

Herm, the Prime Minister of Hagenspan, stole into the throne room at Ruric's Keep, the room that served as the judgment hall of the king. There were actually two thrones in the room; one for the king, and a lesser one for the queen, set somewhat below and behind the other. Herm ignored the lesser seat, and concentrated on the king's splendid chair. It had been months since Ruric Serpent's-Bane had sat on that throne—since *anyone* had sat on it. Herm noticed a light skin of dust beginning to form on the ornately carved arms of the chair, and he took the sleeve of his tunic and wiped it off, admiring the work of the craftsmen as he recognized shapes of lions, dragons, trolls, women—symbols of the conquests of the kingdom. He patted the velvet seat cushion, and flecks of dust leapt into the air like so many tiny quail flushed from their perches. He shook his head, clucked his tongue.

Herm had been responsible for adjudicating the complaints of Ruric's people for most of the past year, ever since Ruric had yielded to this last illness. But he had listened to the grievances and delivered his judgments while standing respectfully to the right of the throne, never seated upon it, for that honor was reserved for the king alone.

Now he furtively glanced behind himself, listened for a moment, recognized that no one else was in the vicinity. Chuckling inwardly, he lowered himself onto the throne. The throne of the King of Hagenspan. Smiling broadly, he settled deeply into the padded cushions, felt how the chair's curved wooden back caressed his shoulders. *This throne was made for me*, Herm thought with delight. *I was made for this throne.*

For twenty-five years Herm had waited for this throne; had plotted, connived, cajoled, had striven for this throne. *For a quarter of a century!* Herm thought. And now it was nearly his. Still there were obstacles, still there were barriers ... but the kingdom was so close now that he could taste it, and the taste was *so* seductive on his tongue, like honey, like salt, like cream. So seductive that he began to salivate.

Somewhere in the periphery of his thought, a faint uneasiness began to stir, a hint of a nightmare not quite remembered. Herm's handsome brow creased in a frown. He started to rise from the throne, his throne, and then forced himself to remain seated.

After all these years, he was still feeling some faint, lingering effects of his possession by the spirit of the dragon, he thought. Though he had been free of that spirit for ages, ever since that boy Willum had undone the magic he had worked by doing something completely unforeseen. He had forced Herm to take into his hands the disembodied scales of his own dragon body. *Wait*—not his own. Not his own. Willum had forced Herm to take into his hands the disembodied scales of the body of the dragon whose spirit had come to torment him. Not his own.

The dragon spirit … the spirit that had come to give power to Herm's magic … the dreadful reply to Herm's incanted petitions. He felt a sudden, unsolicited swelling of lust for that power again, a flaring in his loins that was nearly sexual. A bead of sweat appeared on his brow. Gritting his teeth, he subjugated that urge with a strenuous effort of his will. He was not possessed! He was not possessed.

He was free.

After the time of his dishonoring, when the spirit that gave him power had been violently wrenched from his soul, he had been left empty, drained, stupid. Humiliated. King Ruric had dismissed him from his position as Prime Minister … temporarily. But the king had *missed* Herm, the counsel they had shared, the judgments they had arrived at together (or so the king thought). The sense that Herm could have been the son that Ruric had desired for himself, a son to replace the one that had been claimed by the cruel hands of the gods. And so Herm had been gradually brought back to the seat of authority, and no one spoke of his disgrace, and after a time it was forgotten almost altogether.

And Herm had begun seeking the throne again … patiently, patiently. He made no overt suggestions regarding succession to Ruric. He ingratiated himself to Maygret at every turn. He dispensed sound justice to the people of Hagenspan, and as Ruric diminished, Herm became more and more the face of the kingdom. And, secretly, he toiled in the shadows and alleyways of the city to undermine any potential enemies to his purpose. He surreptitiously fostered an army within the king's army, a force loyal to him, perhaps even surpassing their loyalty to the crown. He hired mercenaries, and bade them wait, at his expense—or rather, Ruric's—until the moment he declared. He even engaged assassins, to eliminate threats that could not be dealt with by bribes or threats.

But he worked no more magic. That place of his soul, which had been twisted and fouled by the demonic spirit of the dragon, remained empty. And he filled that emptiness with his plots and machinations, and whatever emptiness he still perceived, he filled with vulgar encounters with chambermaids and ladies-in-waiting. And whatever emptiness still remained, he filled with hatred … hatred for the ones who had been the closest to those who had foiled his plans of a generation ago. And especially for the last remaining human being who had done the most to ruin him, to humble him. Hatred for the repulsive, nauseating, yellow-haired whore called Hollie, who was named the Lady of Beale's Keep.

Herm felt his nostrils twitch now, felt his lip curl in a snarl, as the honey, the cream he had imagined he savored a moment ago were replaced by the taste of bile, bitter and caustic. He stood to his feet, annoyed, the satisfaction he had experienced a moment earlier now frustrated and agitated. If he had stopped for a moment to wonder why he hated the woman so much, he may have been surprised at the intensity of his feelings, but he was simply engulfed by his hatred, gripped by it, possessed by it. *No!* Not possessed! He was free; he was a free man.

Herm paced around the throne room, paced like a tethered dog, frustrated, confused. But as he paced, and paced some more, the severity of his emotions gradually subsided, the sense of loathing seeping from his body like water leaching from a sponge. Soon he was not angry anymore, just bewildered and a little sad.

Empty. So empty.

He needed something to fill him, something to alleviate his desperate longing, something to console the inconsolable. *What?* he thought abruptly. *Hellfire and damnation! You're going to be the king!* He stomped disgustedly from the throne room, stalking off in search of a chambermaid he could devour.

Chapter Twenty-One

Brette rode up to the main gate at Castle Thraill, his mission to Beale's Keep complete. Now he could report to old Lord Smead, if he yet lived, and then collect Jesi and take her home to Alan. The assignment Alan had given him had taken far longer than the young lord had wished, of that Brette was certain. But Alan figured his friend's anxious disappointment would vanish like the morning dew, once he saw the face of the girl—the woman—he had sent for.

The guard at the gate nodded solemnly at Brette, recognizing him, allowing him access to the castle grounds without challenge. Not like that pompous young captain he had met on his last visit—what was his name? Brette couldn't think of it, decided he didn't care enough to try. He was just eager to present himself to Lord Smead and be on his way as quickly as possible. He wanted to be home.

Once within the gates, Brette dismounted and began leading his horse across the courtyard toward the stables. He looked around for a friendly face, but the few people that were about had their faces down-turned, their manner downcast. Feeling a pang of sadness, Brette deduced that some dark cloud hung over Thraill, and figured that probably old Smead had died. His suspicion was confirmed by the stable-hand who took his horse, who also added, "And you'll never b'lieve who the new lord's to be, neither!"

Reflecting silently that there had been a time just recently when he had been the only person outside of Castle Thraill who *did* know the identity of the new lord, he nonetheless bade the young man, "Tell me."

A few moments later, he headed toward the castle, hoping for a moment with Haldamar Tenet to find out how matters stood—it was likely to be a time of some turmoil at Thraill, even if the transition of authority occurred without dispute.

But before he had crossed the courtyard, he was stopped by that same proud young captain with the long dark hair who had sought to detain him at the outset of his last visit.

"What are you doing back here?"

"I'm sorry, Captain, but I've forgotten your name," Brette said in response.

"It's Bascan—never mind that," he said rudely. "I asked you, what are you doing here?"

Brette shook his head gently. "We may have gotten off on the wrong foot, friend. I am no threat to Castle Thraill or any of her people. I am the designated emissary from Lord Poppleton of Ester, on his business, and I have just come to seek audience with the Tenets."

"Wrong foot or no," Bascan said, jabbing a forefinger into Brette's chest, "it's still through *me* that you go, to get to her Ladyship. Mind your manners around her, and if I find you've come a-courting, I'll kill you myself, and feed you to the crows."

"What?" Brette said, incredulous. What on earth was wrong with this man?

"You heard me," the dark-haired man hissed, and glanced over his shoulder. "And if you tell anyone I said so, I'll deny it, and then kill you when you're not looking."

"How did a man like you ever get to be a captain in Thraill?" Brette demanded, his anger growing. "You must be some kind of idiot!"

"An idiot, is it?" Bascan laughed irritably. "That sounds like a challenge to a duel!"

In response, Brette pulled back his fist quickly and let it fly, smashing Bascan full in the face. Bascan staggered backward, trying to maintain his footing, then sprawled on his back in the dirt. He tried to draw his sword, but Brette quickly stepped over him, pointed his own sword at the prone man's throat, and said through clenched teeth, "Do not attempt it, friend."

"Hold!" came a shout from behind Brette. "Lay down your weapon!" When Brette did not immediately comply, the command came again, "Lay it down!" It was the guard from the castle gate, rushing over to the pair of combatants, his own sword drawn. Hearing the commotion in the courtyard, two more guards appeared from somewhere nearby, and brandished their blades, approaching Brette cautiously.

"Take him, before he kills me," Bascan snapped. "He's come to threaten our Lady."

"That's a bald-faced lie," Brette growled.

"Then drop that sword, and tell us who you are," one of the other guards said. Brette was a fair swordsman, but he recognized that there was no way he could prevail against these odds, so he reluctantly stooped and laid his blade upon the ground.

"Take him to the stockade and put a watch on him," Bascan commanded. "If he tries to escape, run him through."

Brette went compliantly with the guards, but he said to the one from the gate, "Get word to Haldamar Tenet that Brette from Ester is here, and being held in your prison."

"We'll see about that," the guard grudgingly agreed.

They led Brette to a barred cell that was actually an extension of the castle stables, pushed him firmly (but not unkindly) into the room, and locked the door behind him. Two of them took positions at the door, and the one from the gate departed. Brette settled down upon a bale of hay which proved to be the only furniture in the room, and prepared himself to be patient, placidly studying motes of chaff as they floated lazily through the rays of sunlight streaming through his barred window.

ξ

A few hours later, the two guards standing watch over Brette's cell parted, bowing their heads toward somebody who was approaching, and Brette stood up, expecting that it would be Haldamar.

"Allow me to enter his cell," spoke a female voice.

"Are you sure that's wise?" one of the guards asked.

"Nonsense. I've known Brette for years," the woman declared, and the guard said, "As you wish, m'Lady," and opened the barred door to admit Paipaerria Tenet.

Brette knelt before her, for though they had once been friends of a sort, she was now the Lady of Thraill, and he was, well, nothing.

"Brette, son of Jerl," Piper said, "it's good to see you again. Please rise."

"Thank you, my Lady," Brette replied, raising his eyes to meet hers. He was a bit startled to see how lovely she was; he had nearly forgotten. She was dressed all in black—in honor of Lord Smead, he thought—and her auburn curls tumbled down about her shoulders like a gentle golden-brown waterfall. "I'd for—" he began, and then hastily swallowed his words. "Forgive me, my Lady."

"What is it?" she insisted.

"It's just, I was going to say, I'd forgotten you have green eyes," Brette said. "Foolish of me—I'm sorry."

Deftly changing the subject, Piper asked, "What have you done to end up in my prison? Have you accosted one of the young women of the castle?"

Aghast, Brette stammered, "No! No, my Lady!"

For the first time since Smead's death, Piper laughed with delight. "Well, certainly no one who looks as innocent as that could be guilty of anything *very* dangerous!" In spite of his humiliation, Brette smiled weakly. Piper continued, "Jesi told me you had been here, several weeks ago. Why didn't you stop in and see me?"

"It was Lord Smead's wish that I make all haste to Beale's Keep with a message he had given me to deliver. I believe you are aware of its contents, now."

"Yes," she nodded, becoming somber again. "So … what has brought you to my prison?" she asked once more.

"Your Captain Bascan seems to think that I, uh … that I am up to some kind of mischief regarding, uh, Your Ladyship." Brette could think of no way to delicately explain what it was that Bascan had insinuated to him. He had never given a thought to the idea of courting Piper Tenet; they had never been that close. Though, with her dark-shrouded beauty practically surrounding him here in the confines of this dusty cell, he felt a brief surge of regret that he had not.

"Well, are you?"

"My Lady?"

"Are you planning some mischief against me?"

Brette was unsure whether she was serious or only mocking him. So he simply answered, "No, my Lady."

"I thought not. Guards," she said to the two outside the door, who were both listening intently to the conversation, "please release my friend."

"I don't know," said one of them uncertainly. "Captain Bascan—"

"Who is Lady of Thraill? I, or Captain Bascan?" Piper asked reasonably.

"But, my Lady," the guard protested, "he *is* my Captain—"

"Fine," she said a little testily. "I understand completely. Would you please then notify my father and my sister that we will be dining here tonight? And have the cooks prepare something special for our guest. And bring me a chair, if you please."

"My Lady—" the guard objected.

"Choose your course, and be quick about it," she said, her anger thinly veiled.

The guard looked at his companion helplessly, then opened the door and allowed Piper and Brette to pass. Betraying no hint of ill temper, she said calmly to Brette, "You will join me for dinner tonight? Good. I am looking forward to hearing how you have spent the past ten years."

Chapter Twenty-Two

Hollie held this new message loosely in her hands, her arms feeling suddenly drained of strength. Two large drops of water fell upon the parchment with audible splats, and she realized that they were her own tears. She removed the letter from where she held it in her lap, placed it on the table beside her.

The message was from Piper Tenet, and it simply stated that Esselte Smead had died, and that she had assumed the rule of Castle Thraill as he had directed in his will. Hollie thought wistfully that she wished Piper had included some sort of personal note; they had once been very close, back when Cedric was alive, back when Will was alive. Two more tears trickled down her cheeks. Back when Smead was alive.

Esselte Smead. Hollie remembered him now, remembered him as she had last seen him, a dozen years ago or more. In Hollie's mind, he had never aged past that day—he had waited, suspended in time, waited for Hollie to return and take up the conversation again just where they had left it. It would have seemed like no time at all had passed, a seamless garment of relationship that they could put on again as if the intervening years had meant nothing at all. But now that conversation would never happen.

Smead had loved Hollie; she had known that even before Brette had haltingly tried to tell her a few weeks ago. And she had loved him, too, though not romantically. But Smead had been one of the two or three men she respected the most out of all that had remained in the world following the War of the Last Dragon. Heavy-hearted, she sighed, thought for a moment of the others … Keet and Lirey from Blythecairne—Lords in Hagenspan now. Yeskie, who had come to join her in the early days at Beale's Keep, now dead, as dead as Smead. And Hess, too, she supposed—though Hess stirred something else in her besides respect.

It had been years since she had seen Blythecairne, she thought, even longer than it had been since she was last in Thraill … maybe she should take a holiday. Take Owan across the Senns, across the Maur Wain, across the wilderness, and show him the place that his father had resurrected from the pile of rubble it had once been, transformed it into a garden. She thought she would like to see Maryan again, who had been a true friend to her. And Keet's wife, too—what was her name? It alarmed Hollie that she could not bring it to mind, the name of the woman who was once her friend. *Thalia*, she remembered suddenly, and felt a swell of relief, though she did not know why.

She raised her sad eyes toward her window. Everything looked very clear today. Even though her eyes were still blurred with tears. She sighed again. Her mind was wandering, darting here and there all over the landscape, over all the history of her life, when she was trying—she was *trying*—to mourn for poor Esselte Smead. She saw Owan outside in the courtyard, stood to her feet, thought that she might call out to him, didn't, sat down again, watched her son. Owan was walking slowly toward the walled garden, dragging a stick behind him. She wondered where he had gotten the stick. Forced herself to remember Smead again. Watched Joah come up to her son, saw their mouths moving in conversation though she could not hear the words. Sighed.

She said a silent prayer for Smead's soul, though it occurred to her that all that could be done for Smead's soul, probably, had already been done. She prayed a prayer of blessing for Piper Tenet, for wisdom for her, for success, for happiness. She prayed for Lirey and Maryan and Keet and Thalia … prayed that none of them had died already, and she just hadn't known about it. She sniffled, dabbed at her eyes with a sleeve.

She heard a footfall in the corridor outside her room, a heavy tread, and knew it to be her priest.

Aron Millerson cleared his throat, "Lady Hollie—you sent for me?"

"Thank you, Aron. Does the *Iesuchristion* contain words of comfort for the bereaved?"

"Why, yes, I'm certain that it does. Yes," he said, trying to think of something he had read, and cursing himself the hundredth time for his deficient scholarship. "Yes, I'm certain."

"Then," Hollie said, "prepare some kind of a memorial ceremony, please. One of the great men I have known—Esselte Smead, Lord of Thraill—has passed over into Iesu's country. We must declare days of mourning. And a memorial ceremony fitting for a great man."

"Might I have a day to prepare? A day or so?" Aron asked, his furrowed brow betraying his uncertainty over the task Hollie had just assigned him, but she did not notice.

"Yes, certainly," she replied distantly, and turned back to her window. "Thank you, Aron."

ξ

"That was a messenger from Thraill, wasn't it?" Joah asked Owan.

The young would-be Lord's face grimaced in a crooked smile of greeting for his friend. "I think so. I didn't ask."

"Two messengers in a month! What do you think it means?"

Owan shrugged his thin shoulders, and traced a pattern in the dirt with the stick he had trailed along behind him since he had picked it up at the edge of the forest this morning. He didn't know why he hadn't left it behind when he had headed back to the castle, but it had felt good in his hand, and he had been loath to let it go.

"You know what I think it must be?" Joah asked.

"Bet you'll tell me," Owan smiled.

"Yes, I will," Joah retorted, and gave Owan a soft punch in the shoulder. "It must be that old Smead has died."

"Probably," Owan agreed. Then he said, "Does it matter?"

"Well—" Joah considered that for a second. "No, I suppose not. But, still—it must make you feel *something*."

"What's it make *you* feel?"

"Well, nothing much, I guess," Joah admitted. "Just curiosity. But then again, *I'm* not the one who lost out on a lordship."

Owan did not reply for a moment, as several conflicting thoughts chased each other in quick succession through his adolescent brain. "I don't care about the lordship, not really. It'll pass to me someday, I expect. But you know what I *do* regret?"

Joah looked at his friend curiously.

"The letter my father sent to me before he died—he said 'listen to Smead.' As if Smead was somebody worth listening to. I'm just kind of sorry that I never got a chance to."

Joah studied Owan appreciatively. Feeling the tangible weight of the silence as well as the calm insistence of his friend's gaze, Owan glanced up at Joah. Their eyes caught, and Owan, embarrassed, said, "What?"

"My Lord Owan," Joah said in his most courtly manner, "I have a boon to ask of you."

"Don't be foolish."

"I'm not. I really want you to promise me something."

Owan looked at Joah again, wondering if he was being set up for a joke.

"What is it?" he asked warily.

"We're friends, aren't we, you and me?"

"Yes, we are."

"You might even say we were the best of friends."

"Yes," Owan agreed.

"I want you to swear to me that, wherever you go in this world, you'll take me with you. If you ever go to be Lord of Thraill, that you'll let me come along. If you stay right here at Beale's Keep, you'll keep me at your right hand. And if you ever go adventuring in the wild places of Hagenspan, you won't go without me." Joah gazed steadily at Owan's face, and Owan heard his words, respected them, returned his gaze. "You're an uncommon boy, Owan, and you show signs of being an uncommon man. It would be my honor to serve you, though I'm only common myself."

Owan was uncomfortable with these words of praise, but he understood that Joah was being utterly sincere. "You're not common—not at all. And I'd be honored to be your friend forever." He felt foolish, as if he were talking to a girl and not his lifelong companion.

"Swear to me, my Lord."

Owan thought quickly, and then commanded, "Kneel," and Joah did so.

He raised the stick he had carried in from the woods, and laid it gently on Joah's right shoulder, and then his left. "Joah, son of Guthery, I hereby name you the Right Arm of Owan Roarke, both now and till the end of our days. May this branch serve as witness between you and me." Joah, his head bowed, smiled. "Rise."

Owan broke the stick into two pieces, and handed one end to his friend. "Keep this. I will keep the other half. If you ever feel the need to remind me of my pledge, just present your half of the branch to me, and I'll remember."

"Thank you, Owan."

Owan shook his head, smiling away the humiliation he had felt scant moments earlier. "Thank *you*, crazy boy. Can we lighten up a bit now?"

"At your command, my Lord," Joah laughed, and grabbed him by the shoulder. "Here's to many fine days before us."

"Amen," Owan agreed.

ξ

Hollie saw her son break the stick and give half of it to Joah. She wondered what kind of game they were playing now. *But at least he seems happy*, she thought. She liked Joah; he was more like Owan than the other boys that hung around the castle—more somber, more thoughtful. Though she was glad for Tully and Windy, too, for if she didn't quite approve of them, at least they kept Owan from becoming too withdrawn, too morbid. *There are tears aplenty waiting for you, my son*, she thought, hoping she was not prophesying. *Enjoy the laughter of your friends while you may.*

Chapter Twenty-Three

Two fortnights had come and gone since Brette's arrival at Castle Thraill. It had not been seemly for Jesi Tenet Bost to depart for Ester during Smead's days of mourning, so Brette had tarried at the castle, a guest of the Tenets. This was a delay that he initially regretted, being anxious to return home with Alan's prize and be discharged of his disagreeable duty.

But as the days passed and he found himself evening by evening in the entirely agreeable company of the Lady Paipaerria, his desire to hurry home shrank like the waning moon. He was careful to never suggest anything inappropriate to the striking young woman, but he felt certain that his breathless eagerness to sit in her presence glowed from his face like a signal fire. Amazingly enough, she seemed to be comfortable with him as well—perhaps even happy. She was contented to sit and talk with him long after dinner ended, with the candles burning low and her father nodding in his cups, and her sister eager to be off to bed. They talked of the years Brette had spent at Beale's Keep, and the welfare of Piper's Aunt Hollie and young cousin Owan. They talked of Piper's dreams for Thraill, being freshly born in her heart and just starting to become exciting to her. Occasionally they spoke of Alan and Jesi, and what the future might or might not hold for them. And, Brette thought—he almost dared to hope—that sometimes they shared things unspoken, things that bled from their lingering eyes like liquid light.

He shook his head with a smile. Just wishful thinking, he told himself.

And soon Smead's days of mourning would be done, and Brette would be off to Beedlesgate with Jesi in tow, and his next duties for Alan would begin. His next duties for Lord Poppleton, he reminded himself. Brette, perhaps, was not precisely free to just come and go as he pleased …

but he knew that if he asked Alan, the young Lord of Ester would grant him anything he wished. Even if he wished to venture back to Castle Thraill.

How would such an act be received by the Lady Piper? Would she send him away shamefaced, tell him she had just been being polite, and that the things shared by their longing eyes were only in his imagination? *Were* they only in his imagination?

Haldamar Tenet had told Brette that the answers Piper sought were not likely to be found in a man. Or was it that he had told Brette that the answers Alan sought were not likely to be found with Jesi? Brette couldn't remember now; he just remembered that Haldamar had told him something vaguely discouraging back when he had first come to Thraill a couple of months ago.

But Brette did remember vividly one thing that Haldamar had said. It had struck him as curious when the white-haired old man had said it; somehow poignant, a little sad. But somehow triumphant, too. He had said, "You have to at least ask, don't you? Otherwise you'd never know. And you'd always wonder. Asking is better, even if you turn out to be a fool for it."

Brette decided that he was not afraid to be a fool. He would ask. He would ask, as soon as he could figure out what the question was.

ξ

Thirty days of solemnity had been observed for the memory of Esselte Smead at Beale's Keep as well. For one full turning of the moon the people of Lady Hollie's charge had worn muted colors, spoken in muted tones. Aron Millerson had presided over a satisfactory ceremony recalling Smead's good deeds and generosity. Thankfully, he had discovered some fine passages toward the back of the *Iesuchristion* that spoke glowingly of

Iesu's land, and suggested even that Iesu Himself would dry the tears from the eyes of those who crossed that land's bright borders.

By the close of the dreary month, many at the Keep had grown restless, so Hollie declared the end of the time of mourning by hosting a great feast for all her people. Four fat pigs had been roasted on spits over open fires, and the wine and beer had flowed liberally. Many exuberant toasts had been hoisted to the memory of Smead, and many more flagons were tipped back with joy that the tedious days of mourning were concluded. The roistering lasted long into the night, until the only light that remained in the litter-strewn courtyard was that cast by the crackling embers of the fire pits. Hollie had granted her workers the next day to spend at their leisure and recover from their hangovers in peace.

Now she sat at her looking glass, studying her face with a concerned frown. There were lines around her eyes that she had not previously noticed, and her once-golden hair was shot through with threads of white. She looked tired, drained, faded, she thought. A stab of panic pierced her breast; she forced herself to take a deep breath, calm down, calm down.

She considered calling for one of the maidens of the Keep who occasionally used face paints. A little blush for the cheeks and lips, a little color to draw out the blue of her eyes. She was tempted, briefly … but she had not used makeup on her face in many years, not since before Cedric had rescued her from Kenndt's. *No*, she decided. *No.* If he was going to love Hollie, he would have to love the Hollie in the looking glass, not one made up to look like someone else, like some*thing* else. She suddenly wanted to weep, and again, forced herself to calm down.

He would be there soon, and if he had guessed why she had summoned him, he hadn't betrayed that knowledge. She felt lightheaded. Giddy, breathless, terribly afraid. *Terribly* afraid. She thought about sending to him, telling him not to come, that she had made a mistake. She had almost made up her mind to do exactly that, when she heard a vague tune being whistled from down the hallway, and her heart leapt in her breast. He was here!

She turned on her stool to face the doorway, and smoothed down her skirts, brushed back her hair. She drew in a breath through parted lips, and exhaled one last jagged sigh.

She heard the rap on her door, began to speak, couldn't think what to say, felt another moment of panic, blurted, "Yes!"

"Captain Boole, m'Lady," came the muffled reply from the other side of the oaken slab. "You called?"

"Yes, Captain, you may enter," she said. *No!* she thought, but stifled that terrified exclamation before it could squeeze past her lips.

The door opened, and Hess Boole filled the entrance. Stout, balding, still ruggedly good-looking, barely hiding a benevolent smirk beneath his whiskers. Not only did he fill the doorway, he filled Hollie's eyes, filled them like the tears that blurred her vision now. She longed to rush to his arms, have him fold her into the refuge of his brawny embrace. But she sat, hands folded in her lap, her breathing so shallow that she feared she might faint.

"Captain B—"

"Enough of this formality, my love," he said in a soft voice. "This has been a tiresome long month without you, and if you haven't called me in here to give you a kiss, I'll need to go out and kiss my damned horse for desperation!"

She smiled, and her anxiety dissipated a bit. *He* does *love me!* She said, "It may be … but I have something to ask you first."

"Thanks be to God!" he cried in mock relief. "Well, then, ask away, and then get ready to pucker up!"

"Hess, this is something serious."

"I'm sorry," he grinned, "but my very loins have ached for you, ever since old Smead died, and you decreed that wretched moratorium on romancing your poor Captain."

"Hess," she said, smiling sadly, sorry that she had denied him, sorry that she had denied herself. But it had been the honorable thing to do, and it was done.

"Well, my fine Lady, be quick with your question, because I'm longing to touch you." He took a step into the room.

She nodded once, smiled a faint butterfly smile, drew a breath to sustain her. "Hess, do you remember, many years ago in Ronica's garden, when you asked me if … if you might court me?"

"Seems that I can recall something like that," he said, but his grin faded somewhat as he realized that this really *was* something serious.

"Do you … still want to?" she asked, full of hope and fear. She hoped that it didn't sound as if she were pleading.

The perpetual smile beneath his whiskers flickered, guttered like a wisp of flame. "My Lady," he said huskily, kneeling before her and taking her hand, "there is nothing else I've desired for the span of ten years, and half that again." He pressed his lips to her hand.

Hollie bowed her head, breathing thanks to the Almighty. "Are you … are you of a mind to … marry me?" she whispered.

Hess Boole tipped his head back and laughed for joy. "Hollie, my love, my own! What have I ever done that you would see fit to make me the happiest man in Hagenspan?"

"Shh!" she commanded. "People will hear!" She covered his mouth with her hand, and then, on an impulse, covered his mouth with her own, kissing him over and over again as he laughed.

"Oh, Hollie, my own love!" he rasped as he gripped her in his embrace. "I'll marry you just as quick as we can get Aron to find words in his book to make it proper!" He kissed her again. "And, if you're disposed to being a tad *im*proper with your new husband, just let me close that door behind us for a bit."

Gratitude swelled in her breast like a bird taking flight—gratitude to God for giving her this jovial bear of a man to love her, gratitude to Hess for waiting for her for so long. Everything that seemed proper had been done, every decorum observed. She turned her heart loose, at last, turned it loose to love. "Close the door."

Chapter Twenty-Four

Aron Millerson had been trying to increase his proficiency with the *Iesuchristion*, the huge book containing all of the Words of God. The Lady Hollie's request for words of comfort at Smead's memorial service had taken him by surprise, and he had determined that—as much as he was able—he would not be caught off-guard again. Also, he had practically promised young Owan that he would find him some kind of answer that would provide solace for his adolescent trials; he felt that the answer he sought must be in this book somewhere.

He had obeyed the dictates of the Amendicarii not to write out a translation of the book in his own tongue … mostly. At least he had not copied out a word-for-word rendering. But what Aron *had* done was to take selected portions of the holy scriptures and copy them, a paragraph or two at a time, and then add his own thoughts about the words. In this way—he hoped he wasn't committing some kind of blasphemy—he was creating some entirely other kind of work: a commentary on the *Iesuchristion*, not just a translation of the holy words into the mundane. And he did not intend that anyone else should ever see these words. He just thought it would help him study, and remember, and understand, so that the next time Lady Hollie or Owan pinned him down with a question, he would have an answer fit for an oracle of God. Not for the sake of his own pride did Aron desire this; it was an honest yearning to do the work of God in his small, fat, sweaty fashion. He prayed as he wrote: *God, forgive me for my presumptuous ways. If I am in error by writing out your sacred words in my common tongue, forgive me, chastise me, correct me. But help me to serve You and Your people, the best that I possibly can.*

The passage Aron was working on at the moment presented some difficulty for him in translation, and once deciphered, gave him more trouble just to comprehend what it was God was saying in the words. He shook his head, stymied for the moment, and turned back to the

Iesuchristion. Perhaps he had misunderstood. Again he read the words—words that Iesu had once said to His friends:

> *... cum inmundus spiritus exierit de homine perambulat per loca inaquosa quaerens requiem et non inveniens dicit revertar in domum meam unde exivi et cum venerit invenit scopis mundatam et tunc vadit et adsumit septem alios spiritus nequiores se et ingressi habitant ibi et sunt novissima hominis illius peiora prioribus ...*

With a line of perspiration starting to bead along his furrowed brow, Aron worked out his translation again. *When the unclean spirit is gone out of a man ... he walks through dry places, seeking rest*, Aron wrote. *—seeking rest, and finding none.* Aron nodded to himself grimly; that part seemed fairly straightforward.

He continued his interpretation: *So the unclean spirit says ... "I will return to my house whence I came out."* That sounded ominous. *And when he comes ... he finds it swept clean and garnished.* Aron's quill scratched feverishly against the parchment, and his sense of disquiet grew. *Then he goes and takes with him ... seven other spirits more wicked than himself ... and they enter in, and dwell there.... And the last state of that man is worse than the first.*

Aron sat back and blinked into the dimness of his candlelit cloister. He wished he could ask Matthias what these words meant ... though he feared he had understood them well enough. He wished he could at least speak with Gosse or Spence! They were brighter than he; they might know what to do. But they were far away, and he would probably never see them again, not in this world. He sighed, frowned. Maybe he didn't need to do anything. But perhaps he should at least talk to Captain Boole.

ξ

In hushed tones they cackled to themselves, barely able to suppress the delicious maleficent glee that swelled within their spirits like hot, venomous bile within Herm's chest. "Shh!" one would hiss, and then "Shh!" another would answer, and then one again would bark, "You'll wake him!" and then the four demons would giggle and gurgle and hiss like smoke. And in Herm's belly there was a tremulous rumbling, a fluttering, like bats, like the wings of the bats in Ruric's tortured dreams.

There was one of the demons, the one who had been the dragon spirit of Blythecairne for a hundred years of men, who had inhabited Herm's marionette body once before. He had been granted access to Herm's meager mind by the meager magic Herm made, and been exorcised by the undoing of that same magic. After his forcible expulsion from the proud puppet man, the demon had joined the other three, his kindred spirits, in the bowels of the last dragon of Hagenspan.

Such destruction had they made! Such death had they birthed!

But at last, the candle of that dragon had been extinguished, and the four devils had been forced to wander through arid places, as cursed Iesu had said, always within the smell of burning sulfur and the sound of unquenchable cries. And not the luscious cries of frail humanity—no! These were the throaty, hatefilled bellows of other demons, bound and tormented by the servants of the Creator they despised—terrifying portents of the everlasting living death that the dragon spirits too would one day live, and die. But not yet—not yet. *Now* was the time to curse God, to curse God again. Now the time to poke a finger in the holy eye, to belch a sulfurous pong into the holy nostrils. To spoil a bit more of the creation of His delight, to ruin lives of the children of His affection.

Iesu Himself had suggested it. Nay, He had prophesied it, He had granted it, He had even promised it! "Find the house swept and decorated," foul Iesu had said, and so the dragon spirit did. After spending a moment or two or a few years—who could tell?—wandering the flaming desert and listening to the stinking bawls of his own future, the spirit who had been the dragon of Blythecairne floated back toward Herm, suspicious at first for a trick. But then he found his dancing little puppet just as he had left him—empty, but tidy, but *empty.* With the ethereal eyes of his demon consciousness darting back and forth, ever alert for a trap, he entered his little home again. And as Iesu had said—fool Iesu! God of God!—as Iesu had decreed, the demon found little Herm spacious and accommodating.

Room enough for more!

"Seven spirits more wicked than himself," stupid Iesu had granted. Well, the Blythecairne demon didn't have access to seven other spirits—only three. And they were most certainly *not* wickeder than himself, the devil thought haughtily— but they would have to do! *Come and see!* he had cried to his kin, and they had flown across the expanse to Ruric's Keep, to the castle of the king, to little dancing doll Herm. Chortling with mad hilarity barely suppressed, the devils entered their new home, and filled it, never letting Herm suspect that he was anything but empty. *Hellfire and damnation!* they suggested to him. *You're going to be the king!* And they laughed.

"Shh!" one would hiss, and then "Shh!" another would answer, and then one again would bark, "You'll wake him!" and then the four demons would giggle and gurgle and hiss like smoke.

Chapter Twenty-Five

Ruric the King, third of that name, called Serpent's-Bane at his own insistence, woke from a peaceful sleep feeling delightfully refreshed. It was almost as if he had been long submerged beneath the Great Sea and was now rising, rising from the depths, rising to the light. He longed to stretch his arms and was faintly surprised when they did not move. His eyelids fluttered, battling the dim rays that filtered into his bedchamber. Though his vision was blurred, he could make out the form of another sitting beside his bed, crowned in white, and knew her to be Maygret.

He opened his mouth to greet her, or so he thought, and he heard himself utter a muffled grunt. Maygret's head snapped up—he saw the shock on her carelined face as she recognized that he was there, he was not gone. *How are you, my dear?* he asked, and heard one short unintelligible grunt in his own ears. *Who is making that disagreeable sound?* he asked, and then he knew.

"Ruric! Your Majesty!" Maygret whispered, all full of despair and wild hope. "May I get you something? Water?"

Ruric was rising, rising from the depths. He needed no water. With a colossal effort of his will, he forced his lips to part, groaned, looked at his queen through his pale, unblinking eyes, willed her to hear him. *Have I been a good king, my dear?* For some reason, she did not seem to perceive his question.

"I have been singing for you, my king. Did you hear me?" she asked pleadingly, as she motioned for the girl to bring a skin of water.

Ruric found a reservoir of strength from someplace, summoned his voice, whispered, "No," and wished instead that he had said *Yes*.

When the girl tried to hold the skin to his lips, he shook his head slightly. He was thirsty, yes, but not for water. He was thirsty for … what?

Wine? No. He didn't know. But not water. The girl looked helplessly at Maygret, who murmured, "That's all right," dismissing her.

Did you know how proud of you I was? he asked Maygret. *Did you know how much I loved you?* He was rising, rising.

Maygret the queen stared at her husband in horror as his breath seeped from his lungs through his sagging lips, as his unblinking eyes continued to stare back at her. Rising, rising. She reached out a trembling hand and shook his arm, his cold arm.

From somewhere above her, he saw her grip her robes in her fists, and with shuddering limbs attempt to rend them, but she was too feeble, too old, and so she lay her head down beside the still old man on the bed and wept. *Why are you doing that?* he thought happily, feeling especially strong and vigorous. He wondered what was going to happen next.

ξ

"Sound the bell," Herm commanded grimly. "Sound the bell once for every year of King Ruric's reign. Hagenspan must know that a great man has left her shores this day."

"Yes, my Lord," Sir Olefin replied, and soon the sonorous tones of the huge bell of Ruric's Keep began to peal mournfully across the land. In the streets of the city, people's heads were raised, conversations aborted, faces curious and fretful. Five times, then ten. As the bell tolled again and again, the waves of shimmering sound proclaimed the lament for the king. Fifteen … twenty.

Knights outside the castle removed their helms, bowed their heads. Women on Market Street clutched their children to their knees, or dabbed at their cheeks with their sleeves. Dogs howled. And still the dirge played on and on. Thirty … forty. Babies cried, and so did old men, who didn't know altogether what Ruric had meant to the kingdom, but feared where future days might lead them nonetheless. Forty-three times came the hammer of metal upon metal, the elegy of iron and bronze.

Finally the bell stopped, the sound echoing through the distant hills, the clanging din dissipating into an unnatural, uncomfortable silence. After a time, somebody talked, and then somebody answered, and after another moment or two, somebody laughed … but for the rest of that day, nobody forgot Ruric the Third, King of Hagenspan, called Serpent's-Bane. And it was known that a great man was gone, gone forever from Hagenspan's shores, and that somehow, tomorrow, the world would be different than it had been today.

Chapter Twenty-Six

At least his mother and Boo had had the opportunity to have their wedding before this new time of mourning had been declared, Owan thought. Forty more days of mourning! He groaned silently. Would this entire year be wasted wearing dull colors, eating dull foods, making dull conversation? Is that what Smead would have wanted? What the king would have wanted? Well, maybe.

The wedding had been a joyous affair—just a few words mumbled incoherently by Aron Millerson to get the God part out of the way, and then hours of jubilation, filled with loud singing and drinking and dancing. Owan and his friends had been allowed to fill their cups with mead (though Hollie had probably not known how often those cups would be filled!), and soon the room had spun and danced by itself, a blur of lights and sounds and laughter. Joah had danced with rose-cheeked Sirina, and had declared it to be the greatest moment of his life. Tully had had his face loudly slapped by homely Bleuthe when he had attempted to plant a drunken kiss on her cheek, and the handprint had still been visible the next morning. Three of the boys had puked out their celebratory excesses in a dark corner of the courtyard; only Windy had been able to hold his drink, and Owan suspected that he had actually snuck off somewhere and performed the same act himself, beyond the scrutiny of his friends' bleary eyes. It had been a great night.

Oh, and his mother seemed really happy.

Owan felt no bitterness toward Boo for marrying his mother. He recognized that Hollie was a beautiful woman, kind of, even if she was his mother. And she had been alone for an awfully long time. And out of anyone Owan could possibly have picked for Hollie, he acknowledged that Captain Boo would have been the best choice.

Almost surprisingly, Boo had completely renounced any claim to the lordship of Beale's Keep on his part. He had said something about avoiding any appearance of opportunism, whatever that meant, but what it amounted to was he just loved Hollie. So he was still just "Captain Boole," not lord of anything. And Owan thought that was all right, for being a captain suited Hess Boole just right, and merely giving him a new title probably wouldn't have changed much anyway. Except that, now, Owan was still first in line for the succession, and that was all right too. He loved his mother, but he wasn't naïve enough to think she was going to live forever, and with Boo renouncing the lordship, at least there wouldn't be room for any potential hard feelings between the two later on. Of course, Boo was older than Hollie, and would probably die first anyway. But Owan was still a little impressed with the man—his stepfather—that he would decline the lordship of Beale's Keep.

And then, just a day after the messenger arrived from the king's house saying that old Ruric was dead, the guard Kelly had come back from a long time away— nobody seemed to know where it was he had gone. But he had come with a pair of other horseman, and they had a wagon with them, heavy with gold. Hollie had seemed very happy to see him, Owan had thought, and had asked if he had heard anything from Feather—another guard who had mysteriously gone missing. But Kelly didn't seem to know anything about that, and a day later he was gone with the others, and the gold, and they were trudging southward toward Ruric's Keep. Owan had asked Boo what was going on, but the Captain had been evasive. So Owan forgot about it, more or less, but he was a little annoyed that his mother and Boo didn't think he was old enough to care or understand.

Oh, well. He supposed there was plenty of time for the intrigues of court when he got older. Today, at least, there were lessons with Dreo, and swimming, and practicing his archery, and that was enough, enough for one day.

ξ

Billy Clay had begun the great adventure of his life just days ago. He was traveling on horseback from his home in Katarin to the great castle of Blythecairne—the first time his father (or his mother) had ever allowed him to go out all by himself on a trip of anywhere near this magnitude. He had a letter from his father, Padallor Clay, the chief of Katarin, introducing him to the two Lords of Blythecairne, Lirey and Keet, and requesting that he be allowed to spend the winter there and learn courtly ways. Apparently his father was calling in some old favor that the Lords owed him—a fact which impressed Billy Clay greatly.

Billy was heading due east across open land … well, mostly open land. He had to pick his way carefully through the scrub brush and short trees that blocked his path at times. But his father had told Billy that if he kept his horse's nose pointed to the sunrise, and his arse pointed toward the sunset, he would come upon Blythecairne in less than a week, if he didn't dawdle. Billy was trying not to dawdle.

Off in the distance before him, he noticed some crows gathered in a cluster on the ground, squawking and flapping at each other, and he figured there must be a dead animal there. Of course, he had seen plenty of dead animals in his time, but his curiosity was piqued; besides, he liked to bother the crows. So, with a tug on his horse's reins, he headed in the direction of the commotion. His horse, Reddy, shied at the cacophonous cluster of glistening black birds, but Billy patted his neck comfortingly and clucked his tongue in encouragement. The crows protested noisily, but gave way.

What he found unnerved him a bit, and he suddenly wished he were back in Katarin, sharing a pint with his father at The Cold Fish. Mostly bones is what it was, already picked clean by the black-winged scavengers, but the size and shape of the skeleton and some tufts of hair lying about led him to conclude that it had been a dog, a yellow dog. That in itself was not particularly alarming, but the fact that a black-feathered arrow had obviously been the cause of the dog's demise was. For a moment, Billy entertained the ludicrous and chilling idea that the crows themselves had killed the dog, and he involuntarily shuddered.

"Come on, Red," he said in a low voice, and nudged the horse's belly with his heels. The horse seemed happy enough to be on its way again, leaving the quarrelsome crows to bicker over the bones.

Billy rode slowly on for a few minutes, entering a mottled thicket that promised new terrors on every side. And almost as soon as Reddy had stepped into the faint path between the shadowed brush, Billy heard it: the voice of a ghost maybe, or perhaps the challenge of the warrior who had shot the dog with the arrow. A low moan from the bushes produced a startled yelp from the boy, accompanied by the urge to kick Reddy in the flanks and send him flying toward the trees, which was only barely suppressed. But Billy's curiosity overcame his unreasoning fear—and the voice of the ghost warrior did not, in fact, sound all that threatening.

"Who's there?" Billy asked, and his voice seemed to peep like a chick in the large emptiness of the wild.

"A bit of help, if you please?" came a barely audible plea from the bushes.

"Yes," Bill swallowed. "Yessir! Where—where are you?"

"Over here," the voice sounded again. "I fear I can't walk."

"Hang on, I'll find you." Billy dismounted, shuddered convulsively once again, steadied himself, and draped Reddy's reins across some branches. "What happened? Bandits?"

"Of a sort," the voice said weakly.

"Oh," Billy replied, and he wished the other would talk some more, but then he scolded himself. If the man *had* been set upon by bandits and left for dead, he was probably weak with hunger and pain. "Want some food?"

"In a bit."

Billy pulled back some boughs and found the man then, a largish man, ashen-faced, lying on his side with another black-feathered shaft extending from behind his right shoulder. His tunic was crusted with blood, and his legs seemed to be jutting out at wrong angles. Billy fought the urge to retch, and lost that battle.

"Not too pretty, am I?" Feather groaned, with a wry grin on his pasty face.

"I'm sorry, sir," the boy apologized, and began to cry. This was more of an adventure than he had hoped for. "Who done this to you?"

"Black Knight," Feather gasped, and then whatever reserves of strength he had been drawing from ran out, and he lapsed into unconsciousness.

Billy didn't know what to do. Should he ride on to the castle and bring help for this man? He figured there was no way he could lift him onto Reddy. But he didn't know if the man would still be breathing by the time he got back with help from Blythecairne, even provided that the people from Blythecairne would believe his story and come. In the end, he decided to make camp right here, and see if the man would wake up in a bit and help him with an idea. He built a fire, checking over his shoulders for anything that might be a Black Knight. Once a crow came and perched on a nearby branch and squawked at him. He wondered if that might be it, and threw a rock at it.

ξ

Feather's eyes fluttered open, closed again, and he said, "I'm dry."

Billy scrambled to provide him with a drink of water from his skin. He had noticed an empty water-skin lying on the ground beside the man, and wondered how long it had been since he had drunk, but he didn't dare to try to give him water while he slept.

Feather nodded, and Billy took the skin away from his lips. "Good."

Billy squatted on the ground next to the man, and waited for further direction.

"Thanks for the fire," Feather murmured. "It's been cold of a night."

"Welcome."

After a moment more, the wounded man said, "I'd kind of hoped you would've took that arrow out of my back by now, while I slept."

"I'm sorry," Billy replied, horrified. "I didn't know how."

"It's all right," the man smiled feebly.

"I don't think I can," Billy hesitated.

"It's all right."

Billy squatted next to Feather until the muscles of his legs ached. *Not so bad as this fellow, though*, Billy thought. Finally he asked, "Can you talk?"

"I expect so."

"What's your name?" Billy asked, and Feather told him.

"Did the Black Knight shoot you with that arrow?" Feather nodded.

"What—what happened to your legs?"

"He did that, too. Whilst I was layin' on the ground after he shot me ... he come over and stomped both of my legs." He added unnecessarily, "Busted."

Billy nodded sadly.

"He give me that water-pouch, too. Damnedest thing," Feather said, his voice trailing off.

Billy waited respectfully for a moment, and then asked, "Why do you suppose he did that?"

"Said he was tired of killing. Not *too* tired, I guess." Feather coughed weakly. "He said he'd give me a chance to live, and if I died, it was up to me, not him."

"Oh," Bill said, because he felt that he had to say something.

"Best sleep a mite, lad," Feather gently smiled. "We've a sore trial ahead of us in the morn. I'll take the first watch."

Billy was amazed that this man had the strength to attempt a joke in the face of his troubles, even if it was only a feeble joke. He decided that he liked Feather. He said a silent prayer, as he laid himself down under the scrub, that Feather would still be alive at the coming dawn. And that he could help him, somehow.

Chapter Twenty-Seven

Lady Jesimonde Tenet Bost was anxious to be going. What was taking Brette so long? He had said he would be ready to leave with her this morning.

She knew what it was that her old friend Alan Poppleton desired … though she did not yet know how she was going to respond. But she knew that she was going to let him plead his case, and see if he was able to rekindle any desire in her heart. And she already did desire to at least see if those faint embers could be stirred again, as they once had, during the turbulent days when they had courted, once, long ago.

She knew that she could return to the house of her husband, if she wished. And part of her did wish that, for before Tayson's injury, her days at Thrimball had been carefree and full. She had had warm girlish friendships with three of Lord Bost's many daughters—Bennita and Audra and Bessamer, the youngest—and she missed her sisters-in-law, almost as much as she had missed her own sister Piper after Tayson had married her away to Thrimball.

But since Tayson's death, she had noticed a suggestive leer in her father-in-law's eye, and she had begun to fear spending time alone with him. Old Lord Bost seemed to be angry with her for reasons she did not entirely understand, too—it wasn't *her* fault that Tayson had died. She wondered how it was that he could be bitter toward her one moment and yet still lust for her the next, but then, she did not pretend to understand all of the ways of men. She just knew that if she could imagine a crude, base reason to interpret a man's behavior, she was probably correct.

Even Alan had once been that way, she remembered, though he had become a changed man after the Dragon War. But her first encounter with Alan, which had occurred when she had been just a girl, had been an uncomfortable attempt by him to wrest a kiss from her when he thought they had been alone in the stables. She had only been rescued from that clumsy rape of her lips by the sudden presence of her Uncle Cedric, who had been hidden in the shadows; he had sent Alan packing, gently but firmly. Funny, though—it was her wise Uncle Cedric who had later commended Alan Poppleton to Jesi, with what turned out to be the last words he ever spoke to her. That certainly counted for something, Jesi thought.

"Laupra," Jesi called to the attendant who had traveled with her from Thrimball, "would you please see if you can find Master Brette, and see if he's nearly ready to go?"

"Certainly, Miss," Laupra replied. "I'll be back quicker than a lamb's tail. You just sit yourself down and relax."

"Thank you," Jesi said, and she did sit down, but a moment later she was on her feet and pacing again.

ξ

Brette said guiltily, "I should probably be going. I bet your sister is wondering where I am. Probably wearing a groove in the floor."

"I suppose," said Piper softly. She was surprised at how strong the sense of regret was that she felt. "Do you think … you may have occasion to visit Castle Thraill again?"

"I'd like that," Brette blushed. "I'd have been here earlier this morning, but I couldn't think up a proper pretense for bothering the Lady of the castle."

"You need no pretense to bother me," she said, blushing too.

"Then you may be sure that I will be back." He stole a furtive glance at her emerald eyes, and drew courage from the fact that they were gazing tenderly back into his. "Soon, if you like."

"I would," she said simply, but then felt a pang of misgiving. "Brette—"

"Yes, my Lady."

"You know—" She didn't want to say the wrong thing here, but she was suddenly unsure of what the right thing was. "You know that I will … never marry? Probably," she concluded weakly. "Don't you?"

Brette was silent for a moment. He was saddened by her question, but he didn't want to betray that sadness to this lovely young woman, who was still suffering from wounds of her own. "Until a fortnight ago," he began softly, "the idea of marrying someone as fine as you never even entered my mind." He studied the patterns on the stone floor at Piper's feet. "It's an honor to me that you would even be troubled by such a thought."

Piper reached out and took his hand. He drew that hand to his lips and kissed it gently, and once again, she was startled at the poignancy of the response she felt.

"I know I'm a lesser man than Sir Willum, who holds your heart," Brette said humbly, and Piper felt the urge to protest rise in her breast, but held her peace. He continued slowly, "You might also say … that Captain Boole was a lesser man than Lord Roarke. But he persevered. He loved her, and he persevered. And see what a change the years have wrought." He kissed Piper's fingers, and she nearly gasped, swooned. What was happening? "Now, I know for a fact that I'm a lesser man than Captain Boole, and I don't know that I could stand to be around you for fifteen years and never—" he blushed furiously, "—and never, uh—"

"Brette."

"I'm sorry, my Lady. I didn't prepare this speech, it just kind of came upon me sudden."

"Brette, will you give me a year to decide?"

A look of astonishment broke over his face like the sunrise. "Why, of course I will!" he said, and he couldn't help smiling broadly like some kind of a simpleminded oaf. "I—I believe you've made me quite happy!" he blurted, and laughed aloud.

Though her brow was still furrowed with confusion, she smiled a small smile back to him. "I haven't promised anything…."

"I know, I know," said Brette, standing, still lightly holding her hand. "But you've given me—unless I misunderstand—you've granted me a year to enjoy your company and look on your lovely face. And then—who knows?"

"Thank you, Brette," she said, rising as well. For a terrifying moment she thought he was going to kiss her, but instead, he just bowed deeply, released her hand, and turned to go. "Brette?"

"The sooner I get your sister delivered to Lord Poppleton, the sooner I can be back."

"Yes," she murmured. "Brette?"

"My Lady?"

"Godspeed."

"Thank you, Piper," he said with a wink. And then he was gone.

ξ

From the shadows of the stable, Bascan watched as the girl Laupra led his reviled foe to the room where Lady Jesimonde impatiently waited. *If only you'd stayed in your own station*, he thought bitterly. *I told you I'd kill you, but would you listen?*

There had been rumors of a knight dressed all in black, who walked through the north lands as silent as shadow, as silent as death, who served neither God nor king, but committed treacherous acts of brutal terrorism. Bascan had no idea if there really was a Black Knight or if he was but the frightened gossip of peasants, but no matter. Myth or man, he served a purpose for Bascan now.

A day earlier, the longhaired captain had crafted two brace of arrows fitted with crows' feathers, and coated with pitch and scorched to make them black all over. He had hidden them in the crook of a tree along the trail that led from Castle Thraill south to Lauren, which would doubtlessly be the path chosen by that fool Brette to take Jesi and her handmaid to Ester. They would be traveling slowly, of course, for did women ever ride hard? There would be plenty of time for Bascan to leave the castle, retrieve his arrows, and shoot the damned fool in the back without ever revealing himself. Wouldn't the Black Knight do it that way? Then the frightened women would scamper back to Thraill bearing their tale of a black shaft dropping from out of nowhere like the wrath of God descending upon their miserable escort, and the deed would be one more crime ascribed to the mysterious black-clad brigand. Bascan smiled nastily. The Lady Paipaerria could wear her own black for another month if she chose ... but sooner or later, she would surrender. She would be his. He gave a soft snort of presaged triumph. Then another thought occurred to him. *But what if someone wonders why Brette alone was killed, and the ladies left unharmed?* He pondered that idea for a moment.

Perhaps it would be best for me to shoot one of the women as well.

Chapter Twenty-Eight

The Lady Maryan walked alone along the perimeter of the fields of Blythecairne, quite far from the castle. It was one of the concessions she made for the maintenance of her sanity—several times a week she would take a long solitary walk to enjoy the feel of the sun on her face, the breeze riffling her long hair, and the sweet, blessed silence, away from the commotion and clamor of her house, which was nearly bursting with the pulsing vitality of her husband and nine sons. Maryan was growing old—she could feel it when she rose, aching, at dawn, and when she retired, exhausted, at night. There had been a heavy toll to pay for the blessing of birthing nine boys and giving them suck. But she tried not to betray the frailty of her body to Lirey, the husband that she adored. She smiled and worked and planned, and rested when she could. She only hinted at her aches and torments to Thalia, the wife of Keet, who shared the lordship with her husband.

Lady Maryan had been the darling of Blythecairne once. She had been the only woman to travel north to the desolate castle with the little expedition that had set forth from Fairling to reclaim the land from the dragon Roarke had killed. She had cooked meals for them and tended their wounds and sung over their dead; she had been mother and sister to them all. Now, two decades later, she was revered, esteemed among her people. Though Maryan was virtually unknown outside County Bretay—they had not sung songs about her like they had for the Lady Hollie, who had once possessed legendary beauty and had killed the last dragon of Hagenspan—among the people of Meadling she was venerated as much as famous Hollie, who had once also been the Lady of Blythecairne, but had been carried off to other adventures by her husband and God.

Maryan knelt to examine some small purple wildflowers, and a squall of wind whipped her hair in front of her face. She swept the tangled curls from her lips and cheeks with a wave of her hand, and thought to herself that the breeze held the first chilly promise of autumn in its gusts. Suddenly a new sound pierced the relative calm; from somewhere quite nearby she heard the mellow tones of one of the horns of Meadling, which signified that some traveler was approaching the borders of Blythecairne. She rose to her full height, her knees aching, and debated whether to head back to the castle or walk out to meet this visitor.

Hearing a hum of voices being raised in excitement but not being able to discern their words, she decided to see what the commotion was. Cutting through a field tall with brown-tasseled corn, she emerged upon the path that stretched north from the King's Road to Castle Blythecairne. Several workers standing in a worried knot greeted her with nods and waves. Down the road a couple of the farmers were running to meet a boy who led a reddish horse, over which was draped the form of a man. She turned in that direction and began walking briskly. Behind her she heard the horn sound again, and beyond that in the distance, the bells of Blythecairne.

"Lady Maryan!" One of the farmers in front of her had turned around and was jogging back toward her. "Ye'd best not have a look; it's grim!"

She nodded to show that she understood, and thanked the man, but continued striding purposefully toward the new arrivals. She met them quickly; the boy was as young as some of her own sons, and he was weeping. She laid a maternal hand on his arm, and glanced back at the man draped over the horse—it *was* grim. "Is it yer father, lad?" she asked softly.

"No," the boy sobbed. "It's Feather."

Maryan was not sure she understood what he was saying, but she asked, "Is he dead?"

"I don't know," the boy replied, and one of the farmers said, "No, m'Lady, not quite."

She told the farmer, "Take the strap from this boy, an' lead the man an' the horse up to the castle, an' call fer the surgeon, an' see if somewhat can be done fer 'im. Me an' the boy'll follow along presently."

Maryan continued to hold the boy's arm, keeping him back from following the horse, separating him from the tragedy he had brought to her borders. "What's yer name, lad?" she asked with a gentle smile.

"Billy Clay."

"Ah. Would ye be the son o' Paddy Clay o' Katarin, then?" she asked, and he nodded gratefully. "I've knowed yer dad, time past. He's a … surprisin' man."

"Thank you, ma'am," Billy said. "I'm awful sorry about crying."

"No need t' be."

"I didn't cry until I saw the people. I just felt so … relieved, and then before I knew it—"

"That's fine," she said, patting his arm. "Even me own husband's been knowed t' tear up a time 'r two, an' he's a man." She began walking slowly northward toward the castle, still holding his arm. "What brings ye an' yer, ah, Feather, t' Blythecairne?"

"He's not *my* Feather. That's his name," Billy said, and immediately feared that he had sounded disrespectful. "Beg your pardon, ma'am." She smiled at him, though, diffusing his apprehension, and he continued. "I was heading to Blythecairne, with a letter from my father, and I come upon him lost in the wilds. Feather, I mean. It's a wonder that anyone ever found him."

"How'd he get t' be in the state he's in?" she wondered. "Could he tell ye?"

"He said it was the Black Knight."

"Oh!" Maryan unconsciously began to walk a bit faster. She had heard rumblings about the dark-clad knight—who hadn't?—but there had never been any report of him venturing this close to her home before.

"I don't think he's still around, though," Billy said by way of comfort.

"No, o' course not," she agreed. "Ye must be a very brave boy." She patted his arm again distractedly, but did not slow her pace.

ξ

Nat Bene, who had risen from a humble beginning as a guard in Yancey's Brigade to the exalted status of court physician of Blythecairne, examined Feather's wounds, touching and poking and sniffing. His visage became apprehensive and pale, and he said, "Ye'd best call Gosse. We'll be wantin' a prayin' man."

Lirey nodded to one of his sons. "Go find Gosse, Tim, like Nat says." Tim, tall and slender, practically a man, nodded in reply and hurried from the room.

"Ye see where this arrow's stuck into 'im," Nat pointed out, speaking in undertones, "it's all green an' sickly. Oozin'. We got t' get that arrow out of 'im, but it's like t' kill 'im, just t' do it."

"But it'll kill 'im sure if we leave it in there, won't it?" Lirey asked.

"Aye, surely."

"Then let's just do what needs t' be did."

"In a bit—that'll be arright," Nat Bene said. "Let's give Gosse a chance t' get here an' ask fer God's help first."

Lirey looked at the doctor grimly, then nodded.

"Look at the poor feller's legs," Nat continued. "All black an' busted. If he ever walks again, it'll be a marvel."

Feather rasped through cracked lips, "Howdy, gents."

"Ye're awake?" Nat Bene asked in astonishment.

"In and out," Feather replied in a coarse whisper. "More out than in."

"Ye're in a bad way," Nat told him, in case he didn't know.

"I'm looking … for the Lords of Blythecairne."

"Ye've found 'em," Lirey said, bending down to the man. "I be Lirey, an' I can answer fer Keet, in a bind like this."

"I come from … Lady Hollie," Feather wheezed, then he coughed once, and a worried look creased his dirt-streaked face. "Help—" With that he lapsed into unconsciousness.

"Has he died, poor soul?" Lirey asked.

Nat shook his head. "Not yet. But I hope Gosse gets here quick." He laid his hand on Feather's face and forehead. "When Tim gets back, send 'im along for my leeches."

ξ

"Greetings, Sir Herbert," the Lady Hollie said as she welcomed the slender knight into her counsel room. "Tidings again from Ruric's Keep—so soon?"

"Yes, my Lady," Sir Herbert replied with a bow. "And Captain Boole—you are to be congratulated."

Hess Boole smiled thinly and said, "I'm surprised a bit that the news has got all the way to the throne."

"The Prime Minister knows much," Herbert answered uneasily. With something like a guilty look at Boole and Hollie, he said in a lower voice, "He has eyes and ears in most unlikely places."

"Forgive us our suspicions," Hollie said lightly. "We are so isolated here in the northlands, sometimes we forget our manners."

"No, my Lady, the fault is mine. Would that my tidings were pleasant, but I fear that they may prove troublesome for you."

Hollie sighed. Boole said, "Well, be out with it, then."

Sir Herbert apologized again, and produced a scroll from his pack. "Would you care for me to read it, my Lady?"

"All right."

Herbert broke the seal, unrolled the parchment, cleared his throat, and began.

> *To Hollie, Lady of Beale's Keep and widdow of Roarke, Lord Cedric:*
>
> *Payment has been rec'd in the amt. of nine thousand rurics.*
>
> *Due to the untimely death of His Majesty and the need to settle the Royal Accts., the year given most gen'rously by the king must needs be shorten'd.*
>
> *One month from today you must appear in person at the Castle of Ruric's Keep bearing in hand the remanant of your debt to be repay'd, or else to give acc't of why you cannot repay it. If repaymt of your loan cannot be made, the ~~cullat~~ collatterrel for which your late husband borrowed the sum must be turn'd over to the Crown. To wit: whatever Lord Roarke bought with the money loaned*

him by the Crown shall become the property of the King's Estate.

(signed) Herm, Prime Minister, for His Highness Ruric King of Hagenspan

The room became silent. Sir Herbert cleared his throat again, chuckled nervously, and said, "Well, perhaps that wasn't as bad as I'd feared. At the very worst, you'll have to turn over Lord Roarke's purchase to Prime Minister Herm."

"Quiet, man!" Hess Boole snapped. "You don't know what you're saying!"

"Hess," Hollie said softly.

"Forgive me, my Lord and my Lady," said Herbert, humiliated. "Is it very dear, then?"

"Yes," Boole said in carefully measured tones, "it's very dear."

"I am most sorry for speaking out of turn," Herbert apologized.

Hollie said, "All is forgiven, dear Sir Herbert. As my husband noted, you didn't know what you were saying."

Herbert nodded gratefully, and stammered, "What answer, then—what answer shall I give the Prime Minister?"

"Tell him … tell him nothing," Hollie decided. "Tell him you have delivered your message, and that we are formulating our response. Tell him he'll hear from us within the allotted month."

"Yes, my Lady—thank you."

"Captain Boole, will you kindly take Sir Herbert someplace where he can find a meal and a bed for the night?"

"Thank you. my Lady. You're too kind," Herbert said.

"Come along, Sir Knight," Boole said, and he clapped him on the shoulder encouragingly, silently apologizing for his brusque manner toward the messenger. "I'll find you some bread and cheese, and you can eat with me and the men tonight."

Chapter Twenty-Nine

Owan said to Joah, "Can you feel it? It's all tense and jittery around the castle."

"Hadn't noticed," Joah replied cheerfully. "I'll try to pay attention this afternoon."

Tully and Windy were working in the fields that afternoon, and Owan and Joah were on their way to taunt them with prospects of a forbidden excursion to their sanctuary amid the willows, before joining them at their labors so they could get done sooner. But Owan's mind was plagued by dark thoughts that hovered overhead like rainclouds.

"It's coming from Ruric's Keep, I think," Owan reasoned. "First there was the messenger telling us the king's dead, so everybody was gloomy already. And then that other fellow, the skinny one? After he came, my mother shut herself up in her room for a whole day just to pray, and when she came out, you could tell she'd been crying. What was that about?"

"I don't know," said Joah unnecessarily.

"And Boo—he's even more secretive around me than he was before. Used to be, he'd talk to me about most anything, except not about my mother. But now it's like another curtain's been drawn or something. He's preoccupied. You can see he's worried about something."

"Hadn't noticed," Joah repeated. "Sorry, Buds."

"What good are you?" Owan asked, mystified.

"Well ... I can swim."

ξ

Bascan had retrieved his black arrows from their hiding place along the path to Lauren, and was now scurrying to catch up with the oxcart that inched its way slowly southward carrying Brette, Jesi, and Laupra, along with a significant accumulation of baggage for the women. As he jogged along on foot, he bit out blasphemous curses under his breath. This plan was proving to be more difficult to execute than he had imagined. He tried to cheer himself with thoughts of the Lady Paipaerria; he imagined himself as the Lord of Thraill, Piper at his arm.

After giving the travelers a bit of a head start, he had stolen out of the castle grounds unnoticed, leaving his horse behind at the stable so that no one would wonder where he was going. But by the time he had gotten to his cache of arrows, the wagon had made considerable progress, and Bascan had been forced to run under the blazing late-summer sun to catch up. Trotting along the path, half-hiding, trying to stay ready to conceal himself in an instant should the need arise, Bascan's progress was laboriously slow. He didn't see the wagon at all until he was much farther south than he had anticipated, and he was considerably more exhausted too.

Finally he saw the tops of heads bobbing over the horizon and knew that he was close. Urging himself onward, he sprinted over the next knoll, and blessed his good fortune: the oxcart had stopped. Apparently the travelers were discussing whether to make camp or continue the rest of the way into Lauren, or maybe somebody had to make water—he didn't know, but the wagon was stopped. He darted behind a bush alongside the road, and drew the first of his pitch-covered shafts.

First Brette, then one of the girls. He would kill Brette, but if he could manage to merely wound one of the women, preferably the handmaid, that would be best. Brette had just dismounted from the seat of the wagon, and was helping Jesi down. Bascan drew back the bowstring, but he was more winded from his exertions than he realized, and his arm trembled. Relaxing the tension of the string, he paused and took two deep breaths, then drew the string again, steadily now, and let the arrow fly toward his hated foe. *For Lady Paipaerria!* he raised the silent cry.

Perhaps it was the weakness of his arms, or maybe the pitch that coated the arrow had altered its balance—Bascan didn't know—but the arrow flew high and wide of its mark. For a shocked moment, he thought it was going to strike the handmaid Laupra directly in the face, and he involuntarily stood up to warn her, before he remembered he could not. At the last second, though, she turned her head, and the shaft creased her cheek and clipped through her hair. Even as she screamed, a red stripe appeared on her cheek. Jesi's head snapped up and she stared at her friend, but Brett quickly traced the path of the arrow back to its origin and saw Bascan standing there dumbfounded.

"What are you doing?" Brette demanded furiously, and Bascan thought, *Damnation! Now I'll have to kill them all!*

Grabbing another blackened arrow, he drew a bead on the center of Brette's chest, and sent it whizzing on its spinning course. He watched in horror as the shaft sailed through the air and lodged in the flank of the startled ox, which leapt off the ground and began loping southward, spilling the contents of the cart along the path. Laupra leapt from the wagon and landed in a crumpled heap beside the road.

Jesi ran to her friend, and Brette, even though he was unarmed, started sprinting toward Bascan. Even though there were still two arrows remaining, Bascan, shocked at this disturbing turn of events, spun and dashed off into the wilderness. Seeing him flee, Brette halted his pursuit, and went back to see what help he could provide for Laupra.

As Bascan stumbled through the tall grass and fled for the protection of the forest, he cursed bitterly. His mind raced, his thoughts jumbled; could he return to Castle Thraill? Where else could he go? Maybe he could go back long enough just to retrieve his horse and steal some supplies, and then head out innocently, never to return. And then where would he go? Would he find a place to start over? Would he become an outlaw? Would he become the Black Knight? *Wait*, he told himself suddenly. There was still one other way. One other way. He could go back and kill Brette, then Jesi, and Laupra; then no one would know what had happened, and he could return to Castle Thraill ... return for Piper.

ξ

Brette knelt to check on Laupra; she appeared to be bruised and dazed, and it seemed that her wrists had been sprained by her fall from the oxcart. Her face was bleeding where it had been scored by Bascan's black-tinted arrow, but that injury was not serious. The ox had stopped some distance down the road, and was bawling in frustrated pain. "You stay with her," he said to Jesi, "while I try to put our stuff back together. If you see him coming, give a yell."

"He's coming," Jesi said softly.

Brette jumped with surprise, and gazed toward where Bascan had disappeared. The longhaired man was indeed striding purposefully in the direction of the three travelers, though he was still quite far away. Brette pulled the girls to their feet, and said, "Come on!"

Laupra leaned against Jesi and the two shuffled along as quickly as they could after Brette, who sprinted to the wagon. For a moment, Jesi thought with dismay that he was running away, a coward, but she was shamed when he arrived at the cart, rummaged through the cluttered baggage in the back, found his sword, and then ran back in the other direction to meet his foe. As he passed the women, he gasped, "Pray!" and kept on running.

Jesi turned and watched as Brette proceeded toward Bascan. She saw the captain of Thraill's guard stop and raise his bow, and for a moment she wondered, dazed, how this thing could be happening. Then she remembered to pray, and got as far as *Please, God,* when she saw the release of the arrow, and Brette's jagged lurch as it struck home somewhere on the side of him she could not see. She watched as Brette staggered forward, nearly losing his footing, but somehow stumbling on. Bascan hurried to draw another arrow, but Brette reached him before he could fire it, pitching forward into him and running him through with the point of his sword. The two men collapsed on the ground together, a tangle of arms and legs and sharp-pointed weapons, and Jesi feared that they were both dead. Then a new fear struck her: that perhaps Bascan was *not* dead. And she knew that she had to go and find out.

"Wait here," she said to Laupra, who replied, "No, my Lady. I will come with you." Laupra had recovered somewhat from her injuries; though her wrists were still useless, she could walk.

The two women went trembling, hand-in-hand, to where the pair of men lay on the earth in their grisly embrace. They were both alive; Brette was moaning softly, Bascan whimpering and staring at the sky. Jesi rolled Brette over onto his side. A black-feathered arrow protruded from his left shoulder, both before and behind, and his tunic was stained with blood. He seemed confused, barely conscious.

Bascan stirred and tried to rise, but could not. Jesi glared down at him contemptuously, and demanded, "Why would you do such a thing?"

Bascan uttered a dry cough that might have been a chuckle, but contained no mirth. "For love."

"What?" Jesi said incredulously, but Bascan said no more, and Jesi realized suddenly that he was dead, though he still stared toward the sky.

Laupra drew her attention back to Brette. "We'll need to care for our savior, lest he share the fate of our attacker."

"Oh, my. Of course! Yes."

She knelt in the dirt and the blood and tried to get Brette's attention, but he was someplace beyond speech. "We need to get the arrow out of him, and then stanch the wound somehow." She looked up at Laupra, who hovered over Brette like an anxious guardian angel. "Run back down to our luggage and bring a clean garment. I'll try to force the arrow through."

"Are you sure?" Laupra said hesitantly, and Jesi said, "Go!"

While Laupra went to fetch something to use as a bandage, Jesi first stripped the feathers off the arrow—no need to make them pass through poor Brette's body. Then she tried to push the arrow through with the flat of her hands, but it was too hard for her. Brette groaned a painful protest, and she murmured an apology. "Iesuchristi, show me what to do," she breathed, and she saw a flat rock lying nearby. Picking that up, she swung it against the shaft of the arrow like a hammer, and drove it most of the way through Brette's shoulder without much more difficulty.

Laupra returned bearing a shift of white linen, and Jesi said, "Good. When I pull the arrow out, stuff it in the wound." She gripped the shaft behind Brette's shoulder and gave a tug, but the wood was slick with blood, and her hands slipped. Crying out in pain, she stared, dismayed, at her palms, which had been sliced on the sharpened, barbed head of the arrow, her own blood mingled with that of the men. Her eyes filled with tears; her voice filled with despair. "I can't!"

"You *must*, my Lady!" Laupra urged. "Try this." She wrapped the clean tunic around the barbed arrowhead, and gave the two ends to Jesi. "Pull!"

Jesi pulled, and the arrow came out with a slick, moist *pop*. Jesi handed the tunic, now bloodstained, to Laupra, who used it as best as she could to plug the hole the arrow had made, both front and back. Clasping her hands tightly to arrest the throbbing flow of her own blood, Jesi knelt in the grass and sobbed.

Chapter Thirty

There was so much to do. Now that Maygret was both queen and king in Hagenspan, she had begun to pay strict attention to the affairs that her husband had handled until his final incapacitating illness, the affairs that Herm had so skillfully managed during the days of the king's infirmity. There was so much to do! She had never imagined the volume of tedious tasks that demanded the king's attention, the piddling problems of patronage. She wondered how it was that she had not noticed this over the course of her lifetime, had not noticed all of the things that occupied Ruric's attention.

She was tempted to throw it all into Herm's lap and let him just take over.

After all, he *was* the Prime Minister. And he would probably be king when Maygret died, too.... She suddenly realized that this was the one thing that she actually did need to do—the one thing that Ruric had left undone: Declare a successor to the throne.

Of course it would be Herm, she thought. Who else could it be? Once, ages ago, she had thought that perhaps Cedric Roarke, the Dragon-Killer, would be a worthy successor to Ruric Serpent's-Bane. But that thought had been snuffed out like the wick of a lamp, crushed with Roarke beneath the dragon's foot. After the war against that last monster had ended, most of the valiant men of Hagenspan had been spent, along with the king's will to name his successor. But Ruric had endured, through long years, and while he had endured, Herm had always been there, his right arm, his confidence. Of course it would be Herm.

But during these, the days of mourning for the fallen monarch, she would honor her husband by serving his people in his stead. Whatever duties were required of a king during these grim and cheerless days, she would bear upon her own shoulders in tribute to the husband she had lost.

She would not presume to choose a successor for the king during these desolate weeks, for to name a replacement would be to suggest that he could *be* replaced, he who had been the father and glory of all Hagenspan.

Her mind wandered from the stack of proclamations and decrees and pronouncements that lay on the table before her, almost all of which dealt with some kind of tribute or memorial for dead King Ruric. Her mind wandered to Herm.

He had been so … sweet. So kind, patient, understanding; so … *sweet.* The queen sighed, and she chastised herself for her own foolishness. She was an old woman. *Old!* And yet, she was forced to admit, there were times when she felt as skittish as a colt when *he* was in the room. Shaking her head as if to clear her dusty brain of cobwebs, she sought to reapply herself to her work.

She signed a proclamation extending the time of mourning from forty days to forty-three. She read a proposal suggesting the creation of a "publick park for the relaxation of the citizens of Rurics Keep, being named 'The Kings Mannor' in honor of his Most Holy Highnes Rurick the Third," and signed that too. She started to read something else, and after a moment realized that her eyes had been moving along the page but nothing she had viewed had translated any meaning to her brain. Surprised, she realized she had been thinking about Herm again.

As if he had been summoned by her reverie, the Prime Minister appeared at her door, knocking politely on the sill. "Majesty? May I enter?"

"Oh, yes! Herm. Yes," she stammered, mortified at the idea that he could read upon the map of her face the places her thoughts had taken her.

He smiled boyishly at the white-haired woman, and said, "I thought that you might be in need of some refreshment. You have been working so hard."

"Well—"

"I insist, Your Majesty ... if you will permit me to insist."

Pleased at his persistence, the queen answered, "On the condition that you join me. Upon that stipulation, *I* insist."

"Nothing would honor me more," Herm crooned, and he clapped his hands twice to summon a maid bearing a steaming pot of tea and a tray of pastries and fruit.

After the maid had set the table and been dismissed, Herm poured the tea for Maygret, and she thanked him. "Not at all," he replied smoothly. "My only desire is to serve you."

She felt the color rise in her cheeks. "One day soon ... you will have need of learning how to *be* served, as well as serve," she said.

"I cannot think what you mean, Majesty."

"It's just that ... when I die, someone will need to rule Hagenspan."

A look of dismay crossed Herm's handsome face. "May that day be far, far away, Majesty!"

"Perhaps," the queen replied.

A moment of reflective silence passed as the two took sips from their teacups. With a thoughtful tone of voice, Herm said slowly, "If the day ever came when I should be called upon to serve the country as I have served the king ... I would do my best. I would live and die for the glory of Hagenspan, as King Ruric taught me. But Maygret—" here he looked at her earnestly, "—my desire—my great hope—is not that I should serve the country, nor the crown, but *you*. Not you, the queen ... but you, the woman."

Maygret's breath caught in her throat, and for a humiliated instant, she feared that she would choke on her tea, and cough and sputter before her handsome Prime Minister. Could it be that he was actually proposing himself as a suitor? But suddenly the idea struck her as eminently reasonable. How better to transfer the authority and power of the kingdom to Herm than by—than by— She found that she could not complete the thought.

Herm broke the awkward silence. "Forgive me for speaking so boldly, Your Highness," he said shamefacedly. "Perhaps you wish me to leave."

"No," Queen Maygret said softly. "That will not be necessary. Though perhaps we should forego such talk … forego. For the moment."

"Of course," Herm earnestly agreed.

"Perhaps," Maygret ventured, "when the days of Ruric's remembrance have passed … if you wish, we might talk of such things then?"

"Thank you, Your Majesty," Herm said. "May I refresh your tea?"

"Yes. Please," the queen said, looking with longing at the hands which held the teapot.

Chapter Thirty-One

The four friends were staging one of their epic battles: the Defenders of Hagenspan warding off the Invading Horde of Trolls. Tully was pretending to be Brood, the Troll King, and Joah was Kender, the King of Hagenspan. Brood's army, which consisted of Windy, was engaged in a fierce wooden-sword battle with the army of the humans: Owan.

The two warriors parried each other's blows, swiping, thrusting, blocking— neither one gaining a distinct advantage at first. After several minutes of frenzied battle, though, Windy began to pant and blow. Desperately, he took a wild cut at Owan's midsection and missed, spinning uncontrollably and toppling into a gasping heap upon the grass. Owan swatted him smartly on the back with the flat of his wooden blade, producing a yelp of protest. Then he dashed around his trollish enemy and directed the point of his sword toward Windy's throat.

"Well done, Kender's army!" cried Joah.

"Okay," the subjugated Windy wheezed.

"God! He fights like the war was for real," Tully (the king of the trolls) said with a trace of resentment.

"Maybe," Owan said, unsmiling. Red-faced from his exertions, he bent over with his hands on his knees, greedily gulping in as much air as his lungs would hold.

"He thinks there might be trouble coming," Joah confided.

"What for?" demanded Tully. "The land's at peace. Has been as long as I can remember."

"Well, that ain't so long," said Windy from his spot on the ground.

Owan straightened up, stretched the sore muscles of his back. "Dreo told me that peace is a fragile thing. That's how he said it: 'fragile.' He said that everything goes in cycles, and that any land that trusts too much in its peace is destined to lose it."

"I don't know," Tully said sullenly.

"Where's he from, anyway?" Windy said, meaning Dreo, who was Owan's tutor in the matters pertaining to his eventual lordship, but was not in charge of the normal, mundane studies of the other children of Beale's Keep.

"Someplace across the Great Sea—not Lispen, but he's been there too. The place he's from is called Combira, or Cambria, or something like that." Owan felt a twinge of shame that he couldn't remember the homeland of his tutor, which he knew Dreo had told him about.

"Well, anyway," Tully said, "we're at peace."

Joah looked at him quizzically. "You never listen at all, do you?"

"What are you talking about?"

Owan twirled his wooden sword in his hand, then flipped it neatly in the air and caught it by the haft.

Windy said, "I'd like to see you try that with a real sword."

"You must think I'm as stupid as you are," Owan laughed.

"I'll show you stupid," Windy threatened, lumbering to his feet again and taking up his carved plank.

"You're not serious."

"We both are," Tully said, and the two of them advanced on Owan in tandem.

Owan chuckled nervously, and said to Joah, "Are you going to help?"

"What do you need him for?" Windy taunted. "You want to get ready for a war? Let's see how you do, one against two."

"All right," Owan said with a tight smile.

Windy and Tully mounted their attack on Owan then, and he fought them off for a few minutes as Joah watched, impressed. But finally the two larger boys proved to be more than he could handle, and he threw down his sword. "All right! I surrender!"

"Two whacks with the flat of our blades, then," Tully said. "That's our terms."

Grimacing, Owan turned obediently and presented his backside. A moment later, smarting from his defeat and his punishment, he said, "I didn't do too bad for one-against-two."

"Nope," Tully agreed. "Nobody's saying you ain't the best. But count your blessings that there ain't a war."

Owan nodded thoughtfully.

ξ

Piper walked through her mother's rose garden for the first time in several weeks, looking contemplatively at the late-season blooms and noticing traces of their faint perfume carried on the caprice of the breeze. She was suddenly glad for the gardeners that she had employed since her mother's death; she had been briefly tempted to let the garden grow wild, and her father and Lord Smead, perhaps, would not have objected. But now she was grateful that they had kept the flowers trimmed and nurtured, grateful for the beauty they reflected back at her, grateful for their nodding affirmation of the beauty she radiated herself.

She made her way to the stone dragon in the center of the garden, which had overseen the courtships of countless couples at Castle Thraill. It had once cast its baleful gaze over Piper herself, and her beloved Sir Willum, when their trembling lips had met in their first hesitant kiss. She smiled slightly as a long-shut door of her memory opened a crack. That dragon had witnessed *many* kisses.

Once it had been a fountain; Willum had marveled at how the water continually spouted from the dragon's stone mouth. But after the report of Willum's death had reached Thraill, Piper had ordered the water turned off, and Smead had not denied her. Its merry, burbling vivacity seemed to mock the cold weight of death that she carried about in her tortured bosom, and she had silenced it. For a decade and a half, the stone pool had remained empty except for leaves blown there by the autumn wind, and the occasional accumulation of a few drops of rainwater.

Piper seated herself at the edge of the dry pool, and wondered why it was that she ever thought that turning off the fountain would be a gesture of honor for poor Will. Wouldn't he have been happier to think that even though he had ceased to be, the things that he loved endured? Will had always been cheerful and full of hope—the most optimistic person Piper had ever known. If he happened to be gazing down from Iesu's land, if he were watching Piper still … maybe he'd like the fountain turned back on.

She allowed herself to admit a fleeting thought of Brette, and then quickly shooed him from her mind. Drawing in a long breath of autumn-tinged air, she turned her face toward the sky, bathed in the sun's golden stream, shook her head gently, the breeze catching wisps of her auburn hair and caressing them soothingly. She breathed again, slowly, deliberately, and released it with a sigh. "Ah, Willum … I did love you," she whispered. And then she thought of Brette again, and realized with a gradually increasing certainty … that she was happy.

She rose, and strolled along the cobbled pathway of the garden, noticing with satisfaction where defiant tufts of grass had won their tiny battles with the cold undersides of the paving stones. *Life*, she thought, *will not be denied.*

She bent over some velvet roses, dark as blood, and breathed in the scent of their bouquet. She should visit her father this afternoon, and tell him about this new peace, this new pleasure—this new curiosity—that she was experiencing. He would want to know. She heard someone humming a lazy, contented melody, and was pleased to discover that it was she, herself. She nearly laughed, and it surprised her so much that she stopped her tune. When was the last time she had laughed?

Walking thoughtfully through the curving path between the flowers, she pondered this intriguing state of her heart. Was there something special about Brette that had set her free from the bondage of her despair? Or had it just finally run its weary course; had a decade of mourning for poor Will been enough? And, if she had just happened to have finished mourning, she considered, perhaps Brette had just happened to come along at the right time. Maybe her heart was free—free to love *any*one!

She wondered about that for a moment, tentatively trying on other suitors like changes of clothing before the looking glass. She considered Wallace, Forttay, Bascan, and Pelfrey—the four unmarried captains of Castle Thraill's guard. They were brave men, all of them, and at least two of them were quite handsome. But none of them moved her heart, she decided, and she summarily dismissed them. She mulled over the young knights and lordlings she had met; she opened the door to her past a little bit more to see if there might be some lingering wistfulness about Alan Poppleton … but no. Then she considered Brette.

A pleasing sensation of warmth filled her, as if it were warm milk being poured into a saucer. She smiled. She had been cold for a long time. She would tell her father; he would want to know.

Chapter Thirty-Two

Dreo the tutor sat with his elbows on a table in the castle's refectory, solemnly chewing on a crust of brown bread. He was a slender man, well advanced in years, with a tangled shock of white hair and a sporadic white beard. He had traveled to many places in this corner of the world, and had peeked behind the corners too, when he was able. Of knowledge that was available in books, he had perhaps more than any other man living in Hagenspan; of experiences and adventures in the vast world, the same. His face was wrinkled and creased, as if it were a map upon which the cartographer had attempted to draw every tiny creek and rivulet. He had come to be at Beale's Keep because he had heard the song about Hollie's beauty, and had decided to see it for himself. Once there, he had declared that there were six women he had seen in his life that were more beautiful, but she was the seventh, which was no mean blessing. (Privately he confided to Hess Boole sometime later that she may have actually been the fifth.) And Hollie had prevailed upon him to stay and share his wealth of knowledge with her babe Owan, whom Dreo had only tolerated at first, but had grown to love as, perhaps, a cherished nephew. There were days, now that Dreo was old, when his manner was impatient with people that he deemed to be dimwitted. Other times, he welcomed any conversation, no matter how slow and stupid his companion, for he had learned valuable things even from idiots. He noticed fat Aron Millerson walking tentatively into the dining hall and, feeling charitable today, waved him over.

"Blessings of Iesu be upon you," Aron said hesitantly. He was a bit intimidated by Dreo's vast learning.

"And upon you," he said benevolently. Dreo did not believe specifically in Iesu, but admitted the possibility that there might actually be some kind of supreme creator—though he bowed the knee to no superstition.

"I'm pleased to have found you," Aron said. "I'd been meaning to have a word with you."

"Hmm," Dreo replied with a twinkle in his eye.

"I'd like to talk with you about Owan."

"Indeed?"

"He seems … to struggle with matters of faith."

"Excellent! I was hoping that he should!"

Aron, confused, said, "I … don't— Is that wise?"

"Ah! What is wisdom?"

This was why Aron avoided protracted conversations with Dreo; he felt like he was constantly fencing with the old tutor, always defending, never advancing.

"I should think that it would be beneficial for the young lord to trust in the Almighty; to commit his course to His care."

"Perhaps, perhaps," Dreo acquiesced. "But this 'Almighty' that you commit yourself to: who is he?"

"Why, Iesuchristi," Aron said defensively.

"Yes, Iesuchristi is the god of the day here in Hagenspan, but it was not ever thus," the old pedant began. "Other peoples in this very land have called their gods by other names at other times. The first men who came to these shores worshiped Iopeter; when they arrived, they found an indigenous tribe who named their god Architaedeus. Which of these is the master of your Iesu? Or is it he who is first god?

"And in other lands—I have been there—there are other words for the same crumbling deity: some call Him Alleh, some call Him Yhwh; some utter his name not at all. Some worship one god, as do you; some worship many, scattering their entreaties abroad like seed in a field, hoping that *someone* will hear! And some gods are not so kindly as your Iesu claims to be … but is there a difference?"

Aron Millerson stared guiltily at the table. He felt that he should have an answer, but his brain was slow, faulty. He started to open his mouth and make a reply, but he decided it was insufficient, and changed his mind.

"Oh, no, don't surrender so quickly!" Dreo cried. "Here—let me help you." Aron looked at the old man, perplexed.

"Don't fear; I mean you no harm," Dreo laughed. "I have read the book you call *Iesuchristion*—at least some of it. There are parts in that last half of the book—the Second Covenant, I think you call it—that deal specifically with old reprobates like me. There are some parts written by the famous Paulus Apostolus that seem to declare that all matters of faith (as you call them) are decided by decree of the god. That, no matter how learned or quick of mind I may be, I am utterly unable to perceive the truth of the god unless he specially reveals it to me. Conversely, no matter how dimwitted or dull *you* might be—not meaning to offend—if you are blessed by the favor of the god, you are inestimably better off than me. A matter of having your destiny chosen for you, you might say."

Aron was unsure of these matters, but he nodded that he understood.

Dreo continued, "All bosh and nonsense, of course. Why, man's as free as a bird, to chart his own course. Can't you feel it? Doesn't all of your experience shout out that it's so? Still, I mention it only to show that there are other points of view than mine. It's possible I am wrong." He laughed tolerantly.

Aron thought of the thread of an argument, and voiced it. "Men have always believed in a Creator."

"Yes, and that's another point in my favor, isn't it?" Dreo challenged him. "Your Iesu is rather a late comer to the god competition, is he not? There were Bales and Iopeters and Zooces long before your Iesu arrived at the ball. Seems that if Creation is the argument you wish to use, then the oldest gods would be your champions. Perhaps Yhwh, who was venerated in Iuda."

Aron answered, "I believe you misunderstand Iesu. He has existed since before time."

Dreo waved a hand dismissively. "Perhaps. As I say, he has apparently not graced me with his choosing." Aron looked at him, troubled. "But you mentioned young Owan. What is your concern?"

"Yes," Aron said, trying to recollect his thoughts. "I believe that Owan is … angry with God for taking away his father. I think that's the root of his frustration."

"Yes, that is quite perceptive of you, young priest." Dreo tapped the table with a bony finger. "I will give you a gift. I should make you find it for yourself, but you might read that book for years and never see this passage—it's so damned big."

Aron bit his lip; he did want the gift of Dreo's learning, and didn't want to say something that would change the old man's mind.

"There is a little verse buried deep within the songs of the king of Iuda called David. It says something like this, in your tongue: *'God Himself will be a father to the fatherless.'* You might build a tidy little homily around that theme. Perhaps that might be of comfort to young Owan Roarke."

"Thank you, Master Dreo," Aron said humbly, but privately he thought that that was not such a very large gift. He ventured, "Is there more?"

"Oh, I'm certain there must be," Dreo said offhandedly, "but I believe you will have to do the rest of that work for yourself."

Aron nodded. "Thank you again. If you don't object, I will make mention of you to Iesu in my prayers tonight."

"Not at all. Mention me to *all* of them, if you wish. Perhaps the light will shine on this poor benighted soul."

Aron smiled. "Just Iesu. But I will pray for you most fervently."

"Thank you, thank you, young priest." Dreo returned a wrinkled smile at him. "You're a fine lad. You must come to class with Owan one day. We shall debate."

"I will—if you will come to worship." Aron beamed back at him, feeling that he had finally scored a touch in their verbal fencing.

"Ah, you have found my weakness!" Dreo cried. "Well, we shall see … we shall see."

Chapter Thirty-Three

The blood had crusted over on Jesi's gashed palms, and Laupra's weakened wrists had healed enough so that she could help, but loading the wounded Brette into the back of the oxcart the next morning was a pain-filled, tear-filled endeavor. By the time the two weeping women had hoisted the unconscious man into the cart, Jesi's hands were cracked and bleeding again, so they remorsefully left Bascan lying in the open field, his face covered by one of the dresses that had been littered along the trail.

With some difficulty, they got the injured and irritable ox turned back northward and goaded toward Castle Thraill; sometime later in the morning, the two battered women reached the gates of home, huddled together like refugees. The guard who received them immediately saw their distress and raised the alarm, bringing several of the castle personnel running.

"Get my father," Jesi sobbed, and one of the guards sprinted for the castle.

Haldamar Tenet and the Lady Paipaerria sat in Haldamar's room, the sparse apartment that he occupied alone since the death of his wife Ronica. Piper held her father's hands in her own, and was talking softly but urgently, wearing a smile as tentative and hopeful as springtime upon her winter-worn face.

The guard found them there, and hesitated before knocking at the doorsill and clearing his throat; it looked as if the Lady was speaking of things precious to her tender woman's heart. But he realized his duty, and apologetically interrupted their conversation.

"What is it, Debler?" Piper asked the guard.

"Forgive me, my Lady," Debler replied. "My lord. Your daughter Jesimonde begs you to attend."

"Are you sure?" Haldamar asked dazedly. "She's gone to Ester."

"Is there trouble?" Piper rose from her couch, and stepped toward the guard. "Please come, Daddy."

"The two ladies have returned, and they seem to be injured," Debler said uncertainly. "I know nothing else."

"But—where is Brette?" Piper asked anxiously.

"I did not see him, my Lady."

Piper rushed past the guard then, a fresh look of dismay upon her face. Debler waited to provide Haldamar with a sturdy arm to lean on as he descended the stairs, if he wished it. The old man shuffled beside him, thanking him, still confused why Jesi had returned.

By the time Piper reached the cart and its troubled cargo, Jesi and Laupra had been helped from the seat, and were being attended by some of Thraill's women. The castle's physician—Sonnat Timple, a sturdy gray-haired man with a manner that always suggested he was a bit distracted—was clucking and shaking his head at the backside of the wagon. A couple of the guards were with him, awaiting his instructions, wearing grim, perplexed expressions.

"Piper!" sobbed Jesi. "Where's Daddy?"

"Coming," Piper said sternly. "What's happened?"

"It's terrible," her sister cried. "Captain Bascan—for some reason—tried to kill Laupra. He said it was for love."

Piper had no idea what she could mean. But she asked the question closest to her heart: "Where is Brette?"

"When he tried to defend me, the captain shot him through with an arrow," Laupra said, and Piper noticed the neat slice along the young woman's cheek.

"A black arrow!" Jesi said.

"This—this is crazy!" Piper said, fighting to beat back a sudden fluttering terror, but just then the guards carried the wounded Brette past her under the supervision of Sonnat Timple, and she saw his hurt for herself. The doctor was bustling ahead of the guards, snapping orders back to them. Piper started to say, "Take him—" but she was interrupted by the doctor, who said firmly, "Under control, m'Lady. I'll take care of him."

Piper nodded grimly, feeling impotent and out of place. Her father was arriving from across the courtyard, and Jesi ran to his welcoming arms, weeping.

Piper still did not understand the significance of Bascan's actions; she turned to Laupra. "Captain Bascan loved you?"

"I—I had not known of it, my Lady," she admitted.

"Where is he now?"

"He lies in an open field midway to Lauren. We could not lift him."

"He is dead?"

"I am sorry, my Lady."

Piper shook her head, and tried to understand. "Had Captain Bascan been courting you?"

"We had scarcely met. I am baffled by it."

"Well, never mind. It is done now, whatever it is. And you and Jesi are safe." Piper turned to two of the guards who were still milling about, mystified, and asked them to take the oxcart back down the road and retrieve Bascan's body.

"Could it be true, my Lady?" one of them asked.

"Could what be?" she said with a trace of asperity.

"That Bascan was the Black Knight?"

The question stunned Piper, and for a second, for two seconds, she was unable to respond. "Of course not," she said at last, with little conviction. "There's ... no way that he could be."

"Thank you, my Lady," the guard said, ducked his head, and left to tackle his grim chore.

ξ

Queen Maygret had been flitting about the palace like a butterfly, smiling and rose-cheeked and a little absent-minded. She was cheerful and generous to everyone she encountered, from knight to maid to wobbling tot, doling out compliments like gifts, as if she were a cheese vendor at market cheerfully dispensing free samples of curds. The charwomen of Ruric's Keep noticed (of course) and chattered about it among themselves.

"Have ye seen Her Majesty?" one of them asked.

"Of course I have," replied her friend. "What are ye talkin' about?"

The first woman straightened from her labors and brushed a stray strand of hair from her face. "She's happy, I think. She bubbles like a pot."

"You would too!" a third woman joined in.

The first woman said, her tone slightly befuddled, "It couldn't o' been *that* hard bein' wed to old Ruric."

Her friend splashed some water toward her, and said, "It ain't Ruric, ye great ninny! I thought ye knew!"

Embarrassed, the woman said, "O' course I know!" Her homely face was a mixture of defiance and bewilderment. "What?"

"Why, ain't everybody talkin' about it? As plain as the great warty nose on your face, it is! Her Nibs is in love!"

ξ

Queen Maygret was in love; there could be no other explanation. Love! What an amazing, serendipitous, foolish thing to have happened to her! She smiled to herself, thinking it was a secret smile, unaware that she was announcing her coltish joy to everyone who saw her. And, to be fair, if she had known it, she would not have cared. For she was in love!

She had not known that such a thing was possible; this spinning, happy, colorful blur of emotions. What she had felt for her husband had been nothing like this! Her feelings for Ruric had made her compassionate, perhaps, tender and caring maybe. But what she was experiencing now made her want … to dance!

To dance!

She was filled with wonder. Did anyone else feel this way? Were children of mere peasants, right now, tasting this delightful delicacy that she—the queen— had been denied? That she had been denied, due to the design of her parents, who had arranged her indifferent marriage to young Prince Ruric so many years ago? Were children of peasants, lusty young men and fat giggling girls, allowed access into this fairyland that she had been denied? Well, no matter. For now, the curtain had been drawn, and she had been granted a glimpse through the enchanted portal.

Her thoughts were full, full of love, full of her beloved. Was there anyone so kind, so intelligent, so handsome, so trustworthy in all the kingdom? He would make a great and noble king. He would honor Ruric, who had been like a father to him. He would honor Maygret, who had been— who had been like—

She blushed involuntarily—not for the first time, lately! She thought back to the day when Herm had come to her rooms and served her tea. The details of that conversation were etched upon her mind like ink on a scroll.

"My only desire is to serve you. Not you, the queen … but you, the woman," Herm had said, and then, "Forgive me for speaking so boldly; perhaps you wish me to leave."

"No," she had said, trembling. "Perhaps, when the days of Ruric's remembrance have passed … if you wish, we might talk of such things then?"

And so they had not spoken of such things … for about the space of an hour.

But in that brief span of time, their eyes had met, had met and held, had met again … and *held*, and Maygret had fought to keep from swooning. For it felt, when Herm gazed into her eyes, as if she had been stripped bare, all secrets and desires exposed to his bold scrutiny, his tender understanding. Her naked loneliness, her yearning exposed … a door into her heart ajar that had never been peered into before, unlocked by nothing more than the insistent entreaty in the eyes of this handsome, compelling man.

"Your Majesty … I must speak, else I burst," Herm had said, and Maygret had tremulously nodded her consent. Herm had reached across the small table and taken her hand, and—contrary to all decorum—she had allowed him to do so. Herm seemed suddenly tentative, as if he were seeking the appropriate words. Appropriate words to court a *queen*! "I have … watched you … for decades." He smiled, quickly, embarrassed, became sober again. "For love of the father of all Hagenspan—for I loved the king, as you know—I would do nothing to dishonor Ruric."

A smile fluttered, faded, as Maygret struggled to comprehend this. Herm had somehow desired her? He had never betrayed it … how hard it must have been for him! But he was still speaking. "When I thought of the shame it would bring to the throne, if my thoughts were ever discovered …

I could have almost left His Majesty's service altogether. But ... how could I have endured leaving *you*?" His gaze dropped to the table, as if he were unworthy to look upon her face.

Her heart had gone out to him then, as it had been threatening to do anyway.

Since that day, there had been scarcely a waking hour that had passed without Herm looking in on the queen bearing a question, a concern, a condolence. And it was a rare one of those visits that did not include some excuse for Herm to touch the queen's hand, or for his eyes to linger wistfully upon her face. Twice he had been so bold as to kiss Maygret's hand. But other than that, he had been so polite, so discreet ... while underneath their prim conversation there was a pulsating passion impatiently pounding, like the very blood feverishly throbbing through their veins. At least, thought Maygret, that was how it was for her. She hoped ... she hoped she wasn't imagining that it was the same for Herm.

Tomorrow the forty-three days of mourning for Ruric Serpent's-Bane would be at an end. Tomorrow she would speak in earnest of things other than the affairs of court; tomorrow she would find whether there was to be had an affair of the heart. Tomorrow she would offer her body, her bed, her crown—the very throne of Hagenspan—and she hoped that it would prove to be a prize worthy of such a man.

Chapter Thirty-Four

Captain Hess Boole looked across the table at his beautiful wife, whose golden head was bowed in concentrated prayer. She still had not completely decided how to answer Prime Minister Herm's demand for repayment of Cedric Roarke's loan, and today was the last day she had to make that decision in order to provide her reply in the time allotted. So she was applying to the Almighty for wisdom from above, as Boole waited, offering his wordless encouragement. They had already talked their options through, multiplying words upon words, nearly to the point of exhaustion, but had not come to a satisfactory resolution.

If only word had come from Blythecairne, Boole thought. He had kicked himself mentally a thousand times for sending Feather unescorted to the castle in the east. He had not realized how dangerous the journey must have been, or else he had badly underestimated his man. Had Feather gotten sick, gotten lost? Had he simply abandoned his mission? Had he been mauled by a bear or a wolf? Whatever had happened … no help had come from Meadling. Perhaps they were preparing the gift for Hollie at that, but it simply had not come yet, since they did not realize that the time granted by Herm had been shortened from a year to a mere month. Boole grimaced. Whatever … help had not come.

By the time Hollie and Boole had begun to despair of aid coming from Blythecairne, it had become too late to send for more help from Thraill, even if they had been able and willing to provide it. And there was no apparent way that Beale's Keep could raise the money on their own; their meager treasury had been virtually drained of all its resources in order to come up with their share of the ransom.

So what choices had been left for Hollie? She could report to Ruric's Keep as ordered, and surrender herself as the collateral demanded by Herm. *No*, thought Hess Boole angrily. She could send an emissary explaining her dilemma, and plead for more time. But Boole had the suspicious notion that Herm knew precisely about her dilemma, down to the last detail. Hadn't Sir Herbert said that he had "eyes and ears in most unlikely places?" And pleading for more time … that would seem to be an unfruitful entreaty, since Herm had just given them *less* time.

She could defy the Prime Minister openly, but that might invite the prospect of a conflict with the king's soldiers, which Boole shuddered to consider. Even discounting the near certainty that Beale's Keep would lose that battle, the Lady Hollie would scarcely subject her people to the threat of combat, with its attendant dangers—hunger, disease, injury, death. She could ignore Herm's request altogether and just hope it would be forgotten … unlikely, though, and she could soon be facing the same possibility of open battle with the crown.

They could abandon Beale's Keep. They could run away. *Certainly must be considered*, thought Boole, though the idea of fleeing was a foul taste upon his tongue. They could offer to give the holdings of Beale's Keep back to the crown, and return to live at Castle Thraill upon the generosity of Piper Tenet. Also distasteful … also to be considered.

Hollie blinked her eyes, and murmured, "I believe … I know what I shall do."

"You do?" Boole asked, trying to mask the fact that he was a little surprised. Perhaps God had answered her after all. He seldom had received such a response to his own prayers, he thought—but then caught himself short. He was married to *Hollie,* for God's sake; if that was not an answer to his prayers, then what?

"Will you find me a brave volunteer and a fast horse?" she asked.

"Tell me what you're thinking."

She nodded. "I will write to Queen Maygret, and beg her to forgive the loan."

"Maygret!" Captain Boole said. He thought that he had imagined every potential solution to their dilemma, but he was sorry to admit he had not thought of the queen. "But … I did not understand the queen to be your friend?"

"She is not," Hollie admitted. "But she is a woman. And she is the queen."

"Yes," Boole said thoughtfully. He was unconvinced … but it was as good as any of their other options.

"I think it's possible," said Hollie, "that she is not at all aware of this demand. Perhaps it was something conjured up between King Ruric and Herm— perhaps it was Herm alone that concocted such a farce."

"Yes," he repeated. "She might be sympathetic—"

"I don't care whether she's sympathetic or not, though that might help. But doesn't justice—true justice—demand it? This whole scheme has been devised to bring me to ruin. I don't believe there's a scrap of truth to it! Cedric would certainly have paid off that loan, long ago. But with Esselte Smead dead—how would Piper know? And we have heard nothing from Blythecairne! So I have no way to defend myself." She smiled pensively, hopefully. "But the queen … she might at least give me more time."

Boole nodded in what he hoped was an encouraging manner. He didn't feel particularly optimistic about the plan, but he had to admit that it was a better alternative than the others they had considered.

Hollie concluded, "Forgive me if I've seemed short-tempered with you." Boole shook his head, dismissing the notion. "Could you get me a brave volunteer and a fast horse?"

"Kelly's back. I'll see if he's game for another adventure."

"Thank God for Kelly," Hollie said, and Boole agreed.

ξ

The boys were coming around a corner of the castle toward the guards' barracks when Kelly emerged from that building, with his black dog trotting beside him at the end of a rope. "Owan! Boys!" Kelly called.

The four youngsters trotted over to the slender man. They didn't know him well, since he was somewhat older, and was quiet and usually kept to himself—but they liked his dog. Owan greeted him, "Hello, Kelly."

"Lads," Kelly acknowledged with a nod. "Owan, I have a favor to ask, if you're willing."

"Sure," Owan answered, wondering what it could be.

"I have to leave on another mission for your mother," Kelly explained, "and I was hoping you'd watch my Pup for me, you and the boys."

"Ain't you taking him with you?" Tully asked.

"Not this time. I have to ride hard for Ruric's Keep, and the last time the old boy was in the city, he didn't like it much anyway." He knelt and rubbed the dog's head affectionately.

"Didn't you just get back from there?" Owan asked.

"That I did."

"I wish someone would tell me what's going on!" Owan said irritably.

"Well," Kelly said thoughtfully, "I can't say that I know, myself, not of a certain. But it's not my place to tell. Ask the Captain."

"I guess," Owan frowned.

"So, what about it?" Kelly asked. "I need to be on my way."

"Of course we'll watch your dog. It'll be fun."

"We'll all help," Joah added.

"Thanks, boys." He rubbed the dog's ribs, and kissed him on the top of his head. "I'll miss you, Pup—I'll miss you. You be good for the lads, now."

He handed the rope to Owan, and began to walk toward the stables. The black dog strained against its tether, trying to follow him, and whimpered. Kelly turned back and commanded, "You stay, now. Stay!" The dog sat down regretfully, and Kelly turned again, and walked away.

Chapter Thirty-Five

The two horses carefully stepped down between the rocks at the western foothills of the Senn Mountains, making their cautious way across the uneven land. On the foremost mount was a broad-shouldered man in his early thirties perhaps, and following him was a dark-haired youth a dozen years his junior. They were both dressed in ringlets of chain mail, and outfitted with garments of almost regal finery.

As they rode, they chatted softly, but though their manner was casual, there was an underlying urgency to their movements. As soon as the horses were free of the rocky ground and into the open plain, the riders put their heels to the animals, and they trotted briskly toward Beale's Keep, their destination.

The riders were still specks bobbing in the distance when Captain Boole spotted them. His eyes had grown accustomed to searching the eastern horizon for aid from Blythecairne, and now—even though it was too late—he found his gaze still turned often toward the Senns, his mind still wrestling with the question, like a dog worrying a bone: Why had help not come?

He bustled back to the stable to fetch Chancy, and found two of the castle guards loitering there. He beckoned to one of them, a wispy-bearded youth named Jonnefar. "Strap on a sword, lad, and mount up with me." In less than the space of a moment, the two were on their way out toward the eastern border of the Keep.

"What is it, Captain?" the young guard said apprehensively, not perceiving the oncoming horsemen.

"Riders coming," Boole said shortly. "I don't know if they be foe or friend, but there's two coming, and the two of us to meet 'em."

Jonnefar felt that he wished Captain Boole had conscripted *both* of the guards he had found in the stable, and not just him, but he didn't say so. Instead, he just gritted his teeth and trained his eyes upon the approaching men, which he could now see.

Boole pulled back on the reins and turned Chancy sideways, blocking the approach of the two strangers, and Jonnefar followed his lead. The two other horsemen rode directly for the men of Beale's Keep, and reined up a few yards away.

"Greetin's from Blythecairne," the older of the two strangers said guardedly.

"Greetings, and welcome," Hess Boole replied, also with a cautious timbre to his voice. "Might I be so forward as to demand your names?"

"Of a certain. I'm called Yancey Wain, and I'm the Captain o' the Guard at Blythecairne Castle. This lad with me is Davie, and he's the first son of Lirey, one o' the Lords of Meadling."

"Well met," Boole said, still unsmiling. "We had looked for your aid ... but you have brought none."

"We have twenty armed men waitin' fer our signal midway up the Senns, in case strength of arms was yer need. Forgive me—but who are ye?"

"Sorry ... Hess Boole, Captain of the Guard here at Beale's Keep. And this is Jonnefar, one of my men. You have twenty soldiers with you?"

"Yer messenger was waylaid on his way t' Blythecairne," Yancey explained. "All we got from him was 'Help.' Whether he meant help fer hisself, or help fer the Lady Hollie, we couldn't tell. So we sent part of a brigade, in case what he meant was the Lady Hollie was in need."

"Feather—is he dead?" Boole asked grimly.

"I'm sorry," Yancey acknowledged. "He made it t' Blythecairne. But he couldn't deliver his message."

"Didn't you find the letter from Hollie?"

Yancey shook his head. "There was no letter."

Alarmed, Boole asked, "What had happened to him?"

"It's hard," Yancey replied. "He'd been shot in the back with a black arrow, an' his legs was busted, both of 'em. Left to die in the woods. Only the Hand of Providence helped him find his way on in. We give him a hero's burial."

"A black arrow?" Boole considered the implications, thoughts darting like bolts of lightning through the thunderclouds of his mind. He had heard of the Black Knight, of course, but had assumed that the mysterious villain was just a solitary, self-interested bandit, not that he was working for another power. But this offense against Feather … what could the Black Knight have desired from the unfortunate young man save the letter from Hollie? For the first time, Hess Boole conjectured that the Black Knight was working for Prime Minister Herm … for the first time, a pang of terror gripped his heart. Not terror for himself, but terror for his beloved Hollie. What kind of foul, wicked, *evil* force had set its face against her?

"Yes, a black arrow," Yancey was saying. "There have been rumors—"

"Yes, of course," Boole said, cutting him off. "We have no need for strength of arms, not yet. But if you'll call your men down from the hills, we can feed them and bunk them. You and the young lord must come and talk with Lady Hollie."

"We will—but there's no need for ye t' feed the men. Davie, give the signal for 'em t' return t' Blythecairne." Davie pulled a thin horn to his lips and blew three times, a high-pitched rounded tone. In the distance the men could see a faint shadow begin to move back up the mountain, crawling up the rock face like a tiny slow-moving centipede. "Captain—we await yer command."

"Thank you, Captain," Hess Boole replied gratefully. "Please come along."

ξ

"Yancey Wain!" Hollie cried, and hurried to embrace the commander of Blythecairne's forces, which the man accepted and returned bashfully, smiling and patting her tentatively on the back, his face growing warm and red.

"It's a pure pleasure t' see ye again, m'Lady."

"How is Melliss?" she asked, referring to Yancey's wife.

"She's fine, fine—plump as a pear. She's back home with my two wee lads, and a baby girl as tiny as a loaf of rye bread."

"How wonderful!" Hollie gushed, and Yancey had the impression that she really did think so. The Lady next turned toward Davie, asking, "And who is this handsome young man you have with you?"

The younger man smiled gratefully and said, "I'll bet ye'll remember, once he tells ye!"

Hollie recognized something about the youth's smile then, and gasped,

"Davie! Why, you're all grown!" Tears streamed down her cheeks as she gathered Maryan's son into her arms. Some emotional vessel broke free from its moorings within her heart and she cried unabated for several minutes, patting the embarrassed young man on his arms and shoulders, and stroking his hair. "You'll have to forgive me, gentlemen," she sniffled, "but last time I saw Davie he was just a boy."

Finally she composed herself, and noticed Hess Boole standing uncomfortably to the side, wearing a concerned look upon his honest face.

Hollie felt a pang of regret, realizing she had just been drifting down an emotional road that her husband had no access to. Longing to draw him to her, she instead drew him into the conversation. "Yancey, Davie—you've met my husband, Captain Boole?"

"Husband!" Yancey blurted, unaware that anyone could possibly have replaced Cedric Roarke in Hollie's affections. Quickly he recovered, smiled broadly, and said, "Why, congratulations, Captain! Ye must be a man indeed!" He extended his hand to Boole, who took it with a self-conscious grin. "When did this happen?"

"Only just," Boole grumbled, pleased in spite of his misgivings.

"Ye should've sent word," Davie said to Hollie. "We'd've sent a gift."

"Thank you," she smiled. "In fact, that is almost what we did when we sent you Feather."

"Hollie—" Boole began, suddenly realizing that Hollie probably thought the two men from Blythecairne had brought the six thousand pieces of gold with them.

"Where is Feather?" she asked. "He should eat with us all tonight."

"M'Lady—" Yancey said, and Hess Boole finished the thought, "Feather's dead."

"What?" Hollie asked in a small voice, and a fresh reserve of tears burst from her eyes. "How did—?"

"He was attacked along the way," Boole said.

"He got to Blythecairne, though, but the only thing he said was ye needed help," Davie added.

"Yes, we did," she said, dabbing her cheeks. "We still do, probably. Poor Feather!" The men waited patiently, awkwardly, while the Lady mourned. "We must declare a day of fasting for him," she whispered sadly, but then she wrestled her thoughts back to face the task at hand. "You've brought the ransom?"

"Ransom?" Yancey asked.

"I explained in the letter," she said, confused, looking at her husband for support.

"They didn't get the letter," Boole said softly.

"What's it ye need, Lady Hollie?" Davie asked, an earnest plea upon his young face. "Lord Keet an' my dad have give me the say-so t' give ye whatsoever ye need."

"Thank you," she murmured, humbled that she who had once been the Lady of Blythecairne and of Thraill and of Beale's Keep should be reduced to asking the favor of a boy she had once bounced upon her knees. "I'm in need of gold."

"Well, we got *that*," Davie said. "Falconets, rurics, markees, eglons, dorpals—some more, I forget. What d'ye need?"

Hess Boole answered, "Six thousand in rurics."

Yancey Wain coughed once and quickly apologized. Davie's eyes grew wide, but he said, "Aye. We've got that t' spare."

"I'm sorry," Hollie said. "I know it's an awfully lot, and I wouldn't ask if my need was not great—"

"Don't apologize, Hollie," Davie said quickly. "Anythin' Blythecairne has is yers t' command, just about."

"And if you need men—" Yancey added, leaving the promise unfinished but understood.

"Thank you," Hollie said gratefully, gazing unashamedly at her two old friends as yet another stream of tears moistened her cheeks.

"There's something else," Hess Boole said, giving voice to his suspicion about Herm. "I fear that we were never intended to pay off your ransom at all."

Yancey interjected, "Just what is this ransom ye're talkin' about?"

"Forgive us," Hollie said, and then she explained about the letters she had received from Herm, the loan King Ruric had made to Cedric Roarke so many years before, Herm's demand for repayment, her letter to Queen Maygret asking for more time.

"Ye mean," Yancey said thoughtfully, "the loan weren't never repaid?"

"I don't know."

After a moment of silent reflection, Yancey asked Boole, "Captain, what d'ye mean that it weren't intended fer ye t' repay the loan?"

Boole answered, "I don't know how he would have carried it out … but I believe the Black Knight may be a servant of the Prime Minister. I think … the Prime Minister wishes Hollie to be at his mercy. Such mercy as it is."

The room fell silent again for a moment, and then Davie asked, "What must we do?"

Hollie said, "I don't know. Wait for word from Queen Maygret, I suppose."

"And we can bring ye six thousand in rurics while ye're waitin'. *Seven* thousand, in case they're mad that ye're late."

Hollie raised her eyes toward the young man again, a hesitant, grateful smile brightening her tear-washed face.

Chapter Thirty-Six

"Why won't you visit him?" Jesi asked her sister, the Lady of Thraill.

"I will," Paipaerria Tenet said testily.

"He doesn't understand," Jesi pleaded. "I've had to lie for you. But he knows it."

"I said I will!" Piper snapped. "This isn't your concern."

"Before we left for Ester, you spent time with him every day! It was hardly a secret. I'm your sister!"

Piper frowned and turned away.

"You were the happiest you'd been in years, I thought!" Jesi continued. "I thought—I thought maybe you *loved* him."

In a whisper, Piper said, slowly, "So did I."

"What?"

"Nothing."

"Piper, *please*!"

The auburn-haired woman bowed her head of curls and sighed. Then she turned toward her sister and said, "This is going to sound foolish. I loved Will, and he died." She stopped, afraid to continue lest a sob escape her throat.

"Piper—"

"And as soon as I dared to love another—"

"Piper, Brette didn't die."

"As soon as I dared—"

"Brette didn't die!" Jesi's eyes flared with anger. "I know what it's like to lose a husband, you know! But Brette is alive, and he's confused, and he's sad! Go to him!"

Piper looked into her sister's flashing eyes, and said, "I should."

"Go now!"

Yet she hesitated. "I will … later."

"Come with me." Jesi took her sister by the arm and led her from the room.

ξ

Trumpets blared a fanfare; drums thrummed and cymbals crashed. The great hall of Ruric's Keep was filled to capacity and beyond, since the entire population of the city had been invited to join the celebration. As many of the citizens as possible were crushed into the hall, hoping to catch even a glimpse of the festivities. Those who could not gain entrance to the castle's interior milled around in the courtyard, breathing in the mouthwatering aromas of the feasts that were being prepared for the celebration.

Far to the forefront of the hall the dignitaries were gathered: chosen knights, many of the southern lords, and priests of several gods. Of the lords, none from the north had been invited—neither Keet nor Lirey, not Pallmer, Hollie, Bost, Paipaerria, or Centenaery, not Grice or Poppleton or Sylmer. But if the lords that had been invited noticed the slight of their northern brethren, they did not mention it. The priests were a fearful-looking lot; some were garbed in bones and beaks and furs, wearing necklaces of fang and talon, wielding staves of wood engraved with angry carvings; others wore regal finery, gold and purple and haughty condescension. The only representative of the Amendicarii was Matthias in his simple brown robe, but it was not clear whether he had actually been invited.

The crowd, noisy and restless, pushed against each other and craned their necks in hopes of seeing what was going on, which, at the moment, was nothing. Children were hoisted onto the shoulders of their fathers, and mothers held their tots close to their breasts, shielding them from the press of the throng. Tempers flared briefly as toes were stepped on and ribs elbowed, but the crowd was, for the most part, orderly and well-mannered.

"Sh-h! Sh-h-h!" The command for silence made its way from the front of the multitude toward the back, sounding like the susurration of a wave breaking along the waterfront. A scarlet-clad herald was striding toward the center of the dais. He took a position to the side of the two thrones, raised a trumpet to his lips, and blew a complicated call. Then he shouted out in a piercing tenor voice, "People of Hagenspan! Your Sovereign Monarch—Maygret the Queen!"

As the white-haired woman in her royal robes and glittering jewels crossed to the center of the stage, the crowd, which had been temporarily silenced, roared an appreciative exclamation; some cried out her name, some shouted *hurrah*s, some stomped their feet or thumped their hands together enthusiastically. When Maygret reached the thrones, she nodded to the herald, turned and curtseyed toward her admiring people, and seated herself upon the larger throne—the one formerly filled by her dead husband, King Ruric—signifying that she was the ruler of the land.

After sitting there for a moment and smiling benevolently, maternally, at her subjects, drinking in their adulation like wine, the queen rose to her feet and lifted her hands in the air for silence. "Beloved people of Hagenspan! Thank you for your service, and your faithfulness, and your love for me for so many years. Thank you for your love to King Ruric, who rests now with his fathers!" Another cheer went up from the throng, and she waited for the noise to subside. "As your sovereign, it is not necessary for me to explain my actions to anyone but the gods. But because of my great love for you, my people, my heart begs me to reveal all."

A cry of appreciation rose from the people again, and again Maygret waited, gazing lovingly at the citizens of Ruric's Keep, who were more convinced than ever that they adored the gracious woman who stood before them.

"My people, my beloved!" Maygret raised her arms again, and the people hushed each other to hear her words. "Hagenspan must be strong!" She smiled again, with a hint of apology upon her upturned lips. Continuing in a slightly softer tone, she said, "I am old. I am but a woman." A murmur of dissent began to hum through the crowd, but was quickly shushed. "An old woman, I say without regret. But … Hagenspan must be strong!" She took a step toward the audience. "The gods and I have chosen for you, beloved citizens of Hagenspan—the gods and I have chosen your new king! And I wish you to know that, though I could have chosen any man my heart desired, and been answerable to no one, my heart was ever longing for the best choice for you, my people! The best king for *you*!" A loud roar of approval sounded from the crowd and lasted several minutes.

When the shouting had finally died down, Maygret continued, "Though there are scores of knights and nobles in the land, many of whom could provide competent leadership for our land—" here she nodded benevolently to the lords seated in the front, "—I wholeheartedly believe that the man whom I have chosen to be your king is the wisest … the noblest … the *best* man in all of our country. He it is, who is the one that my heart loves right well." She blushed modestly. "Today, with all of you serving as witness, we shall be wed. And great Hagenspan will have a king once again, and not a queen only. Of course, it is no secret to whom I am referring! My people—my beloved!—ready yourselves to raise the cry now for your new Lord and Sovereign! He has served faithfully as Prime Minister; now he shall serve you as King! And you shall love and serve *him*, as you have loved me, and as you loved Ruric your King before me."

She raised her frail voice, shouting as loudly as she was able, trying to be heard over the swell of the crowd.

"And because one syllable is not nearly enough to name the name of one so virtuous, so noble, I bestow upon him today—after the manner of kings—another name! Because the first of his conquests has been the conquest of the heart of a queen—no mean feat!—I give you now, your Ruler, your Benefactor … your King! King Herm the Conqueror!"

The people of Ruric's Keep shouted, cheered, stamped, clapped, roared their approval. "Long live the King!" "Herm the Conqueror!" "King Herm and Queen Maygret!"

Then Herm strode out of the wings to the center of the dais, receiving the adulation with his arms outstretched, as if welcoming the whole of the assembly in his magnanimous embrace. His silver-black hair shone, but no more than his smile, which dazzled and charmed both man and woman, lordly and common.

Maygret beckoned to a pageboy, who followed Herm from the shadows, bearing the crown and sceptre of King Ruric on a tasseled satin pillow. The boy walked over to where Maygret stood, and knelt before her. She took the sceptre and handed it to the herald, who still stood behind her with his trumpet. Then she took the crown in her two hands, and nodded to the boy, who stood and departed with the pillow. "Kneel," she commanded Herm, and she placed the crown upon his head. Again she commanded him with a single word, "Stand." And she placed the sceptre in his hands.

Then Maygret returned to the two thrones, and seated herself once more—in the lesser throne. The crowd continued its frenzied cheering as Herm, sceptre nestled in the crook of his arm, and crown balanced lightly upon his noble head, raised his right hand to them as if in benediction, beamed upon them with the golden light of his smile. "My first act as your king," he shouted over the din, "will be … to kiss your queen!" Then he stepped to where Maygret waited on her royal chair, raised her hand to his lips and kissed the veined, loose skin, to the boisterous approval of his people. His people! Then he turned and seated himself upon the throne of Hagenspan. *His* throne. And the people of Hagenspan cheered until they were fairly hoarse with celebration.

Chapter Thirty-Seven

The black dog bounded after the stick, running so swiftly that he nearly caught it in the air before it thwocked to the earth. Picking it up gingerly with his powerful jaws, he loped back to Owan and Joah and deposited it at their feet.

The boys were taking turns throwing the stick for the black dog, sending the short branch whirling through the sky like a pod dropped from an oak tree. The dog, for his part, was enthusiastically chasing it down and returning it to his young masters, though perhaps not as enthusiastically as he had at first.

"Why do you think he just calls him 'Pup'?" Joah wondered.

"That's his name," Owan replied sagely.

"Aye, but it's not too much of a name for such a grand dog," Joah said appreciatively. "He ought to have a bigger name—a grander name."

"Like what?"

"How about … how about 'Joah'?"

"Why don't I throw the stick and see if *you'll* chase it?"

"Okay, okay … how about 'Boaz, Mighty Dog of Valor'?"

"Good name," Owan admitted, "but it's not his."

"Nope." Joah picked up the stick and sent it on its way again. "If *I* had a dog, I'd name him 'Boaz, Mighty Dog of Valor'."

"What if he was just a rat-tailed cur?"

"Wouldn't matter. He'd still be a mighty dog of valor to *me*."

The dog, Pup, brought the stick back and dropped it a few feet away from the boys, and sat down, panting. Owan reached for it, and the black dog growled, not threatening, just grumbling.

"Maybe he's tired of playing," Joah said.

"I wouldn't think he'd get tired before *we* would." Owan sent the stick on its spinning circuit once again. "Go get it, Pup!"

The dog trotted obediently after the stick, got to the spot where it lay in the grass, lifted up a hind leg, and urinated on it. Then he jogged back to the laughing boys and sat down imperially, resolutely.

"Maybe he's tired of playing *now*!" Joah laughed, wiping a mirthful tear from the corner of his eye.

Owan gleefully slapped his friend's shoulder. "Gosh—do you think?"

ξ

When Kelly had arrived at Ruric's Keep several days earlier, the city had been abuzz with the preparations for Maygret's wedding to Herm, and Kelly was uncertain that he would be granted access to the queen in order to deliver Hollie's message. Still, he had his duty to discharge, so he drew a deep breath and boldly presented himself at the castle, requesting an audience with Her Majesty. The guard who had received him at the gate had bid him wait, and had disappeared back into the castle. But when he had returned a few moments later, he did not escort Kelly to Queen Maygret; instead, he and three of his companions had forced Kelly, at the points of their swords, to descend a dank, narrow stairwell into the very bowels of the castle, where they had locked him in an iron-barred cell.

Kelly could still hear the clang of the cell door, could still see the expressions on the faces of the guards who had deposited him there. One man had seemed almost apologetic, one vaguely malicious, and two were stoic, virtually expressionless, almost as if they were not men at all but some kind of impassive, soulless creatures inhabiting bodies that had been drained of blood, of tears, of compassion. Kelly had tried to plead his case with the apologetic man, but it had been the malicious one who had been in charge, and his protests had been bootless.

Part of the reason Kelly could still hear the door and see the faces was that he could see and hear virtually nothing else. When the four guards had retreated back up the stairs, they had taken the only source of light—a torch—with them. Since then, Kelly had had no contact with any human, nor any food. There was a trickle of water dripping down the outer stone wall of his cell, which he had found early on, so he had not suffered much from thirst, but his belly was a tight knot for want of bread. From time to time he felt a spider or some sort of insect crawl across his flesh, and he hurried to brush the offending creature from his skin, remembering too late that he might have been wiser to have stuffed the thing into his mouth instead. When he closed his eyes, red spectral figures danced on the back of his eyelids, and when he opened them again, they were still there, so he began to lose track of whether his eyes were open or closed, blinking only when his eyes were gallingly dry. Once he had thought he heard something slither across the passageway outside his cell door. Other than that, it was only dark and silent. Kelly wondered why the guards hadn't simply killed him, if they were only going to leave him down here until he died anyway. He stretched out on the clammy floor of his cell and waited for something to happen, and waited more. He thought wistfully about his dog, and hoped Owan was taking care of him.

After a time—he had no idea how long—he heard a kind of rhythmic slapping in the distance, and realized the sound was drawing nearer. Instead of the red spectres dancing in the blackness in front of his eyes, he saw that his chamber was becoming gray—a gray as dark as charcoal, but not black at least. Someone was coming down to his dungeon domicile.

Kelly fought to sit up, and was vaguely dismayed at how difficult that action proved to be. The sound of footfall ended on the other side of the door, and he could see dimly that the door shivered once, twice, as if someone were pushing against it but that it was heavier than the person could manage. He heard a soft voice curse on the far side of the moldy wood, a frustrated clattering, and then the door burst open and bright golden light flooded his world, temporarily blinding him.

"Are you dead?" a female voice whispered, and when she saw that he was not, "Ah! Good."

Blinking his gritty eyes with difficulty, squinting against the light, Kelly said, "Who are you?"

"It's not important. I can't stay. But I've brought you food from the queen's party, and I'll leave you the torch. I'll come back if I can. God's mercy be upon you!"

And with those words, the woman was gone, the heavy wooden door pulled shut behind her, and Kelly was alone again. But she had left the torch in a sconce on the wall, so he was finally able to inspect his surroundings, and—more importantly—a platter with meat and vegetables and bread, and a small flagon which proved to hold an excellent mead. Kelly began to eat some of the food quickly, ravenously, then realized his error and forced himself to eat more slowly. When his small, tight belly was almost uncomfortably full, he set the rest of the feast in an inside corner of his cell for later.

Now that his world was visible again, he was cheered somewhat, but only briefly. As he looked around the dungeon where he was being held, he became fully aware how small and cheerless, how utterly finite, his surroundings were. He thought with bitter irony that when his world was black, it was infinitely large, at least in potential. But now that he could see again, he had borders … he had bars.

And it was small. And he was utterly alone.

A scratch on his cell wall caught his eye—something too patterned to have been a random notching on the stone. He knelt to inspect it, felt it with his fingertips, peered at it through the flickering light. Someone had engraved something on the wall … when? It could have been years ago. Straining to read the writing, which had been painstakingly carved into the stone some day in the dark past—just so that, seemingly, Kelly could read it today—he mouthed out the words as he discerned them.

"I … will … trust." He repeated the words in a hushed tone. "I will trust." Kelly wondered if the person who had determined to trust had been here under circumstances like his own. He felt with his fingertips to see if there might be any more to the message, and made out only two more letters. "C … R."

C. R.? Could this have been the very cell where Cedric Roarke had been held so many years before, when he had first run afoul of King Ruric's advisor, Herm? Kelly experienced a startled moment of wonderment, when he realized that the Herm who had imprisoned Lord Roarke all those years ago was the same Herm who was now becoming the King of Hagenspan! How could he have failed to make that connection? It was almost as if some bewitching fog had settled on his memory, blurring his ability to clearly recall what he had heard about those earlier days.

"I will trust." Kelly repeated the words again, reverently as a prayer. He tried to remember what he had heard about the God Iesuchristi from Aron Millerson, but he had not paid overly much attention. But he knew that Roarke had exercised a strong faith in Iesu, and with nothing left to do in his own world, he decided that he would, too. "I don't know too much about your God," Kelly prayed to Roarke, "but if you'll help me somehow, I'll commit the rest of my days to Him. Though it's as like as not that there won't be too many of them left."

He waited expectantly, as if listening for an answer. He glanced around the cell, looking at the walls both high and low to see if there were any other messages to be revealed before the light guttered and failed. But he saw only the one he had already found, and decided that it would have to be enough. "I will trust."

Chapter Thirty-Eight

Glassrood had stowed his black armor in a thicket far from any snuffling dogs or snooping farmboys, buried under a mess of fallen leaves. He did this sometimes when his hunger for human companionship became too much for him to bear, when he felt absolutely compelled to venture into some hamlet or another for a woman-cooked meal and a few tankards of ale.

He walked from the wilderness on foot into the small city of Goric, and wound through the litter-strewn alleys, staying mostly out of sight. Covering his nose with a sleeve as he stepped past stagnant pools of sewage buzzing with flies, he emerged onto one of the town's main streets and swiftly made his way to an establishment he had patronized several times in the past, a tavern called Buster's.

Finding a spot at the dining board that was somewhat sheltered by shadow, he ordered beef and beer and settled in to listen to the scuttlebutt. Several other men were eating sloppily and gossiping without undue enthusiasm, and a doxy was earning an extra coin or two by waiting on the customers. It cheered Glassrood just to listen to the banter between the men, and to watch the plump woman sashaying back and forth between the kitchen and the board. One of the men at the table was a soft-spoken fellow named Carlie that Glassrood knew to be one of County Bretay's magistrates. Glassrood did not figure that he had reason to fear the local authorities, though; no one in these backward northlands was acquainted with him from his former days at Ruric's Keep or Celester. But he had concocted a cover story in case it was needed, just to be safe.

Carlie the Magistrate was conducting the business of Goric in a relaxed and cheerful manner, lightly granting some requests, deferring his decision on others, and Glassrood drew pleasure from watching the man at his work. He thought it odd that so much business was being transacted here in the tavern as opposed to the magistrate's office, but he found that he approved of Carlie's easy manner, and he decided that when he became Lord of Celester, he would hold informal hearings around a food-filled table as well.

While Glassrood was still musing about this, though, two men came banging through the door looking for the magistrate. "Carlie! News!" barked one of them, a beefy, grizzled man with a booming voice.

"Well, sit yeselfs down, an' have Lita draw ye a mug," Carlie smiled serenely, "an' then ye can tell me yer tale."

The two newcomers were eager enough to comply, and waved at Lita, who acknowledged them with a coquettish grin. "Ye'll ne'er guess," said the second man—an eager man, younger than his companion.

"Well, when ye put it to me like that, I don't know that I should even try," Carlie drawled. "The moon ain't fell down from the sky, has it?"

"No!" the younger man blurted as Lita clapped a mug down in front of him. "Nothin' like that!"

"Well, then, why don't the two of ye just go on ahead an' tell me."

The grizzled man shook his head at his partner and said, "Ye ain't got the sense of a goose." Turning to Carlie, he said, "We was just a-talkin' to some folk what come from out'n the westerlands." He took a lengthy draught from his tankard for emphasis. "An' what it was they said was, th' Black Knight was dead."

"Well, that *is* news," Carlie said, impressed.

"The Black Knight's dead, is what they said," the younger man repeated earnestly.

"Ye don't say!" Carlie acknowledged.

"Yep," the younger man said, as Glassrood sat listening, stunned.

"How'd they know it was the Black Knight? Was he wearin' that black armor?" Carlie asked.

"Yes, he was," the younger man affirmed, and his companion nodded too, but then the older man interrupted, "Well, they didn't say that, exactly. But he shot some feller with a black arrow, so they knowed it was him. He parbly did have that black armor on—" the younger man nodded enthusiastically, "—but they didn't say, precisely." The younger man shook his head solemnly.

Glassrood's head was swimming with the possibilities. The Black Knight dead! This was so much better than the Black Knight just disappearing, an idea which he had been contemplating with increasing regularity. Perhaps … perhaps there was someone else that all of his misdeeds could be ascribed to, who would never be able to deny that the crimes were his own! And then Glassrood could begin making his way back to Ruric's Keep and home at last to Celester. Celester! How he missed home.… The possibilities! Now that Herm had ascended to the crown, perhaps it was time to see if he might make good on his promise to give Glassrood the long-awaited lordship. He had to know more. In spite of his wish to remain anonymous, he ventured a question. "Who—who was it? The Black Knight, I mean."

The others at the table looked at him, surprised that he had spoken. But the younger man, ever eager to please, said, "He was a captain at Thraill Castle, an' he shot a feller from Ester with a pitch-black arrow, an' a couple o' women too. An' a horse—two horses—an' he stole a big batch o' gold, I expect."

"Remarkable," Glassrood murmured, and Carlie asked, "How'd they get him?" Glassrood was curious about that, too.

The grizzled man said, "Seems the feller from Ester, he didn't kill him, not at first anyways, an' the feller from Ester run him through with his blade."

One of the other customers listening to the story asked, "What'd he want t' shoot at wimmin fer?"

"Just a bad one, he was," the eager young man said. "His heart, when they saw it—'cause the feller from Ester ripped it clean out'n his chest—his heart, they said, was just as black as his armor. An' his blood was just as black as his heart."

Men all around the table shook their heads gravely. A cold caprice of the autumn wind blew through the crack in Buster's door, and several men shuddered—it was as if the icy hand of the evil dead had traced its finger across their flesh, making their hair stand on end. Two of the men hurried to draw their cloaks closer about their shoulders. Glassrood was sobered by the realization that these men with whom he had just shared meat and drink regarded the Black Knight as evil ... would have thought that *he* was evil, had they known who he was. He had recognized for ages that somewhere back along the way, he had crossed a line into a world of great darkness—a kind of moral shadowland—but he had never considered himself *evil.* He knew he had sacrificed his integrity for the sake of his ambition ... but he still thought of himself as the benevolent future Lord of Celester.

Carlie had just asked something, and the grizzled older man was answering. "—riddance to him, is what I say. There's somethin' aboot old Blackie that was wrong, all right. Back in th' old days, ye'd have a boss like Belder Payn or someone. An' he'd have his faults an' his tempers, to be sure. But he'd sit an' drink a beer wi' ye, too, an' he'd lay down th' coin fer it, too. But this Black Knight—he was just a terror, just a devil." He hoisted his tankard into the air. "Let's raise a glass to old Blackie, lads. To th' Black Knight! May yer soul roast in Hell for a thousand days!"

The men around the table all lifted their mugs. "To the Black Knight!" And they tipped back their heads and drained their glasses. After just a fraction of a moment, Glassrood drank too.

ξ

Sonnat Timple, the court physician at Thraill, finished his inspection of Brette's wound. "Hmm," he hummed distractedly, "you seem to be mending satisfactorily, if a bit slowly." He covered Brette's chest with the quilts again. "Perhaps we shall try getting you on your feet tomorrow. Have a bite of solid food tonight along with your broth. A wedge of bread."

Brette nodded wearily, listlessly. What did it matter? He supposed that he might as well be on his feet rather than here on his back … but what did it matter?

For the hundredth time—the five hundredth—he wondered why Piper had not come to call on him. After the moments they had shared, the things they had spoken of. After he had saved her sister's life. After the way they had touched….

After— After—what the hell. It didn't matter.

He would get well. He would follow Sonnat Timple's orders and get well. Then he would deliver Jesi to Alan, and then he would travel. Perhaps he would seek his fortune on the seas, leaving Hagenspan forever. He had been out on the great creaking ships a few times, though never out of the sight of land. But the seamen had told him tales, of vast monsters that rose dripping from the waves, grander and fiercer than dragons. Of naked brown girls on islands who bore gifts of sweet and scandalous fruits clutched next to their naked brown breasts. Of gold and drinking and fighting. He would get well, deliver Jesi, and then he would travel. He would travel, and he would forget that he had ever heard the name of Paipaerria Tenet. He would forget that he had ever touched her hand … gazed into her eyes. Heard her gentle voice, dreamed his reckless dreams.

Why had she not come?

He closed his eyes and tried to sleep, but sleep would not come. He tried to entice himself with daydreams of brown girls, but he could not, no matter how salacious a fantasy he tried to fashion. He cared nothing for brown girls; he cared nothing for gold or fighting or drinking.

He must have dozed for a time, for the next thing he was aware of was the sound of a whispered voice from across the room. "He's asleep—we should go."

An ecstasy of terror—a panicked, joyous soaring—occurred in Brette's chest then, causing his wound to throb, to ache. He opened his eyes, half-fearing that he had been mistaken ... but no—she was there.

"Brette!" Piper said, feeling humiliated and sorrowful. "You're ... awake."

"Hello," he said cautiously. He wanted to shout at her in anger; he wanted to gather her into his arms; he wanted to weep.

"May I ... visit you?"

"Please."

Jesi excused herself. "I'll see you at dinner, Piper." Smiling encouragement to Brette, she turned and left the room.

Piper took a step toward Brette's bed, and he struggled to sit up. She said, "I'm ... sorry, that I ... haven't—"

"Why didn't you?" Brette asked quietly.

"I don't know." She took another step nearer. "Are you ... will you be well?"

"Your doctor thinks so." She looked so sad, Brette thought.

"Timple said—?"

"He wants me to try to get up on my feet tomorrow."

"Really!" Something like hope struggled within her, struggled to gain a foothold against the mountain of humiliation and despair she imagined she had created. "Brette, I'm so sorry!"

Brette was still troubled, still wounded by her long absence. "Why didn't you come?"

"I—don't know." She felt that she was pleading; she felt like she was lost. In a tiny voice, she asked, "Do you still want me?"

"Why would I not?" Brette said warily, almost afraid to hope, but almost beginning to hope in spite of his fear.

Tears sprang to Piper's eyes, and she blinked angrily. "I thought you were going to die," she said, and she sniffed defiantly. She took a step toward him again. "I thought you were going to die, because I—"

She sat down upon the bed next to him, head bowed, and took his hand, looking at his fingers, not daring to look at his face. A tear trickled down her cheek; nearly hidden by the tangle of auburn curls.

"Why?" Brette asked. A moment passed, and he repeated his question.

She whispered, scarcely audible, "Because … I loved you."

He pulled her to him then, and buried his face in her hair, and let her weep against his wounded chest.

Chapter Thirty-Nine

Aron Millerson lay on his back on his pallet. He was fatigued from his studies, and at the moment, he didn't mind if God saw him whiling away a few lazy minutes or not. He thumped the rhythm of a drumbeat on his ample belly; the sound was like the thump of a ripe melon in the quiet of the afternoon. To say that Aron was bored would not be a fair representation. But he had studied long, and with unusual success for him, and he felt that he had earned a moment to rest his eyes, his neck, his brain.

Aron had begun with the idea given to him by Master Dreo: *God Himself will be a father to the fatherless.* Upon that small but sturdy foundation, he had attempted to build an edifice that he could present to Owan Roarke, a house where his faith could reside. Aron had spent hours in prayer, hours more racking his memory, and more hours yet studying the *Iesuchristion.* And he had succeeded in mining three more gems from the earthy depths of the holy book.

One of the friends of Iesu, a gentle and poetic man named Iohannes Apostolus, had once written these words: "Consider the manner of lovingkindness the Father has granted us—that we should be named *filii Dei*—the sons of God." Encouraged and excited by this discovery, Aron studied on with more confidence.

Next he examined the works of Paulus Apostolus, the great expositor. And shortly Aron found a letter that that venerable saint had written in which he exhorted, "God has not given you a spirit for you to be bound by fear, but He has adopted you as His sons." And there was more: "God's Spirit Himself declares that we are *filii Dei.*" Sons of God again!

Finally, Aron had chanced upon one of the oracles of the First Covenant, a fiery prophesier named Isaiae. Buried in the midst of Isaiae's thundering rants against the offenses of God's people, he had found this tender passage:

> *"... numquid oblivisci potest mulier infantem suum ut non misereatur filio uteri sui et si illa oblita fuerit ego tamen non obliviscar tui ..."*

Aron had struggled to translate the words—he had noticed the "filio" half-hidden in the heart of the phrase and had felt that it might be pertinent to his search. So he had worked out the words: *"Can a woman forget her own baby, failing to have pity on the son of her womb? Yet even if she might forget, yet I will not forget you!"*

Aron pondered the implication of these words as he lay on his back, drumming absent-mindedly on his melon-ripe belly. *Sons of God....* None of the other gods he had learned about, however incidentally, had ever offered to transform the sons of men into sons of gods. There had been stern rules for behavior, demands for bloody sacrifices, occasional acts of benevolence ... but never adoption as sons! What could it all mean? Suddenly Aron felt a tangible warmth steal over him—a warmth of acceptance, a lovely warmth of *loved*ness. His Amendicarii masters had been men of faith, yes—men of humility and service, yes. But they had not suggested to Aron that he should consider himself to be ... a son of God! Their view of the Almighty had been high and holy, awesome and dreadful and majestic ... but here He was now, stooping low to the earth, to remember the babe forgotten by his mother, to adopt the orphan as his own, to pour out a Father's love like a baptism upon the head of a child. A Daddy's love! Did he dare to suggest such a thing? He wished he could ask Gosse or Spence, or Matthias.

But Aron felt excited by his discoveries, energized. He had to tell someone.

Owan? He hesitated. Maybe not Owan, not yet. Dreo? Perhaps. The Lady Hollie? Well ... yes! She would appreciate his thoughts about the Fatherhood of God. Perhaps she might even share some insights that she had gleaned from her own days with the Amendicarii, quite a few years back. She had known Matthias, before he had grown gray and stooped with age—Aron thought he remembered that Matthias had even performed Hollie's wedding ceremony, her first one, to Lord Roarke.

Yes, Hollie would be the one who might understand his discovery, his conjecture, his hope. She would be sympathetic, and caring. And, he reminded himself, she was always pleasant looking, and smelled nice too—though he should probably not be noticing such things. With a final satisfied thump on his belly, he rolled over and sat up. He would talk to Hollie.

ξ

It was cold in his dungeon cell, and dark again—the torch left behind by the woman had long since gone out, and his food was gone too. Kelly sat with his back against the rusted bars of his cell, his knees drawn up to his chest. Though the metal rods pressed painfully into his back, it was marginally warmer that way than leaning against the clammy stone of the outer wall. He tried to calculate how long he had been sitting in the dark, but found that he had lost all perception of time.

He thought he heard a sound shuffling through the bleak silence from the other side of the wooden door, looked, and noticed a trickle of light seeping through the beams. Fighting not to shout out for joy, he released his knees and tried to stretch his legs to stand. The woman! Coming with more food? Freedom?

The door groaned irritably as it opened, and Kelly blinked in the invading light. He climbed to his feet, stiff-jointed, and as his eyes focused, he realized that his visitor was not the woman. It was a tall, stern-jawed knight who held the torch, and that knight stepped back deferentially to let another pass.

"Prime Minister!" Kelly said in astonishment as he recognized Herm's cold, handsome face, which immediately contorted in an affronted scowl.

The knight who held the torch barked, "He's the *King*, you bloody fool!"

"Forgive me," Kelly said, abashed, as he bowed low to the stone floor. "Your Majesty!"

"Yes," Herm sniffed in a deprecating tone. "You are from Beale's Keep, are you not?"

"Yes, Your Majesty—Kelly of Lady Hollie's guard," Kelly replied respectfully. "I fear there must be some sort of misunderstanding—I've done nothing to warrant this prison cell."

"We shall see," the King answered. "You are most privileged, Kelly, though perhaps you had not known it. You are the first of our subjects to receive a private audience with us, your King."

"Thank you—thank you, Your Majesty." Kelly strove to sound grateful in spite of the clanging alarm of misgiving that he felt.

"Indeed." Herm turned partway toward the knight. "Sir Olefin, you shall serve as witness."

"Of course, Highness."

"Then. We shall begin. Kelly—" Herm fixed him with a discriminating gaze, his eye dark and unblinking like a bird of prey. "Do you know why you were detained?"

"No, Your Majesty."

"Of course not." Herm spoke with a sort of weary pedantry, as if to a recalcitrant child. "Your mistress, the Lady Hollie Roarke, owes us a particular sum."

Kelly said nothing.

"You, her messenger, do not appear to have that sum with you."

"No, Your Majesty."

"The time for repayment of her loan is past, and you have not brought her recompense." Herm spoke in softly measured tones, but his eyes held no kindness. "Why then have you come?"

"If you please, Your Majesty," Kelly stammered, "I bear a letter from Lady Hollie to Her Majesty the Queen."

Herm smiled tolerantly, enduring this man's bald stupidity as graciously as he could. "We are the King of Hagenspan, are we not? And as King, are we not also Queen, and Judge, and Sovereign, and God Almighty!" He fought to keep the swelling emotion from exposing itself in his voice, and continued in a more muted tone, "Deliver the message to us now."

Kelly saw no option but to comply. Retrieving Hollie's crumpled letter from its hiding place within his tunic, he handed it to Herm, looking uneasily at the King's face.

Herm tore open the seal and scanned the note, wearing a widening smirk as he read. "Mercy," he snorted. "She begs mercy." Turning to Sir Olefin, Herm remarked, "She is desperate. And she cannot pay." He tore the note in half, tore those halves in half again, and tossed the pieces to the dungeon floor. Turning his attention back to Kelly and fixing him once more with his eagle gaze, the King asked, "Are you ready now to renounce all fealty to your penniless mistress, and swear to serve us alone?"

Kelly stared at Herm, mute. He had not been prepared for such a question, such an offer—if indeed it *was* an offer—though he was quite certain that he could not have sworn any such thing anyway.

"We thought not," Herm said impassively. "We made the mistake of leaving someone behind down here in this cell once many years ago—someone who came back to do us much harm. That is an error we shall not make again."

"Lord Roarke," Kelly murmured.

"Yes … Roarke." Herm frowned briefly, then breathed a resigned sigh. "Sir Olefin! Do you know what to do?"

"Yes, Your Highness."

"Then carry on." Herm the King stepped past the tall knight and began stalking up the winding stone stairwell. As he ascended, he could hear sliding sounds behind him: the metallic sound of Olefin's sword sliding from its sheath as it was drawn, an almost liquid whisper as the same blade slid into Kelly's midsection … and Kelly's labored groan as his spirit slid from his body and began its fragile ascent to the unfathomable country of God.

Chapter Forty

Owan woke, startled, from a dream that he could not remember. He could not remember any of the details of the dream, but whatever it was, he knew that it had disturbed him. He suddenly wanted to be with his mother—a curious thought for one so mature as he. He almost rose from his bed and crept to the room where she slept, probably in Boo's arms, but the thought that he now had a stepfather with which to share her affections made him draw his bare feet back beneath the covers.

He blinked at the ceiling of his room for awhile, waiting to fall back asleep, but sleep seemed to have abandoned him. He almost succumbed to the urge to pray, but successfully subjugated that unwelcome impulse. *Because of my father*, Owan realized. *Maybe Aron Millerson was right. Maybe I'm just mad at God because of my father.* He wondered if his father had ever stared at the ceiling, unable to sleep. *He* probably would have prayed. Well, Owan would not.

The black dog, nearly invisible where he had been sleeping next to Owan's bed, must have sensed somehow that Owan was awake, for he sat up, looked at the boy intently, and then laid his head upon the bed next to Owan's face. Tentatively, tenderly, he reached out with his tongue and gave Owan a doggy kiss. The boy whispered, "What's the matter, Pup? Can't you sleep either?" The dog sighed dejectedly. "You miss Kelly, don't you?" Owan reasoned. "He'll be back soon." Pup licked his cheek again.

"Come on up here," Owan said, patting his covers. Pup took a step backward, then leaped up onto the boy's bed. The dog lifted his feet gingerly on the mattress, unaccustomed to the soft, spongy footing, turning around and around in a circle. "Lay down, now," Owan commanded, and after one more circle, he did so. Laying his head upon Owan's thigh, the dog uttered another long, mournful sigh. The boy said, "Me, too."

ξ

Hollie was not asleep. She was sitting at a desk near her bed, her hands clasped and worried, her golden head bowed, a faint trail of tears glistening upon her candlelit cheeks. Hess Boole lay on his back in their bed, just beginning to snore.

Kelly should have been back by now with word from the queen ... unless something had happened to detain him. And whatever that might mean, it wasn't good. Hollie's stomach churned with nameless dread. She who had faced the dragon, she who had suffered the loss of her husband, who had endured humiliations and abuses for years, and had come through all of those trials intact ... this noble woman was now afraid.

Boole stopped snoring, and Hollie wondered if he had awakened. "Hess?" she pled softly.

Boole drew a deep breath, shaking off his weariness, and yawned. "What is it, love? Are you coming to bed?"

"Will you talk to me for a moment?"

"Of course I will. Why don't you talk, and I'll listen," he said drowsily, rearranging his pillow and nestling back into the quilts.

"I'm serious."

Boole was silent for a few seconds, and Hollie was afraid that he had already fallen back asleep. But with an effort, he threw off the covers, exposing his skin to the bracing chill of the night, and sat up on the bed. "I'm awake, love. What is it?"

"Hess, I'm afraid."

"Come over here, and let me hold you."

With a puff of breath, she extinguished the candle that sat on her desk, then rose and allowed herself into the dark sanctuary of his arms. She laid her cheek against his bare shoulder and rested there, feeling the gentle rise and fall of his chest as he breathed. For a moment—just a moment—she was safe, and the world was warm and welcoming, and threats were far away.

"What is it you're afraid of?" Boole asked softly, and the night became bleak and perilous again.

"Hess, you know I love you."

"Mm-hmm." He stroked her hair absently. "I didn't know that made you afraid."

Ignoring his joke, she continued. "I need something from you."

"Good."

"Be serious. I need you to promise me something."

"Anything within my power to give is yours. You know that."

"I don't know if you have the power to give what I'm going to ask. But I need you to promise anyway." She pulled away from the warmth of his embrace so that she could look at him face-to-face. "Promise me."

"When you ask like that, I don't know if I can." Boole studied Hollie's features, her pleading eyes—just as if every line, every freckle were not imprinted already upon his memory.

"But you will," she said, and after a brooding moment, he agreed, a single solemn nod.

"Maybe it's nothing," Hollie continued. "Maybe what I fear will never come to pass at all. But if it does—you have to obey me in this."

"What *is* it? Obey you in what?"

She drew a long breath. "It's Herm." She looked deeply into her husband's eyes, imploring him to understand. "First he demanded repayment of Cedric's loan. Then—I think—he tried to prevent me from repaying it; he had Feather killed, I think. Now he is King, and—" She struggled to sound logical, like a man, hoping Hess would hear her. She fought to keep from sounding like a panicking, hysterical woman. "Where is Kelly? Why have we no word?"

A shadow darkened Boole's countenance. He had nothing to say … so he said, "What do you want me to do?"

"If the day ever comes when Herm moves against me, or against Beale's Keep … I want you to take Owan away from here."

"But—" Boole sputtered, "Move against you? It's not possible!"

"You must promise."

"But, if such a thing were ever to happen, my place will be *here*, with you! Leading my—leading our own troops in your defense!"

She just shook her head gently, the liquid pools of her blue eyes continuing to gaze into his.

"Then you'll come with us! We'll go together!"

She continued to shake her head sadly. "No."

"We should leave now, the three of us. We could go back to Thraill."

"No, Hess." She frowned, concentrating, tried to explain. "I am the Lady of Beale's Keep, and there are a hundred people and more that depend upon me for guidance, for leadership … for inspiration, protection. I belong to them; my place is here."

"And mine is with you!"

"I know," she said sorrowfully. Again she attempted to explain. "You remember when I told you about Mara Dannat, and the words she spoke to me?" He nodded. "I don't know what they meant altogether … but I cannot risk Owan's life."

"All right, we can't risk Owan. We'll send him away. But let Dreo take him. Or Aron!"

"No," she protested. "How could I trust them to guard my dearest treasure? The only one I could trust with Owan's safety … is the one who thinks that *I* am *his* dearest treasure."

Hess Boole regarded his beautiful, sad wife, and his own eyes filled with angry tears. He pulled her to him and heatedly, regretfully buried his face in her hair. "Damn it, woman," he breathed. "Hell and damnation," he whispered. "God Almighty!" he pled, he cursed, but he had no words to pray.

Hollie stroked the back of his head, kissed his shoulder, waited for his impotent wrath to subside. "Maybe—" she said, "maybe—" she prayed, "maybe it won't come to that. Maybe the queen has received my letter, forgiven the debt, and Kelly is on his way home to us even now. But if not…."

"Where would you want me to take him?" Boole had grudgingly defied his own dissent, angrily forcing it into subjugation, and now his natural qualities of leadership and planning were beginning to bleed past his rebellious emotions. "Thraill?"

"No!" Hollie said quickly. "If Herm moves against Beale's Keep, Thraill will not long be safe. I want you to take him to the Amendicarii."

"What? I don't even know how to get there!"

"I'll tell you."

"Why, we'd have to go right past the King's city itself! He'd probably just gobble us up along the way, if he was coming with war in mind!"

"I know. You'll have to start by going north, and then cross the mountains, and when you get to the river, get a boat somehow and sneak around him to the south." Her plan sounded stupid and hopeless in her own ears. "Maybe we can talk about that later."

Boole thought for a moment, his imagination full of forbidding notions. "We probably don't have to worry about this now ... not right now, with winter so close at hand. Unless—" he stopped abruptly.

"What?" Hollie asked.

"Nothing," Boole replied. "Just trying to think of every possibility."

"What is it?"

"Nothing," he repeated. "Hollie ... why don't we just give Beale's Keep back to the crown, and go home to Thraill?"

She considered that thought. "I fear ... that it won't be that simple."

"May we try?"

A cloud drifted across the face of the moon, making the candleless night seem very black. "Maybe." She gave his shoulder one last kiss, and said, "I am so weary. Can we sleep?"

Wordlessly, he released her, and they lay down on their bed. Boole stared through the murky dark at the imperceptible ceiling of their room for a time. He glanced sidelong at his wife, and realized that she was staring blindly, blearily, in the direction of the heavens as well, but he said nothing. Occasionally one of them sighed ... and eventually they released their troubled, wounded thoughts into the comforting abyss of slumber.

Chapter Forty-One

"Alan."

It was his father, looking in at the door. Alan Poppleton sat in conference with Brison Cairl and Hallna Bennker, debating how to respond to the proclamation of Prime Minister Herm's marriage to Queen Maygret and his ascendancy to the throne. It was clear that some kind of gift was in order, and undoubtedly some kind of oath of fealty as well.

Alan heard his father's brittle voice from the doorway, and was surprised that he had spent his strength to walk to his chamber, instead of sending for him.

He half-rose, and said, "Father! Come in and join us!"

Sir Charles shook his head, and said, "I wanted to be the one to tell you. She has come."

She? Alan stared at his father for an uncomprehending moment, and then his heart leaped. It could only be Jesi Tenet! "Jesi?" he said in a voice suddenly dry.

"Yes, my boy," the old man said in his crackling voice, smiling. "She is with your mother."

Alan drew a deep quaking breath, and was mildly surprised at the sudden surge of terror that engulfed him. "Gentlemen," he addressed Cairl and Bennker, "will you excuse me?"

ξ

He strode down the chilly corridor toward the hall where his mother was receiving the Lady Jesimonde and her contingent. He wondered, as he had so many times over the past several weeks, what had taken Brette so long to get here; he would have to ask him about it when everything quieted down tonight. But right now he was impatient, eager to see the girl he had pined for, for years—not a girl any longer, he reminded himself. She was a woman now. Self-consciously, he wiped his palms on his pant-legs.

Turning the corner and entering a broad room warmed by two fireplaces, he saw his mother, white-haired and beshawled, smiling graciously at six people whose backs were to him. His mother turned the warmth of her smile toward him, said, "Ah! Here he is now!"

The six turned to greet the young Lord of Ester. Alan noticed peripherally that there were four armed guards, but Brette was not among them. There was a young woman who had a faint pink scar across her cheek; he nodded politely to her. But the focus of his attention was riveted on Jesi, who flooded into his eyes like a dream, like the memory of a dream.

She bowed her head and extended her hand to him. "Lord Poppleton," she said, and then in a softer voice, "Alan."

"Welcome to Ester," he said, taking her hand and kissing it politely. "My Lady. I have long awaited this day." His cheeks grew warm, and he hoped it was not too obvious.

"Yes," she replied with a gentle smile. "I regret that it has taken so long."

Alan studied her face. She was older than he had anticipated; foolishly, he had underestimated the passing of the years. He also decided that she was a little less lovely than he had recalled—a little plainer. He wondered if she was thinking the same thoughts about him. He felt a brief stab of remorse that he had missed those years … those years when she had ceased being the flashing young spitfire he had loved, and had become this calm, polite, rather plain woman. But almost as soon as he had recognized the thought, he dismissed it. He looked into her eyes, and thought he saw something like an apology mingled in with the curiosity and excitement, and perhaps a bit of a challenge as well. He looked into her eyes, and saw … Jesi.

Laughing abruptly, giddily, for joy, he said, "Welcome, to all of you! I pray that you will find Beedlesgate pleasant and accommodating. We will feast tonight!" Turning Jesi by the elbow, he said, "Mother, will you please see that these two ladies are properly cared for? And I will find a place for the gentlemen to rest and refresh themselves." Before he released Jesi's hand, he said softly, "Thank you for coming."

ξ

"He seems quite kindly, and affectionate toward you," Laupra said to Jesi when they were alone in a richly furnished bedroom. "He is handsome in his way."

"Do you think so?" Jesi replied. "Oh, I feel as if I were a child again," she complained. "As if I were a girl wondering whether I should give away my first kiss."

"Isn't it grand, Miss?" Laupra said dreamily. "How kind of God to give you another chance to live those glorious days, after your sorrows."

Jesi wasn't sure whether it was kind of God or not, but she smiled at Laupra indulgently.

ξ

"If I may—where is my man Brette?" Alan asked the ladies' four bodyguards, after he had them settled down with mugs of ale, loaves of brown bread, and a platter of cold beefsteak.

One of the guards, a grim, full-bearded man named Irit, said, "Beg your pardon, m'Lord. We should've told you before this, but there weren't an opportunity. He sends his greeting, and we have a letter for you." He motioned to one of the other guards, who began rummaging around in a pack, looking for the letter. "Fact is, your Brette found himself a spot of trouble, but I believe it's working out for the best."

"Trouble?" Alan asked, alarmed.

Irit explained, "He'd set out with the ladies nigh unto a month ago, but didn't get so very far." He frowned. "This next thing I say to Thraill's shame, for it seems we had a blackguard in our midst, and didn't even know it. One of our captains, a Bascan by name, attacked your man with arrows and wounded him sore." He blinked twice, and continued. "It's said that he did it for love of Missy Laupra, which you just met. It's Bascan what painted that stripe acrost her cheek, out of a fury that she was going off with Lady Jess, and leaving him behind. Some also says that he was that famous Black Knight—though I don't see how it could be."

"Yes, he was," one of the other guards insisted, but Irit shook his head, his moustaches plummeting in a frown.

"Here it is," said the guard that was looking for the letter, and he handed it to Alan, who took it with a *thank-you* but did not break the seal.

"Where is he now? Is he well?" Alan asked Irit, concerned for his friend.

"You might say!" Irit replied, and nearly chuckled. "Your Brette is somewhat of a hero at Thraill, my Lord. It's him what's broke the long winter of Our Lady's tender heart, and we're mighty grateful."

"You mean—the Lady Paipaerria?" Alan asked.

"Aye," confirmed the guard who had said Bascan was the Black Knight. "It's a rare moment that finds them apart. She dotes on him." Irit nodded his agreement.

"Well ... isn't that something?" Alan said wonderingly. "How do you like that?"

"We like it all right," Irit said, "but what we like ever so well is that Our Lady likes it, too."

ξ

A bit later, alone in his own study, Alan remembered the letter. He snapped the cold brown wax into splinters, brushed the crumbled bits from his lap to the floor, and unfolded the crackling parchment.

To Alan, Lord Poppleton:

My friend—I never would have left you, and my arm should never have serv'd another—but now it seems that my heart has chose another course for me, and I would follow it if I may.

Amazing thing! We have been as brothers for lo these many years, you and I—but once you were call'd upon to be Lord in Ester, you became Master and I became Servant. Now—bless'd whim of the Almighty!—it seems likely enough that we may become brothers again—not only in spirit but in law!

I shall come and see you in the Spring if I am able. You remain my dear'st friend in God's vast world, and my heart's only sorrow in Thraill is that you are not here to share my joy with me.

Brette

Alan smiled faintly, and said aloud, "Well, what do you know about that?"

Chapter Forty-Two

"Thank you for coming so quickly, Aron," Hollie said. She was sitting in what had once been the throne room of Beale's Keep, at the round oaken table that had been pieced together by Yeskie, the table that contained some of the wood fragments of old Lord Beale's throne. She was wrapped in heavy furs to ward off the cold, for there was no hearth in this hall. One chilly white hand extended from the wraps, and had been idly stroking the aged gray wood from the throne.

"Not at all, my Lady. I had been hoping to have a word with you anyway." Aron Millerson could see the phantom of his breath as he spoke the words, and he fought to keep his teeth from chattering. His worn brown robe was ill-suited for winter, but he had denied himself the comfort of additional cloaks as a means of self-mortification, which, he hoped, would earn him some kind of favor from the Almighty.

"Good," Hollie nodded, noting his frigid discomfort. "Won't you take one of my robes?"

"Oh, no, my Lady! I am quite comfortable," Aron demurred. "How may I be of service to you?"

"Yes." She drew her icy fingers back within the warmth of the furs that surrounded her. "Will you help me pray?" she asked. "I am ashamed to be so weak—and I would never speak a word of this to anyone but my husband, and you—but I am afraid."

"Of course! Anything I can do to help! But, my Lady—what do you fear?"

She smiled sadly at Aron, and said, "Perhaps nothing. Perhaps everything. I don't know. But … I fear King Herm." Her smile faded, became a frown of concern. "I fear what he may have planned against me. I fear for my son."

Aron agreed with a somber nod, but felt, somewhat breathlessly, that God may have prepared him for this visit with an answer already. Aron had translated a bit of the *Iesuchristion* just a few days ago that seemed to speak to this very issue. Tentatively, he said, "If I may?"

"Please."

"I have recently come across some words from Iesu Himself that may be of some comfort to you. May I share them?"

"Of course."

"Iesu once said, 'Do not fear those who are able to kill the body, but powerless to kill the soul. Rather fear Him who is able to destroy both soul and body in hell.' I believe He meant, in essence: Do not fear King Herm; fear God alone." Aron stopped, swallowed. He hoped he had not been presumptuous; now that he had spoken his thoughts aloud, they seemed inadequate, insubstantial.

Hollie considered this for a moment. Her face did not brighten with any sense of optimism or of release, but she did nod thoughtfully. "I see … I think." She raised her blue eyes to look at Aron. "The very worst that Herm could do would be to kill us. He might have that much power over our bodies … but he has no power over our souls. The worst he could do would be to prematurely release us into the eternal lands of Iesu. Where Cedric and Smead and Will are waiting with open arms to receive us … I think. I hope."

Aron nodded his shivering encouragement.

Hollie continued, "Your words are good." Her eyebrows lifted wistfully. "I confess, they have not much lightened my spirit … but perhaps they will, upon reflection and prayer."

"I hope so, my Lady." Aron's teeth chattered, and Hollie looked at him curiously. He was not certain whether his body's trembling was because of the frigidly bracing air, or the ominous responsibility he had undertaken—that of voicing the very words of Iesuchristi.

Hollie asked him, "You said you had wanted to speak with me?"

"Oh!" Aron said, remembering. "Yes, my Lady. Unless you wished to pray first?"

"Tell me what you wanted to say to me, and we will pray together afterward."

"As you wish." Aron took a hesitant breath and gathered his thoughts. "I believe … God may have revealed something to me as I studied. I thought it may have been … significant. The only person I could think of to discuss it with was you."

"I am flattered," Hollie smiled faintly. "Please tell me."

"Many of the old gods of Hagenspan," Aron began, "were harsh, cruel … stern. They required sacrifices of blood. Virgins. Children. They promised nothing but an occasional abatement of their dour anger. Little more than devils, I believe. And some have viewed the One True God—the One we now know as Iesuchristi—as essentially the same." He looked at Hollie to see if she was following his reasoning, and she nodded patiently for him to continue. "It is truth that the Almighty did command a blood sacrifice. But He also fulfilled His own obligation, clothing Himself in flesh like a man, and offering Himself—His own Blood—as His own recompense."

Hollie said, "Cedric understood something about that, too. But he didn't have the chance to study the holy words that you have."

"Lord Roarke was a remarkable man," Aron agreed. "He was a man full of grace."

An interesting choice of words, Hollie thought, and realized that it was so.

"I have been searching for some way to encourage your son. I believe that he still grieves the loss of his father. Master Dreo started me in the right direction, but the things I have since discovered in *Iesuchristion* have frankly astounded me.

"It seems that the Almighty—the Great King of the Universe—has long desired little more than this: simply to *love* us, the people of His choosing. To love us, as a father loves a cherished son."

Hollie tilted her head, listening intently. Aron went on to recount all of the passages he had found in the Words of God that suggested and supported his premise. The longer he spoke, the more enthusiastic he became in his exposition, and the more fervently he preached, the more his body shivered. It was just about all he could do to keep his teeth from clacking together whenever he paused for a breath. He clasped his hands tightly to keep them from shaking, absorbed as he was in his discoveries and their implications. "God longs to be a father to the fatherless; to adopt us as His own sons and daughters! To make us, as it were, sons and daughters of God Himself!" He shook his head wonderingly. "Amazing!" Aron's gaze, which had become faraway, as if he were seeing worlds beyond the stone-cold room in which he sat trembling, slowly refocused. He saw the Lady Hollie—his attentive congregation—and smiled tentatively.

"Aron," Hollie said, since it appeared he had reached the conclusion of his extemporaneous homily, "your words seem to ring with truth—if you have found them in the holy book itself." Aron nodded that he had. "Do you believe them?"

Aron was taken aback. "What—what do you mean, my Lady?"

"Do you believe that God loves *you* like a father would love his son?"

"I—" He paused, and thought for a moment, vaguely surprised. He had mostly confined his thoughts about his grand proposition to Owan's point of view—Owan, the orphaned son of a great Lord. What, in fact, did God think about Aron Millerson, the lowly priest of the Amendicarii? Fat, undisciplined, common Aron? Then he remembered the warmth that had filled him when he had first discovered these words about the Father-characteristics of the Almighty, the tender flood of acceptance … and he believed. "Yes, my dear Lady," he said, as tears filled his eyes. "As astounding as it is to consider ... I believe that the Great King loves me as His own son."

Hollie smiled softly, and her enemies—her sadness and fear—seemed to retreat a pace or two. "Then, Aron, my friend," she said, "do you not think that God, your loving Father, would be pleased for you to have a coat to cover your arms while you pray?"

A smile broke across Aron's broad face, and he said, "Perhaps he would at that!"

"Then, as your Lady, whom you are beholden to obey, I command you to take one of these furs! Then, dear priest, you may help me come aside to a peaceful place with you in prayer, so that I might, too, believe in a Father's love, that it might drive my fears far from me."

ξ

Alan Poppleton looked at Jesi's face, softly illumined by the firelight. He gazed at her in wonder, for the sense he had experienced two days ago, that she had looked plainer than he had remembered, had been displaced by the thought that she was vastly more beautiful than he had ever recalled. He wondered what trick of his mind caused these vacillations of his regard, and chided himself for his foolishness. She was lovely, and she was here, and this was the moment he had longed for.

"My Lady," he began, and then was unsure how to proceed. "Jesi."

She turned her eyes toward him. She was full of conflicting emotions herself, warmed by the comfortable proximity of Alan, her old friend and beau, but still feeling a lingering pang of sadness for her dead husband Tayson—a sorrow which was only intensified by Alan's nearness. She smiled at him, somber and subdued, but encouraging him to continue.

"I … um," Alan began again, "I think you understand … why I asked you— why I *begged* you to come to Ester."

"I have the ring you sent with Brette."

"Oh, yes. I wondered if he had given it to you." Alan felt a twinge of embarrassment, though he tried to tell himself that it was probably not necessary.

Jesi said nothing, waiting for Alan to speak.

"I am unsure of…." He faltered, and then tried again. "You're a widow, Jesi. Are you even interested in … having me?"

She looked at him for a long moment. Even though the forces of melancholy were still battling within her, she found that she was pleased by his discomfiture. It reminded her of days long past, days when she had loved Alan with all the fierce ardor of adolescence. "I won't make this hard for you," she said tenderly. "Alan, if you truly want to marry me, I will be your wife. I will be faithful to you, and respectful, and obedient, and I'll give you sons if I may. All I ask is just one thing."

"What?" Alan asked huskily. He felt quite certain that he would be willing to promise her the moon itself should she demand it.

"I would ask that you please be patient with me, if, from time to time, I feel the need to grieve a bit for Tayson."

Alan's fluttering spirits were abruptly deflated at this mention of the rival to which he had once lost Jesi, the rival he had never even met. But he suddenly felt the intimidating presence of Tayson Bost almost as if he were physically lurking in the room, threatening again to steal away the heart of the woman Alan loved.

Jesi, sensing this silent injury to Alan's confidence, whispered, "Alan?"

He smiled weakly, but his eyes bled pain. "Will you … ah … will you love me?" he said tightly, sounding helpless as a boy.

"Oh, yes!" Jesi laughed softly, and took his face in her hands. "I will love you! I swear that I'll love you like scarcely a woman could ever love a man!"

Alan's eyes closed in blessed reprieve, and he smiled again faintly, selfconsciously, and bent his cheek into the coolness of her caress. He whispered, "I've never stopped loving you." He kissed her hands, faintly, where they still cupped his face, then he reached up with his own hands and took hers in his. "Will you, then—will you be my wife?"

"Yes, Alan, I will." She smiled at him affectionately, willing herself to betray none of the irrational regret that suddenly threatened to overwhelm her. It would pass. It would pass.

"Thank God!" Alan said, genuinely relieved. "How soon—how soon … could we?"

"I'll marry you tomorrow if you can manage it," she beamed, glowing like an angel in the golden firelight. "Just as soon as you want."

"I'll talk to my parents, then, and Fuller, the priest—" He reached out and pulled her to him, hugging her ardently. "Thank you, Jesi!"

She returned his embrace, holding him tightly, grateful that he could not see the tear that rolled down her glowing golden cheek.

Chapter Forty-Three

Maygret the Queen of Hagenspan curled up like a kitten in the soft pillows and quilts of her royal couch. She was happy—so happy! She had scarcely imagined that she could feel such a warmth of contentment at her age, when she had already experienced all the pleasures and pains that a lifetime could afford. But after the lingering anguish of Ruric's last illness, when she had imagined all earthly enjoyments to have been put behind her at last, happiness had come bursting in upon her like an epiphany, like a cloudburst, like a jester!

Herm the Conqueror, King of Hagenspan—*her* king—had been gallant and noble and romantic and tender … all of the things that Ruric had not been for so many years. He had won her heart, and had won the throne. At first, Maygret had feared that his fondness for her had been only a ruse to help him gain that throne, but—she reasoned—he was the clear choice to be the next king anyway. Why should he not bear the sceptre now? And if he were to show the old queen kindness, even romance … how wonderful! It was a bargain she was prepared to make.

But the thing that made happiness cling to Maygret, warming her and caressing her even more tenderly than the quilts she hugged to her shoulders now, was the fact that Herm's ardor had not waned. If anything, he was even more attentive, more amorous than he had been during the heady days of their courtship. In fact, he had just left Maygret's couch a short while ago; the memory of that encounter produced a pink blush on the queen's cheeks, and she nearly giggled. Scandalous! She was turning into a wanton.

She rolled over onto her back and sighed deliciously. *What a marvelous feeling*. She felt as if she were girl again, even though she knew the count of her years to be somewhat more than seventy. But what did it matter that her skin was not as firm as it once was? What did it matter that there were lines upon her face, and that her limp breasts sagged? She was loved! Loved! And the one who loved her professed a resolute blindness to those corporal flaws that she knew that she owned. He said she was beautiful. Beautiful! Maygret would scarcely have believed him, had it not been for the earnest adoration that shone from his eyes whenever he looked upon her.

For a moment, she wished that she had not been quite so faithful to Ruric— that somehow Herm had dared to speak of his love for her during the protracted decades when he had been so invitingly close, but so very proper. *But no*, she thought. *It was better this way.* She had not betrayed her husband's trust; she had maintained her integrity. And the compensation for those years of denial—denial of the desire that she hadn't even known she carried within her—was this enchanting, exhilarating emancipation now. This culmination, this climax. This hot girlish blush upon cheeks creased with age.

She sighed again, and closed her eyes dreamily. Loved! She was loved....

How wonderful...!

ξ

King Herm the Conqueror slunk soundlessly from his own lavish bedchamber, past his drowsy guard, Sir Olefin. The knight, suddenly crisply awake, nodded grimly at his monarch. Tomorrow morning he would be able to vow that the king had never left his bed that night, in case anyone should ask.

Gliding as silent as a shadow across the corridor into Queen Maygret's bedchamber, he found the white-haired, shriveled crone rasping noisily in a drooling stupor. He shuddered as he remembered her touch—

the icy prick of her claw-like fingers. He despised her for her clinging neediness—her fawning, adolescent fatuity. He marveled that he had been able to maintain the charade as long as he had, and congratulated himself once again for his masterful hypocrisy.

He picked up a pillow that had fallen to the floor … but no. It was too big, too soft. He wanted her to see. Moving suddenly, he jerked one of the quilts loose from her grasp, and clamped it down over her nose and mouth, pinning her arms underneath the covers.

Startled, terrified, Maygret awoke. And she could not breathe! Through the charcoal gloom of the night, she could barely make out the gray form of her attacker. *Who?* her fearful eyes demanded. Herm saw her questioning glare, and bent closer so she could see, smiling grimly.

Maygret saw. And all of the sadness she had ever experienced in her seventy-odd years, if it had been stacked neatly in a heap—the death of her son, the long and empty years, Ruric's deterioration and departure—all of that sadness was little more than an anthill compared to the mountain of heartbreak that she experienced in the moment she recognized her beloved, her Herm, sneering over her with his iron hand clamped over her face. Her heart failed her; her heart broke.

Why? her eyes desperately pled.

Herm's leer broadened as he saw her recognize her utter desolation. Maygret's eyes fluttered as the features of this world began to fade beyond her ability to see, and Herm, unsatisfied with this solitary draught of sweet despair, relaxed his grip for a moment to allow one more brief gasp of air into his wife's straining lungs.

Against all reason, Maygret took that gasp … her eyes brightened momentarily. But they no longer bore any question, only sorrow. Not loved. She was not loved.

Herm clamped his hand back over her mouth and nose again, pinching hard enough to cause the queen pain, but not enough that there would be any mark left behind in the morning. But this pain was inconsequential compared to the break of her heart. Unloved. Unloved.

She gazed steadily into Herm's eyes and waited as patiently as she could, willing herself not to struggle as her lungs screamed for air. It was enough. The room, which had been dark, gradually filled with a slow, bright light, until the leering face of her beloved, her Herm, faded from her view.

ξ

Herm straightened up from the bed, his night's good work accomplished. He tucked the offending quilt back down about her shoulders again, and gently closed the queen's staring eyes. She looked as if she were peacefully sleeping. He bent over her pale, still form and kissed her cheek. It was as if she were bathed in moonlight; the very room seemed to be softly glowing.

He stood up and took a step toward the window, then another, wondering that the moon should be uncovered by cloud. Early winter in Hagenspan was usually heavily overcast; often, days at a time would pass with no break in the cloud cover. Startled, he instantly perceived that the unnatural light did not emanate from outside the window. He turned quickly back toward the dead queen, wary of some kind of trickery.

What he saw caused him to shudder with fear; he—Herm, the Conqueror King—had to fight against the urge to drop to his knees.

Standing sadly next to the sleeping form of Maygret was the source of the room's ethereal illumination. The creature was tall, grim, beautiful as a woman, but strong and severe as a man. Perhaps, thought frightened Herm, it was a seraph.

The being seemed to be clothed in brown and orange and gold; perhaps they were the leaves of autumn, dried and crackling and dusted with snow. His head was encircled with bare twigs, which were twisted together to make a kind of crown, and set therein were jewels, veiled by the natural darkness of the night, but faintly glinting in the light—the light which came from his face itself.

"Who are you?" Herm croaked. The majestic creature ignored him. "Have you come to kill me?"

At that, the terrifying presence turned his glowing face toward Herm, the pitiful king, and said in a voice as deep as a river, "Were it up to me. But no. I have come only to witness."

"Witness what?"

With a glower of disgust, the other said stiffly, "The passing of the last child of Kenyan the Prince, and Réchetthaerielle of the Feie. You have cut off a noble line."

Struggling to gather his courage, Herm challenged, "And you seek no redress?"

The room seemed to grow both darker and brighter at once, and Herm quailed again before the terrifying apparition. A rumble of thunder sounded in the distance.

"I would reach into your soul and squeeze it until it bled your foul essence dry. I would tear it from your body and cast it into the flames unquenchable, but it would scarcely kindle a spark. I would! But apparently Architaedeus the Inscrutable has purposes for you yet." He had indeed appeared to be growing angry enough to reach into Herm and crush his soul … but the mention of Architaedeus appeared to pacify him. He laid a radiant hand upon Maygret's brow, and said softly, "Back to a warmer day will I fly. I will go to Kenyan and tell him that I have seen his daughter pass away gently, and that she was a queen."

Herm did not understand everything the other said, but he did understand that he apparently was not going to be punished for his crime. Drawing himself up to his full height, he said, "I am Herm—King of Hagenspan. Surrender yourself to me now!"

The luminous creature smiled. "You are not the King that I serve." In a blinding flash of argent light he was gone, leaving Herm to grope sightlessly about the queen's bedchamber until his vision gradually returned some minutes later.

Chapter Forty-Four

There was change coming. Owan could feel it.

He could hear it in the mournful whine of the winter wind—the wind that scooped up armloads of swirling snow in its haphazard embrace, then dashed it carelessly against the castle walls, the trunks of trees, the beardless faces of boys. As the snow turned to droplets of biting cold water upon his red, wind-blasted cheeks, Owan thought to himself that he had seen snow before … but not like this snow. He had heard the wind before … but not like this wind.

There was change coming.

He could see it in the tentative, hopeful face of his mother, and in Boo's pensive, brooding glower. He could see it in the movements of his tutor Dreo, always darting and sure, but now somehow even more nervous, more taut. And when the import of Dreo's pedantry drifted away into insensible chatter, the old man did not chide his student for inattention as had previously been his wont; he just kept on jabbering, as if scurrying to reach the end of the lesson … before *it* came. Change was coming.

Owan could feel it. He could feel the nervous prickling in the air during the still of the night, when the black dog would hear something in the hallway or the courtyard, something Owan could not hear, and would lift his head expectantly, hopefully, his brow furrowed with confusion. And when it became clear that the sound—whatever it was—did not signal the return of his lost master, the dog would lay his head back on his paws and sigh, but would not close his eyes. And Owan could feel it in the air, an electric tingling that caused his heart to flutter like a moth.

Now that it was winter, Tully and Windy didn't come around much; they had wood to split and fires to stoke and unpleasant indoor chores to do under the peevish supervision of their mothers. When they were able to enjoy some scant free time, they did not venture long out of doors, for this winter promised to be unusually cold, and neither of the two big boys were favorably disposed toward discomfort. Joah, though, came into the castle nearly every day; he and Owan had sworn oaths of friendship. Occasionally they bickered at each other like common stable hands, when the hours moved slowly and the castle walls were confining. But most of the time they were inseparable companions—weighing the merits of various pretty serving girls, chasing each other through the corridors, dreaming about the future.

"Can you feel it?" Owan asked Joah, not for the first time.

"Sometimes, Buds. Sometimes."

"It feels like I'm seeing and hearing things that I never could before. Even though they were there the whole time, I guess I never noticed them." He paused for a moment to see if Joah had any thoughts of value to contribute.

"Maybe," Joah said slowly, "maybe you're just growing up."

Owan thought that that explanation was unsatisfactory for the amount of turmoil that he was experiencing, but he said, "Maybe."

Joah was still talking, something about Sirina smiling at him, but Owan was lost in thoughts of his own. Something was in the air. Change was coming.

End of Book Six

also by Robert W. Tompkins

The Hagenspan Chronicles

Book One

Roarke's Wisdom: The Defense of Blythecairne

Book Two
Roarke's Wisdom: The Courtship of Hollie

Book Three
Roarke's Wisdom: Going Home

Book Four
Roarke's Wisdom: The Last Dragon

Book Five
Kenyan's Lamp

Book Seven
Owan's Regret: The Dragon King

Book Eight
Owan's Regret: Into the Wilds

and coming soon:

Book Nine
Owan's Regret: Peace of a Kind

non-fiction:

Disease and Faith

The Last Trumpet

and coming soon:

Enemies of God